SARNIA

HILARY FORD

SARNIA

THE SYLE PRESS

Published by The SYLE Press 2014

First published in Great Britain in 1974
by Hamish Hamilton Ltd

Copyright © Hilary Ford 1974

No part of this book may be reproduced or utilized in any form or by any means, electronic or mechanical, without prior permission from the Publisher.

All rights reserved

Cover design by Anna Kövecses

ISBN: 978-0-9927686-0-7

www.thesylepress.com

I

THE BANKING HOUSE of Merton, unlike most of its competitors, was situated not in the City but some distance west: in Magpye Alley, hard by Fetter Lane. This was an advantage of which Sarnia Lorimer was particularly aware on a day like the present with the wind, intermittently rain-filled, gusting fiercely along Holborn as she walked to work from her lodgings in Red Lion Square. Even half a mile was unpleasant on so miserable a May morning. If her destination had been Throgmorton Street, she would have had three times as far to go.

But she would not, of course, have obtained a position in one of the City banks – not in any except the house of Merton. Daniel Merton's employment of lady clerks was universally deplored by his fellow bankers. A man who indulged in such ridiculous whims must, they agreed, be heading for disaster. So far, though, his credit had remained good and his business continued to expand. The crash, they decided, when it did come, would be spectacular.

It was Sarnia's habit to cross the road by the entrance to Chancery Lane, where the sweeper was Gimpy Jimmy. He was a tall thin white-haired man who had left a leg in Spain, fighting under the Duke's command. He would never accept a coin from her, and she had ceased to urge it on him. He was puzzled, she knew, by the fact that, although a lady in appearance, she went to work. He himself was not in need of money. The position was a good one, and he had lived frugally and saved over the years. She had met him once on Sunday in the park, dressed in a suit of good sober serge, the rags of his trade put aside.

Before she crossed she heard the rattle of hooves on granite, the warning halloo of the driver, and paused to watch the yellow and red omnibus dash past in the direction of Liverpool Street. It came from Paddington, and brought to mind the little house there in which she had lived with her mother. The memory of bereavement still had power to shock; a cold hand on her heart. But she would not dwell on it – she had steeled herself against that.

'A good morning to you, ma'am,' said Jimmy, his broom musket-erect.

She smiled. 'Good morning, Jimmy.'

'Not but what it's a dirty one. Though I have never known a lady to handle her dress more delicately when the road is muddy.'

She accepted the compliment with another smile, and passed on. In fact it was a familiarity – he would not have spoken of her manner of carrying a dress to a true lady – but she did not mind it. He meant it kindly. She reflected with annoyance as she stepped up from the pavement and dropped the hem of her coat that, however deftly she managed the crossing, on a day such as this her petticoats were bound to be dirtied. But her coat and dress at least were unstained.

The porter at Merton House was white-haired like Jimmy and of much the same age, but he offered no friendly greeting. Like Daniel Merton's banking colleagues, he disapproved of lady clerks. A male clerk, Mr Dobinson, followed Sarnia in and was given the cordiality she had been denied.

The young ladies had a separate room on the second floor, and Mrs Mallay as their chaperone. She was already in place, seated in her black leather chair, spectacles on nose, ledger open on the table in front of her. The temperature of her greeting lay between those of Jimmy and the porter. She was not unamiable, but a woman of great reserve.

She was the widow of one of Mr Merton's senior clerks who had died suddenly and left her in distressed circumstances. Sarnia had wondered occasionally whether the notion of taking on lady clerks had not originated, in part at least, from a desire on his part to assist her. She could imagine that Mrs Mallay might be unwilling to accept a more open charity.

Whether the venture had been motivated by generosity or a progressive outlook, Sarnia was forced to conclude that it offered support to the doubts expressed by other bankers. The young ladies were paid only a little less than the male clerks – as much in fact as men got in some other houses – and Mrs Mallay's wage, for the supervision of only three girls, must render the operation unprofitable.

But that, she thought with relief as she went to her desk, was Mr Merton's concern. She was only grateful for the opportunity that had been put her way. Her circumstances, too, on her mother's death, had been straitened and the prospect gloomy. Her mother's income had come from a family trust and ceased with her death. Sarnia had tried for situations as a governess, but she had not been trained for that calling. She could sing prettily and play the piano and sketch fairly well, but her French was poor, her Latin almost non-existent, and she could scarcely do a sum to save her life.

Once, during the last few months when the severity of her illness could no longer be ignored, her mother had spoken of the future. Lying on the sofa under the window, her face showing the marks of the pain that racked her almost constantly, she had said that she had once thought of sending Sarnia to the new Queen's College for Women in Harley Street. It had not been the expense that deterred her but a reluctance, selfish perhaps, to be deprived of her daily companionship.

'And of course,' she said, 'I was always sure you would marry young, so pretty as you are.' She drew gasping breath, and Sarnia held the phial of salts to her nose. 'And that is true.' She spoke more strongly, as though to convince herself. 'You are eighteen now. You will be married before you are twenty-one – much before.'

Sarnia had laughed, understanding her fear and the need for reassurance.

'I promise I will do so, if you wish it. But not just yet. Give me time to review my suitors, and make a choice!'

She had been thinking, she supposed, of the two Johns, though not at all seriously. John Fuller was tall and dark and quite old – almost thirty. John Merritt, fair and shorter, was only twenty-four, and she liked him better. John Fuller had a fine tenor voice and she accompanied him on the piano when her mother had a musical evening. John Merritt neither played nor sang, but he was eloquent in praise of her voice, and turned the pages for her with hands that sometimes brushed against her hair. Yes, she decided, she had liked him much the better, though her heart had been safe from either.

Which was just as well, because John Merritt, after a single visit in the week following her mother's funeral, had not called again. John Fuller had drifted away rather more gradually, though with equal finality. Neither, she realized, had known that her mother lived on a pension, nor that on her death Sarnia would be virtually penniless. And for all the differences between them, they were both practical men. If they were to seek a woman as a wife, she would need to have at least a modest dowry. That being so, it would be unwise to seem to pay attentions to an orphaned girl.

She had had no word from either since removing to her new lodging; and little contact with any other of her old Paddington acquaintances. One or two had written with invitations to soirées. In the smart, perhaps, of understanding the motivations of the Johns, she had declined them. Better to change her way of life and acquaintanceship entirely than watch for pitying glances.

Her new acquaintanceship was so far a limited one; though it included, of course, Michael Dowling. She smiled slightly; then bent her head to the copying of a cargo manifest. Currants from Greece, olive oil from Italy, oranges from Spain … Her mother had spoken of their taking a holiday in Italy, providing her illness did not run away with too much money. Her spirits fell as she applied her pen to paper.

The luncheon interval was from twelve-thirty till one-thirty; and punctually at twelve-thirty-one Michael Dowling appeared at the door of her office. He went first to Mrs Mallay and solicited her permission to address Miss Lorimer, and his request was granted with a stiff nod.

'Will you do me the honour, Miss Lorimer, of taking luncheon with me?'

'Why, thank you, Mr Dowling,' Sarnia replied. 'I shall be delighted to do so.'

They went to Stone's Chop House in Holborn, and sat at a table at the rear. The place was full of its usual mid-day bustle of activity: waiters jostling down the narrow aisle with plates balanced perilously along their arms, orders for porter being yelled to the potboy, gruff male voices talking business or politics – all noise and flurry and tobacco smoke. She could not possibly have dined in such a place by herself. Even with Michael beside her, her presence had initially provoked glances that made her feel not quite comfortable. But Michael overrode her doubts. One or two old fogies might think a lady's presence unsuitable, but no one minded them.

'We are in the second half of the century,' he had reminded her. 'The world is going forward. You have quite as much right here as they. Will you take the boiled beef or the steak pie, Miss Lorimer?'

She realized the sense of what he had said. Having accepted a post as a lady clerk she must face the obligations of that occupation, and an occasional frown was no great matter. In fact after the first few days there had been few frowns, and smiles from some surprising quarters: from the old gentleman, for instance, who sat in the corner opposite and always dined off poached halibut and a pint of ale. He nodded to her now in an entirely friendly fashion.

A group of men at the next table were talking in loud voices, and she noticed Michael glance sharply at them. Their discussion centred on the papal aggression. One of them proposed an anagram: War, Sin and Malice. When the others could not solve it, he provided the solution: Cardinal Wiseman. They roared with laughter.

Michael quietly asked Sarnia to excuse him. He rose to his feet and walked across to the table. The man who had offered the anagram, a thin dark fellow, looked at him in inquiry. Michael said:

'Gentlemen, I am an adherent of the Catholic faith. I do not seek to limit your freedom of speech or discussion. But I would hope you might find it possible to conduct your conversation more quietly.'

There were four of them. They stared up at Michael, and for a moment she thought they might be going to jeer at him – even that there might be a brawl. But Michael stared them down. The dark man said:

'I beg pardon, sir.'

Michael returned to sit beside Sarnia. He said:

'I beg your pardon, too, Miss Lorimer, for taking such action in your presence. I did not wish to cause you embarrassment, but …'

She shook her head. 'I'm not embarrassed.'

The men were talking again, but in low voices. Michael's own voice was low also.

'We have not discussed the matter, but am I right in believing you do not share the prejudice against Catholics?'

'I think everyone has a right to the exercise of his religion.'

'This talk of aggression … it is to misunderstand the situation. Through ignorance in many cases, though in some I fear from malice. The restoration of the hierarchy, making Wiseman a Cardinal – none of it is directed against this country's sovereignty, nor against the English church. It is merely a matter of administration.'

'I understand it scarcely at all,' Sarnia said, 'but I am sure you are right.'

'People think of Catholicism as belonging to the Dark Ages. But there are progressive elements within the Church, and I am confident they will prevail as they are doing in the world in general. Science is changing the way in which men look at things, and very rapidly. When I was a boy trains were scarcely heard of, and look how they now whisk people about the land!'

'Mr Merton was talking the other day of the turnpikes – how they are falling into decay since so few people use them and the tolls do not bring in sufficient for their upkeep.'

'Just so. The roads will turn into cart tracks as the railways multiply. Except in towns, of course – though I would not put it past the capabilities of the engineers to run trains through the streets as well!'

Sarnia watched him as he talked. He had a broad face, calm in repose but capable of showing emotion, grey eyes with wrinkles of laughter at their corners, thick brown curly hair. And she liked his hands: the nails large but well-tended, the hand itself heavy and capable. Their eyes met, and he said:

'Miss Lorimer ... may I ask a favour?'

'Of course.'

'That you call me Michael, and allow me to address you by your Christian name.'

She smiled. 'By all means.'

'Sarnia.' He looked at her. 'A sweet name, and one that I have never heard before. What is its origin?'

She shook her head. 'I do not know.'

'And it does not matter. It is enough that it is your name. And so pretty – almost pretty enough for you. Though no name could be. I was wondering ...'

'What?'

'Whether, if you have no other engagement and the day is fair, you would let me take you out this coming Sunday? We could make an excursion by train, to Staines perhaps. The river is very pleasant there.'

Sarnia nodded. 'I should like that.'

The house where Sarnia lodged was kept by a couple called Wilkinson. He was an affected and idle man who tormented his wretched wife with sarcasm. She was a woman of great industry but little capability. She cajoled her servants and was continually losing them. She was inclined towards nervousness in any case, and her husband's unremitting persecution aggravated that tendency. Sarnia returned in the evening to find the house in confusion and Mrs Wilkinson in one of her states. The cook, it appeared, had walked out in the middle of the afternoon.

During a supper of cold meats followed by gluey rice pudding, Mrs Wilkinson sniffed and sobbed while Mr Wilkinson sniped. Sarnia was glad to escape at the end and go upstairs to her room. But she was called back by Mrs Wilkinson, who had followed her out into the hall.

She turned unwillingly. There had been previous sessions in which Mrs Wilkinson had poured out her troubles to her, and she suspected another might be proposed. She was not unsympathetic to the older woman's plight, but she could not help feeling that it stemmed from feebleness of spirit. She should stand up to her husband instead of weakly enduring his bullying.

Male domestic tyranny was not a condition to which Sarnia herself had ever been accustomed. She had previously lived alone with her mother; and her mother's attitude towards that tyranny, as observed in other households, had been more one of scorn than indignation. It might be the case that a wife was legally the chattel of her husband, but that did not, in her eyes, excuse women who tamely submitted to a man's domination.

But Mrs Wilkinson was not, on this occasion, seeking a confidante. It appeared she had only now remembered that there had been a caller that afternoon for Sarnia, and a card had been left. She unearthed it from beneath a clutter of objects on the hall table, and Sarnia looked at it with surprise. The legend ran:

>D. H. Jelain Esquire
>Les Colombelles
>Guernsey.

'Mrs' had been entered by hand in front of the name, 'Esquire' crossed out.

Mrs Wilkinson said: 'The lady asked when she might find you in. I took the liberty of suggesting tomorrow afternoon, since it is Saturday and your office closes at mid-day. She said she would call between three and four.'

'But she did not say what business she had with me?'

'Why, no. And since she inquired for you by name, I took it she was a friend of yours – an acquaintance, at least.'

Sarnia looked at the card. 'She is no acquaintance. Guernsey – is that not an island?'

'Near the coast of France,' Mrs Wilkinson said. 'I have heard my uncle speak of it. He was a sailor.'

Sarnia said: 'I know no one in France or its islands. It is a mystery. Tomorrow afternoon, you say? At least I do not have long to wait for the unravelling.'

The following afternoon Sarnia waited for her caller in her room. She had the latest copy of *Household Words,* and when that palled she took up her square of Berlin woolwork, which she had scarcely touched since joining the bank. She was called down by Mrs Wilkinson shortly after three o'clock, and informed that her visitor was in the sitting-room.

She found Mrs Jelain seated in an armchair by the window, under tall plumes of pampas grass that nodded in a draught from the opening door. She was a handsome woman in her fifties, with strong clear-cut features and elegant clothes. Under her open coat she wore a wide-sleeved dress of blue grenadine over a white chemisette, and her neck was encircled by a string of large garnets. She rose and greeted Sarnia with a warm smile.

'Dear cousin, I am so happy to meet you!'

Sarnia was enfolded in an embrace from which, astonished and disconcerted, she withdrew.

'Cousin? Is there not some mistake, ma'am? Perhaps you seek another Miss Lorimer?'

'Not if your first name is Sarnia, as I believe it is.'

'Why, yes.'

'And do you not have an Aunt Maria in Gloucestershire? It was through her we learned your address. I perceive she did not warn you of this call. In fact I asked her to allow me the pleasure of surprising you, but I could not be sure she had not let something slip.'

There had been a letter from Aunt Maria some days earlier, and Sarnia tried to recall its contents. She remembered one sentence. 'You have had grief and unhappiness, child, but better things lie ahead.' A pious hope, Sarnia had supposed. Her aunt had previously written, after her mother's death, offering her a home; but with such a lack of enthusiasm as to make the refusal both satisfying and easy.

She shook her head. 'My aunt told me nothing. And I have never heard of relations on the island of Guernsey.'

'Your mother did not speak of that?'

'Never. Of what was there to speak?'

'She would not. I understand it.' Mrs Jelain sighed. 'A most unhappy affair. And having changed her name, she would wish to draw a veil over it.'

'Changed her name?'

'Rather, re-taken her old one. Lorimer was your mother's maiden name. Did you not know that?'

Sarnia felt giddy, unbearably confused. She said:

'I did not know. If it is true.'

'Your mother had no brother, of course, and both her sisters married. And she was orphaned early in life. But I am surprised it did not emerge in intercourse with your aunts.'

Aunt Charlotte Poskett lived in the north of Yorkshire, further off than Aunt Maria Webb. Meetings with both had been few and formal. In a family lacking a father or brothers or sisters, the absence of the friendly visiting aunts and uncles, of which other girls might boast, had been no more than a minor additional deprivation.

She had stayed silent. Mrs Jelain continued:

'And your father? Your mother never spoke of him?'

'Only to say that he died while I was a baby.' She recalled the occasional unhappiness in her mother's face; at an early age she had been sensitive to it, and quick to turn from a subject which seemed to provoke it. Growing older she had envisaged a romantic but tragic love, whose memory was best left sleeping.

It was Mrs Jelain who now was silent. As moments passed, Sarnia felt a constriction in her breast, a stifling apprehension. She cried:

'What is it, ma'am? What do you wish to tell me?'

'Your mother had her reasons, and I would not decry them. But then you had her with you. I must tell you, child: your father is not dead. He still lives in Guernsey. His father and my husband's father were brothers. You had our name. You were not born Sarnia Lorimer, but Sarnia Jelain.'

She shook her head quickly. 'It cannot be so!'

'How can it not be? Is not your name itself a proof?'

'Lorimer? I do not see ...'

'Not Lorimer. Sarnia. Did you never ask where it came from?'

She had a sudden memory of doing so, as she stared, one wintry afternoon, at the stitches she had made on a half-worked sampler. It was a name, her mother had said, that belonged to her father's family. She had seen constraint again, and sadness, and asked no more.

She asked now: 'From where does it come?'

'Why, from Guernsey! Sarnia is the ancient name of our island, the name the Romans gave it. Your mother chose it for you, from love of her adopted home.'

They were interrupted by the appearance of Mrs Wilkinson with a tea tray. She fussed and talked interminably. When she had gone at last, Sarnia asked in an agony of impatience:

'Will you tell me it all, ma'am? My father is alive – and I was born on Guernsey? What happened, to cause my mother to leave that place and change her name? Why did she never speak of him?'

Mrs Jelain sipped her tea. 'It was an unhappy affair, as I said. To put it in short, your mother left your father and the island, taking you with her, when you were little more than a year old. There had plainly been great bitterness between them, but I do not know what caused it. Your father did not talk of it, and your mother, of course, had gone.'

'Did my father not seek after her?'

'Most likely he did, but England is a very big place compared with Guernsey. It would not be difficult for someone who wished to lose themselves here.'

'Yet you have discovered me now.'

'Only because your Aunt Maria wrote to your father after your mother died, telling him that you were left alone in the world.'

'And so he sent you?' Her feelings were strange and confused, but she was aware of disappointment. 'He did not choose to come himself?'

'He is a sick man. He was much older than your mother. He is now close on seventy, and has been in poor health for years. My husband and I were intending in any event to come to London to see the Great Exhibition. It seemed proper that we should take the opportunity of visiting you.'

'He could have written, surely! He is not too sick to hold a pen?'

'Your father is a man of substance, but he has made his own way in life. He can indeed read and write, but not fluently. He would find it awkward to pen a letter, especially to you. And he must have doubts of your reaction. You say your mother never spoke of him, but she might have done so; and with a bitterness which could have fixed your mind against him. You understand this, surely?'

Sarnia put a hand to her head. 'I do not know what I understand – or if I understand anything.'

Mrs Jelain said: 'This has been a great shock. Perhaps I myself should have written to you in advance, but it seemed better to break the news in person.'

Her look as she spoke was one of compassion and sympathy, and Sarnia said quickly:

'I am glad of it, and deeply grateful for the trouble you have been to. But I do not know …'

Mrs Jelain stopped her. 'There is no need to think of the future yet. It is enough that we have found you, and in such good health and looks. Your mother was very beautiful, but I think you surpass her.'

This too was said with warmth. Mrs Jelain went on:

'My husband and I will stay two weeks in London. He is anxious to meet you, but left the introduction to me. Will you permit us to call on you tomorrow?'

'You are most kind, but I am afraid I must refuse for tomorrow. I am already engaged.'

Mrs Jelain smiled. 'It does not surprise me. A girl as pretty as you is bound to have many engagements. Will you be free on Monday evening?'

'Yes.'

'Then you must promise us that. We will get seats for the opera. I have heard wonderful things of Signora Angri. Living so far from the culture and amusements of London, we are greedy for them. It is different for you, who live here all the year round. May we solicit your kindness in showing the town to your country cousins from across the seas?'

'Of course, ma'am. But …'

'Not "Ma'am", please, child. If the difference in our ages makes "Cousin" too hard a word, call me "Aunt Jeanne".' She raised her finger above the tea-cup. 'And promise me you will limit your other engagements while we are here. I know the request is selfish, but I make it all the same.'

II

On Thursday, when Michael took Sarnia to luncheon, he said: 'I have a capital idea for next Sunday. We will take the train to Brighton, and bathe in the sea.'

'I am afraid I cannot.'

'You think the sea may be still too cold? We could paddle, at least. Or walk along the shore and watch the waves breaking. I always feel there is such grandeur in the sight. And the sound, too – that lion-like roar of the surf.'

'I cannot because I am engaged. My relations wish me to go with them to the Zoological Gardens. They are anxious to see the hippopotamus.'

'Can they not go by themselves? You have been engaged with them all week.'

'They like to have a companion. They are not used to the bustle of London. And they are only in England for a short time, so I feel obliged to fall in with their wishes.'

'I had been hoping we might go and see the hippo together.'

He spoke with a touch of resentment. She smiled at him over the arm of the waiter who was putting down plates of soup in front of them.

'We can do that after they have gone back. The hippo will still be there.'

He said unwillingly: 'I suppose so. When did you say they were returning to their island?'

'On Wednesday week. They will take the evening train to Southampton and travel overnight by mail packet.'

'And does that mean you will be engaged with them a second Sunday?'

'I fear it does. You must understand, Michael, that they are being wonderfully kind to me. Mrs Jelain has insisted on making me a present of a new dress, though I tried to refuse. They are very generous.'

'I will try to think of that. But I doubt if I shall weep over their departure.'

She laughed; his face was comically indignant.

'Nor shall I! But I like them and am grateful to them. The world is not so full of kind people that one can be excused failing to appreciate those one encounters.'

On the Sunday afternoon they strolled through the gardens of Soyer's Symposium. Mrs Jelain chatted and Sarnia made appropriate responses, but her thoughts wandered. She wondered what Michael was doing, and if he had recovered from his disappointment about Brighton. Not entirely, she hoped.

They found seats near the Grotto of Ondine: music from a string orchestra came faintly through the air from the Doge's Terrace. Mr Jelain sat down with a sigh of satisfaction.

'We seem to do a prodigious amount of walking in London,' he observed.

'Do you not walk much in Guernsey, then?' Sarnia asked.

'That we do,' he chuckled. 'And climb as well. Our town is built on the side of a steeper hill than I have found here. And our pavements, of Guernsey granite, are as hard. No, I must put my fatigue down to nothing but my good lady's resolve not to miss a single pleasure London can afford.'

'He is worse than I,' Mrs Jelain said. 'We have already been twice around the Crystal Palace, and he plans a third visit tomorrow.'

'It is a Shilling Day, which will be a great economy.'

Mrs Jelain shook her head indulgently. 'You can go by yourself to your Shilling Day. I will take a hackney coach to Bond Street, and more than make up for your economies.'

He roared his laughter. 'I dare swear you will!'

The sun came out from cloud, and the ladies put up their parasols. Mrs Jelain said:

'Sarnia, my dear, there is something I wish to ask you.'

'What is that, Aunt Jeanne?'

'It is simple enough. We should like you to accompany us when we return to Guernsey.'

She was startled. 'Accompany you?'

'And stay with us for a time. The holiday will do you good.'

'I thank you for the offer, most heartily. But I could not.'

'Why do you say so?'

'I do not … It is difficult to explain.'

Mrs Jelain smiled. 'We shall not take that for an answer. Do you think you would not be happy with us – that you would find our island ways too dull?'

'Indeed, no! I am sure I should love it. But … my mother chose to leave, and come back to England. I cannot think it right to renew a connection which so distressed her.' She added quickly: 'It has nothing to do with you, you must realize.'

Mrs Jelain leaned towards her. 'Your scruples do you credit. But consider, all that unhappiness took place when you were an infant, a very long time ago. And the island itself had no part in it. Your mother loved it so much she gave its name to you. Are you not curious to see the land of Sarnia?'

'The island may have played no part in her misery, but my father did. And he lives there still.'

'Yes. An old and sick man. Even if he wronged her, she gave him no chance to make amends. He can no longer ask your mother's forgiveness, but he might ask it from you on her behalf. Would you think that disloyal to her memory? She was not so hard of heart, I am sure.'

Sarnia shook her head. The words were persuasively spoken, the argument reasonable. She was conscious of the awkwardness of her refusal. It was with relief that she discovered a more practical reason for saying no.

'In any event, I could not accept. I began my employment with Mr Merton too late to be granted a holiday this year. Perhaps next summer it might be possible. I am to get a week of leave then.'

'We had no thought of a week! It is scarcely worth the sea voyage for that. A month, say.'

'Then I fear that rules it out completely.'

'Could you not give up your post with the bank?'

'And what would I do, on returning? If you knew the difficulties I had in securing employment, and how fortunate I am to have been the object of Mr Merton's kindness ... I know no other employer who would find a use for lady clerks.'

'Nor I,' Mrs Jelain said. 'And while I understand your feelings, I am not really sure I think it suitable. I may be old-fashioned, but it is not something that seems entirely proper for a young lady of your quality.'

'I do not share your view. And in any case I must work to live. My mother, through no fault of her own, was not able to leave me anything.'

'There are others who could assist you, and would be very glad to do so. Is that not so, Mr Jelain?'

He stared up at the sun. He was a coarse-looking man, with a complexion red enough for a peony, and his speech was somewhat rough. But his manner, though awkward, was warm. He said:

'It is, indeed.'

Sarnia said: 'I am grateful for the thought. But I could not allow myself to become a charge on anyone, however kind their intention. If I were a child it would be different, but I am a grown woman.'

Mrs Jelain said: 'A woman, indeed, and plainly one of sturdy independence. We admire you for it. You are firm in your judgement, and that is a good thing. But we shall not let it rest there, shall we, Mr Jelain?' She saw Sarnia's expression and added: 'But leave it for the present. I thought we might take a box at the theatre again tomorrow. Tell me what there is good that we have not seen.'

It was Mr Merton's unvarying custom to have luncheon at his club in Pall Mall, leaving the office at a quarter to one and returning punctually at two-thirty. But it was a quarter to three one afternoon when the ladies in Mrs Mallay's charge heard his footsteps on the stair, and saw him in profile as he went past the frosted glass of the door of their room.

A minute or two later, the office boy brought Mrs Mallay a message: Mr Merton desired to see Miss Lorimer.

The boy took her up and showed her in. Mr Merton's room was unusual for a banker. It was light in colour, almost gay, the lower part of the walls dark green but in a shade of lime from a few feet above the floor. His desk was walnut, covered with red leather, and the fireplace, during the summer, held a vase of flowers delivered each morning from Covent Garden. Today the display was green and yellow: acacia and laburnum, mixed with sprays of glossy myrtle. On the walls were several daguerreotypes – Mr Merton practised the art himself – and a couple of bright canvases of the pre-Raphaelite school.

He was in his late fifties, a man of commanding figure but unhandsome features. He had a thin craggy face, a bulbous nose, small eyes deeply recessed. His voice, though, was a warm and strong one.

He said: 'I have a great aversion against being accosted without due notice. That is why I fixed my office on the third floor; it makes it easier to avoid unexpected callers. But this is something one cannot always escape. I had such an encounter today at my club, with a stranger who sent in his card by the steward. I need not have seen him, of course, but the address intrigued me. He was a man called Jelain, hailing from the island of Guernsey.'

Sarnia felt herself colour. Mr Merton went on:

'He apologized, very properly, for approaching me in this way, but said he was in the neighbourhood and, desiring an interview with me, thought the occasion might be appropriate. I believe Mr Jelain is related to you, Miss Lorimer?'

She could remember speaking to the Jelains of Mr Merton's

mid-day routine. Mr Jelain had asked to which club he belonged and she had told him, thinking the inquiry casual. She said:

'I beg your pardon, sir, if you feel I have been too free in speaking of your affairs. I assure you I had no notion that Mr Jelain might approach you. I hope …'

He raised a hand to silence her. 'Your concern is unnecessary. I do not accuse you of indiscretion, and Mr Jelain assured me you had no foreknowledge of his call. Though I imagine you may now be able to guess its purpose?'

She said faintly: 'No, sir. I cannot.'

Up to this point she had thought he was displeased, but did not know how greatly. She was annoyed herself: it had been quite improper of Mr Jelain to do such a thing without mentioning it to her. But Mr Merton now smiled.

'Mr Jelain tells me that he and his wife have asked you to return with them to Guernsey, but that you have refused because of your desire to keep your position here. He wondered if you could be relieved of that anxiety.'

He looked at her keenly, and she dropped her eyes.

'I am glad that you are happy in your work with us. For my part, I am very pleased with it. You copy neatly and accurately. As it happens, business is fairly slack at this moment, and is likely to be so for another couple of months. I have assured your cousin that there will be no difficulty in sparing you for any period up to that limit, and that your post will be kept open for you, if you so wish.'

'You are most kind, sir,' Sarnia said, 'but the indulgence was not necessary and I would not have asked for it. I do not ask it!'

'Mr Jelain told me a little of his acquaintance with you and the circumstances surrounding it. I understand that your father lives in Guernsey, and that you may have expectations from him.'

'Mr Jelain is kind. Too kind, perhaps. I have never seen my father, or not since I was so small as to have no memory of him. Whatever expectations might lie in that direction, and I would doubt there being any, I do not want them.'

She had spoken warmly. Mr Merton frowned.

'I can see how such a feeling might arise but, my dear Miss Lorimer, you must accept some counsel from older heads.'

She stared in stubborn silence, and he went on:

'The position of women in our society is a thing that troubles me deeply. For all the progress we have made and are making, for all the advancements of science, there are respects in which even mid-nineteenth-century England is a dark and barbarous land; and its treatment of the female sex is one of these.

'Until a few years ago, women were made to work in coal mines, harder than a liberal man would work an animal. But though that brutality has been suppressed, there are many others. I met a lady last evening who was very proud of her dress. Almost twenty yards of silk, she declared, had gone to the making of it! And how many hours of soul-destroying labour, I wonder, by some wretched girl, ruining her eyes in a garret for a pittance of reward? You know Mr Hood's poem, "The Song of the Shirt"? The Secretary of a philanthropic society in which I have an interest tells me that during the present season girls work eighteen hours a day to keep up with the trade's demands – some even longer. It is little wonder that many of them, rather than continue in such heart-breaking toil, turn to a life of shame.'

The remark startled her. Mr Merton said:

'I beg your pardon, Miss Lorimer, for speaking of such a thing in your presence, though I am not sure that I should. My own daughters, had Fate willed things differently, might have been such girls as these. You yourself might.'

She said: 'That may be so, sir, and I pity them. I have told you of my gratitude to you for employing me. But if my work is satisfactory, this post suffices me. Surely it is better to thank God for my good fortune than to seek after legacies.'

He looked at her in silence, and she grew uncomfortable again. He said:

'Did you know Mr Andrews, who banked in Cheapside? He often came here. Yesterday afternoon, leaving his office, he fell and died of an apoplexy. He was a younger man than I. I must tell you, Miss Lorimer, that if anyone other than myself were proprietor of this bank you would not retain your employment here, however good your work.'

She did not know what to say to that. Mr Merton did indeed seem old to her, very old, but old people could live on for many years, and he did not strike her as the kind of man likely to have an apoplexy. Her marriage, and the consequent retirement from her present occupation, seemed on all counts a much nearer likelihood than his death.

Mr Merton continued in an urgent tone:

'A young lady ought to seek security wherever it offers itself consistently with virtue. In an ideal world this would not be necessary, but the world, while manifestly improving, is far from ideal. I cannot advise you too strongly against spurning the possibility of financial betterment, whatever your sentiments.'

He looked at her expectantly, and she said:

'I am grateful for the advice, sir, as much as for your past help.'

'Then consider it seriously. I shall be sorry to lose you, even for the period of a holiday. We shall all miss your pretty face, Miss Lorimer, and your charming ways, quite apart from your penmanship.' He smiled. 'But I join fully with your cousin in urging you to accept their invitation. And now you may return to your desk.'

When Sarnia saw the Jelains that evening, she reproached Mr Jelain for his intrusion, but gently: since it so clearly arose from generosity she could not be too indignant. Mrs Jelain, for her part, scolded her husband, but expressed her satisfaction that it had turned out so well – that Mr Merton had proved both understanding and accommodating.

They both took it for granted that the last objection to her returning with them had been removed. She did not dispute this, though she was far from agreeing with it. That night she dreamt of her mother. She was bright and cheerful as she had been before illness wore her down, and Sarnia was telling her of Michael and she was listening and smiling. Sarnia awoke in the night, at first happy and then miserable. She would not go to Guernsey with the Jelains, she decided: she would tell them so firmly at their next meeting.

Although she had made the decision, she had not meant to speak of it to Michael, but over luncheon the following day he quizzed her about her interview with Mr Merton: it was common knowledge that she had been called to his room. Sarnia did her best to put him off, but he persisted; and in the end she told him something of what had taken place.

His indignation over Mr Jelain's action was far greater than hers had been, and almost violently expressed. It was intolerable, he declared over his steak-and-oyster pudding, that a man should be accosted in the seclusion of his club: quite intolerable!

'It was merely a matter of sending a card in,' Sarnia said. 'Mr Merton need not have seen him.'

'Mr Merton ought not to have been put in the position of having either to tolerate or reject the presence of a total stranger. He is a very tolerant man, as his employment of both of us bears witness, but your cousin was not to know that. His interference might well have hazarded your position. The man was entirely callous of your welfare.'

Although Sarnia agreed in part, she disliked the extremity of Michael's opposition and the strength with which it was expressed. She fell into a defence of Mr Jelain's motives which provoked still stronger condemnation from her companion. He was angry with Mr Jelain, but a little angry with her, too, she realized, for defending him.

They left the chop house in an atmosphere of estrangement, and walked in silence. Sarnia did her best to recompose her feelings. If Michael had been angry with her, it stemmed from affection; she already knew he was jealous of the way the Jelains had monopolized her.

He said suddenly: 'At least, after such insolence, you have good cause to refuse their offer. You could not possibly return with them.'

It was a dry blowing day. A four-in-hand, furiously driven close by, roused a swirl of dust which stung her face. She said sharply:

'I can very well go if I choose.'

'To see this father of yours, whose abominable behaviour drove your poor mother away? His cousin's insolence shows something of what she must have had to endure.'

The control which she had been putting on her temper snapped.

'I must remind you, Mr Dowling, that the man you describe as abominable is my father. It is not for you to set yourself up in judgement on him.'

He looked at her, white-faced, and said ironically:

'I beg your pardon, Miss Lorimer. Or would Miss Jelain be the more proper title? You are quite right to reproach me. Doubtless even an ogre can be tolerable, providing he is a rich ogre.'

They were close by the door of the bank. Sarnia stared coldly at him.

'Thank you for taking me to luncheon, Mr Dowling. I shall not trespass on your kindness in future. Good day to you.'

She mounted the stairs without looking back. She did not weep until she was safe inside the ladies' cloakroom.

III

THE EVENING of a clear summer day was darkening when the carriage conveyed them into Vauxhall station. The gas jets flared high up but were little needed still; even under the shadow of the platform roof one could see what was going on without artificial aid.

And there was so much going on. Sarnia had been in railway stations often enough, but never for so important an occasion as the departure of a boat train. The bustle of passengers and their friends, of porters and hawkers and entertainers, was unlike anything she had witnessed. A group of three officers swaggered past, brilliant in their scarlet uniform, and Mrs Jelain whispered that they were of the 54th, at present garrisoning the island but due soon to be relieved. Sarnia keenly felt the excitement of it all, and the misgivings she had suffered during the day were completely banished. It was unthinkable that she might have missed this!

The opulence of the First Class carriage was another welcome novelty: Mr Jelain installed them in it and departed. The oil lamps were already lit, and the guard himself came to check that they were properly trimmed and burning well. He affected to remember Mrs Jelain from the inward journey, and inquired after her holiday in London. He was a merry-looking, portly man, with curling white side-whiskers, and he promised them a good crossing to the island. The sea that morning had been calm as a pond, and there was no sign of the weather breaking. Then, touching his cap, he passed on down the train.

Mr Jelain returned, bearing things he had bought for them: fruit and sweetmeats, magazines and books. One little book described the sights to be seen on the way to Southampton, which amused Mrs Jelain.

'We shall see precious little on this trip. It will be night before we are out of London.'

He laughed. 'Why, then, you can read it afterwards, and take note of all the wonderful things you saw on the way up, providing you can remember them. Have I brought fruit enough?'

'A sight too much, since for our supper we have this huge hamper from Fortnum. We shall not eat the half, and what is left will scarcely tempt us in Guernsey, where our own fruits are so much better.' She spoke confidingly to Sarnia. 'I suppose all men have their faults, but I would rather have extravagance than meanness.'

'I perfectly agree,' Sarnia said. 'Meanness and coldness – they are much the same thing – those are the qualities that are truly hateful.'

She was thinking of her farewell to the Wilkinsons, and Mr Wilkinson's sarcastic expression of hope that she would have a good holiday. Mrs Wilkinson, adding her own sincerer compliments, had said they would be looking forward to seeing her in fine health and spirits on her return, and that her room would be kept for her. Mr Wilkinson had raised a weary but decisive hand.

'We must not engage Miss Lorimer with thoughts of her return. She will not wish to dwell on anything so dismal, when she has so bright a prospect before her. And I am sure she realizes that, as humble lodging-house keepers, we could not undertake to keep a room empty if a prospective boarder solicits us for it. In fact, I have had inquiries already.'

He had looked from his wife to Sarnia with a small tight smile of satisfaction. It was Mrs Wilkinson, she realized, that he was most concerned to wound. How dreadful, she thought shuddering, to be so dependent on the good will of a man utterly lacking in that quality. She pitied Mrs Wilkinson, but could not help despising her a little. It had been a failure in judgement not to have come to a truer estimation of the man's character before she consented to marry him. Yet she had paid heavily for that failure, and must go on paying.

The guard's whistle was blown and the engine chuffed into life. The train moved out of the station's gloom into the brighter ambience of the city's dusk. Overhead the sky was deep, almost violet blue; ahead the horizon was lemon and orange. They rattled past along rows of little houses bordering the railway line, newly built or still building, and out into the country as the twilight darkened. In fields close by, dim shapes of cattle grazed while horses, more nervous, ran from the fiery monster as it approached.

Mrs Jelain read a magazine by the oil lamp's light, while Mr Jelain dozed in the opposite corner. Sarnia had no desire to read and was too excited for sleep. She thought of Mrs Wilkinson at her never-ending never-rewarded tasks in Red Lion Square. All of that came from her decision to accept an offer of marriage. There could be no decision in a woman's life more crucial.

More happily, she thought of Michael.

For a week the estrangement had persisted between them; they had passed on the stairs with cool nods and blank faces. Then, when she entered the office building on the morning of her last day of work, she had encountered him at the foot of the stairs. She realized, even without the explanatory smirk from the porter, that he had been waiting there to meet her. He was nervous, and stumbled over his words.

'Miss ... Miss Lorimer, I – that is, I would deeply – most deeply – appreciate it if you would have luncheon with me today.' She looked at him in silence. 'Please. Please, Miss Lorimer.'

She smiled, but with constraint.

'Thank you, Mr Dowling. It is very kind of you.'

On the way to the chop house he apologized for his behaviour. When she accepted the apology, he said:

'I would have begged your pardon before, but I dared not speak. Your manner was so cold towards me.'

'At any rate, I am glad you did speak.'

'Do you really mean that?'

'Of course I do. I should have been sorry to see our friendship ended.'

'You travel to Guernsey tomorrow evening?'

'Yes.'

'But I shall not see you tomorrow?'

She shook her head. 'Mr Merton has given me the day's leave, to complete my packing.'

He was silent, then said: 'I hope you will have a very happy time. How long do you plan to stay?'

'A month.'

He put a hand lightly on her arm. 'Will you write to me, Sarnia?'

She smiled. 'Yes, Michael.'

'I depend on your giving me an address to which I can send letters. Miss Lorimer, Guernsey, might not be enough. Though "the beautiful Miss Lorimer" should suffice: there could be no question who was meant.'

He hurried the waiters during luncheon, and afterwards led her to the gardens of Lincoln's Inn. The day was fine and attorneys took the air, sunning themselves like plump blackbirds. They sat on a bench in a quiet corner, and he turned to her and clasped one of her hands between his.

'Have you truly forgiven me my rudeness?'

'Truly. It is quite forgotten.'

'It is not by me. I could not justify it, and would not seek to excuse it, but I must explain … something of my feelings.'

He spoke in a low voice and she guessed what must follow. The slight fluttering of heart she felt was disturbing but not really unpleasant.

'I know you have been aware of my admiration and affection for you. But admiration and affection do not give rise to rudeness. It takes a more violent emotion for that. And such an emotion explains my conduct, even though it does not excuse it. I behaved as I did through fear of losing you.'

'All that was proposed was a few weeks' holiday.'

'In the first place, yes. But these relations of yours are clearly much taken with you, and it seems to me more than possible that they plan to hold you if they can. They would do so on their own behalf, but in addition they act as agents for your father. He wishes to recover the daughter lost so long ago. It is a natural thing. He will seek to keep you with him in Guernsey.'

Sarnia said firmly: 'There can be no question of that. It is not even certain that I shall see him during my visit. If I do, it will be formally and in brief. There can be no question of reconciling with a man my mother sought to forget.'

'I know these are your present feelings. But there are persuasions that might be applied.'

'Do you mean financial persuasions?'

He said quickly: 'That was not in my mind.'

'I hope not. Any wealth my father might have to offer should have gone to my mother. If she did not choose to have it, there are no circumstances in which I could possibly accept anything from him.'

'I know. And I admire you for it. Lord, I am putting everything badly! I am making a fool of myself.'

He looked so woebegone that she felt like laughing; but at the same time was moved. She touched his hand.

'No, you are not. And if you are, I like it in you.'

'Do you?' He brightened. 'Yet only like …'

She smiled. 'There is no one I like so well. No one.'

'But I do not like you, Sarnia.' She arched her brows, mock-indignant. 'I love you, which is a far different thing. I should like to make you my wife. There – am I not a fool?'

'No. You do me a great honour, Michael.'

'But do you have an answer for me?'

'I am fond of you. I have said: there is no one I like better.'

'Is there a hope that you might feel something more than liking? I do not ask you to engage yourself to me. Only to allow me the hope.'

She said slowly: 'There are problems, as you know. Your religion presents one.'

'I would never ask you to give up your own faith. And I realize that to an ordinary person there might seem too great a barrier. But you are not ordinary. You are warm and sympathetic, above all intelligent. And one can see a bright future, not only in fields of science but in religion. Despite the present agitation I am sure the churches are moving towards union. And even if that should not come during our lives, there is no reason why we two should not live together in happiness and good will – in love. It need not come between us that we attend different places of worship on the Lord's day. We could pray for each other, and return to a home where the prayer was made real in mutual comfort. Do you not agree?'

She looked seriously at him. 'I am glad of your proposal, Michael. And I promise I will think deeply of it.'

'I cannot offer you luxury – at any rate for the present. I am only a bank clerk, as you know, and have no independent means. But Mr Merton thinks highly of my abilities, and has promised me promotion within a year or two. And rest assured I would work twice as hard for a future which I could have the joy of sharing with you.'

What she was thinking of was children, who could make a difference of religion far more acute. The Romans, even if they sanctioned marriage with a non-Catholic, insisted on maintaining power over the issue of such a union. She could scarcely speak of this to Michael – it would be too indelicate – but it was in her mind.

He said: 'Then may I hope?'

'Of course, you may.'

'And you will not marry someone on this island of Guernsey without giving me a chance to advance my plea further?'

Sarnia laughed. 'I am only to be there for a few weeks! Do you reckon me so flighty in my fancies? I am committed to nothing more dreadful than a seaside holiday. "This island of Guernsey"

– you make the place sound almost infernal by that dismal tone!'

'It does sound so to me. No, I will not attack the island. After all, you were born there. And I rely on your undertaking to write to me, not to forget me, and to return at the month's end.'

'I will do my best to observe all three points.'

'Do your best?'

'I will perform them, then. Does that content you?'

He kissed her hand, his lips warm on her skin.

'It contents me.'

The engine's whistle shrieked, and they plunged from night's blackness to the thicker starless dark of a tunnel, the racket of their progress magnified by the confining walls. Then out again into the open, and she saw in the distance a glow that proclaimed the rising moon.

No decision more crucial: there was no denying it. She allowed her mind to form pictures of what it might be like to be married to Michael, to share his life in an intimacy so much greater than that which she had known with her mother. And he so much more a stranger! It was not only the scarcely thinkable image of their two bodies side by side in one bed, of that light touch of lips on the back of her hand transformed into a holding and deep embracing of nakedness, a yielding up of secret flesh, that alarmed her. It was the surrender of more ordinary privacies, the wider sharing. To live always together within the confines of some small house, to see the same face each morning on waking and each evening when he returned from the day's work, to lose all elements of surprise – how was that to be borne? And yet in return it must yield felicities that now could only be guessed at: the confidence of affection confirmed and renewed by that very familiarity, the security of knowing that one was the mistress of a home, not a lodger under risk of being given notice by such as Mr Wilkinson.

In fact, as her first thoughts had urged, all turned on the quality of the man; and so on one's own assessment of his character and nature. How did Michael figure in such a calculation? She liked him for his looks, except in some trivial points for his manners, for his light-heartedness, good sense and humour – not least for his attachment to her.

The question must follow: what vices lay beneath the virtues of which she was conscious? What difference might there be between the present lover and a future husband? Had Mrs Wilkinson – incredible thought! – once reckoned Mr Wilkinson an amiable man?

But Mrs Wilkinson's weakness of judgement need not make her pessimistic about her own. Michael did have defects of temper – the outburst which led to their estrangement was an example – and she had marked them. She could be confident, though, that in essence he was warm-hearted. And that he had courage. He proved that by speaking up in public to name himself a Roman. With criticism of his church so harsh and widespread, it showed a staunchness that was wholly admirable.

Yet all this mattered less than another thing of which she was convinced: that in ruling his heart she would rule him altogether. There were women who enjoyed subservience to men; far fewer in these enlightened days, but they existed. Mrs Wilkinson very clearly was such; but she, Sarnia, was not. If she were to marry Michael she would pay due respect to his standing as a man, but she would not bow down to him as though he were an idol – nor would he expect it. She smiled to herself. No, she was confident he would expect no such thing.

She permitted her thoughts to stray from his character to his person. His way of smiling crookedly, like a boy … She had a sudden longing for the sight of him, followed sharply by the realization of how long it would be before they met again. She had grown used to their daily encounters. Even during the week in which they had not been speaking to one another she had seen him pass on the stairs, and known he was in the room below.

There was no doubt that her liking could without much difficulty pass into love: she felt she was a little in love with him already. Perhaps their separation would serve a purpose in making her feelings clearer.

She stretched, smothering a yawn. It was warm in the carriage and she was weary from the excitement of the day. She was glad she and Michael had made up, and glad of his proposal. For the rest there was no hurry. There was a holiday to look forward to. A strange island, and yet her birthplace, lay only a few hours' journey away. She let herself drowse in sleepy anticipation.

The transfer from train to mail packet was effected without difficulty, which was just as well, for by that time she could scarcely keep her eyes open. Mr Jelain took them to the main cabin, where the steward provided reclining chairs. Sarnia settled in hers and in almost no time was asleep. She was awakened briefly to feel the ship shuddering underneath her, followed by a dull clunking sound. The paddles, she realized, and drifted back into slumber.

When she awakened again it was light, and Mrs Jelain was smiling down at her.

'The steward is bringing tea, *chérie*. And then it will be time for your first sight of Guernsey.'

IV

Sarnia went up on deck with the Jelains and stared about her. The morning was blue and still, the sea a deeper blue, with only the gentlest of swells on which the mail packet rocked, her paddles silent and motionless.

They were less than half a mile from shore and she gazed with eager interest at the island. The sight it presented was captivating. Behind the small harbour a town stretched away on either side and up the slopes of the hills behind. At the centre the houses, tall and thin, were packed close, but further off there were villas with gardens, a patchwork of white and green bathed in the slanting rays of early sunlight.

Mrs Jelain asked: 'How do you like your first view of St Peter Port?'

Sarnia said: 'I don't think I have ever seen a place so pretty.'

Her praise delighted them. Mrs Jelain said:

'That is our house.' She pointed to the northern outskirts of the town. 'On the hill there. No, a little further that way. Just above the group of small houses – do you see?'

Although a long way off she could see that it was a big white house, built in the Regency style, with a long terraced garden beneath it and an imposing conservatory to one side, reflecting silver sunlight. The Jelains pointed out other landmarks: the town church, the Assembly Rooms, higher up the square shapes of Elizabeth College and Castle Carey. Then they directed her attention the other way, towards the offshore islands, identifying them by name: Herm, Jethou, further off the long line of Sark with the sun above it, and south and north the shadowy outlines of Jersey and Alderney.

'We are at the centre of things here,' Mr Jelain said. 'Jersey and Alderney are both nearer to France, but we are better off where we are.'

'Can one see France?' Sarnia asked.

'Sometimes, but at present the haze hides it. You would see the coast along there, to the north of Herm. Near enough – too near for our liking. We have had enough trouble with the French in the past, and with this new Napoleon they are making so much of we may have trouble again before long.'

'Do not mind now about politics,' Mrs Jelain said. 'The boatmen are coming out for us.'

A number of small boats were being rowed out from the shore. Mrs Jelain cried:

'Look, there is Edmund!'

She waved, and from one of the boats a figure waved back. This was the son she had spoken of so often and so fondly, their only child. Sarnia looked at him with great curiosity as the boat drew nearer. A first impression of dark hair and side-whiskers became a man who seemed not handsome, but not ill looking: thick-set, heavy of jaw, somewhat swarthy. No, she decided, not at all ill looking.

The boat drew in under the lee of the packet and the young man seized hold of the rope ladder that hung down from the deck. He climbed up, powerfully but without haste, and hauled himself on board. His mother embraced him, while his father watched and smiled: a happy picture of family reunion. Then his mother drew him towards Sarnia.

'And see, we have brought you your pretty cousin, as I promised you. Do you not thank us for such a gift from London?'

He was of middle height, a couple of inches shorter than Michael. His voice was deeper.

'I am most grateful for it.' He held her hand with steady firmness. 'I am very glad indeed to meet you, cousin Sarnia.'

The journey to shore was scarcely comfortable, the boat being crowded with passengers and their luggage. Mrs Jelain commented that it was disgraceful, and due to the fact that the boatmen worked on a fixed tariff, packing in as many people as possible for each trip.

'But you are fortunate,' Edmund said to Sarnia, 'in arriving on so calm a day. When I returned from England last year our boat was well-nigh swamped by the breakers.'

The landing place, Deschamps Causeway at the Roque St Julien, had a number of carriages waiting nearby. The Jelains' was a landau, old but well painted and equipped, and in it they were taken first along the paved road of the Esplanade and then uphill by way of a winding narrow thoroughfare. The condition of this road was not good to start with, and got steadily worse. They were jolted considerably despite the coachman's care, and once Sarnia found herself thrown into Edmund's embrace. She was aware of the strength of his arms as he set her back in her place.

The Jelains grumbled about the potholes in a manner that spoke of long familiarity. Sarnia was more interested in staring at her new surroundings. There were cottages clustered together higgledy-piggledy, mean in size but with exteriors bright in washes of pastel shades: pink, yellow, blue. Many had garden plots dense with summer flowers. An old man, sunning himself on a low flat-topped wall, straightened up and touched his forehead as the carriage passed.

They turned off at last, between stone pillars, into a drive that ran beside a large well-kept lawn. Their progress was smooth now, with red gravel crackling under the wheels and the hooves of the horses. Servants were assembled to greet them at the main entrance, headed by a small plump woman in black silk. There was a high portico with wide stone steps, newly scrubbed, and beyond the open door the hall, sunlit from a round window at its end.

Inside Sarnia had a confused impression of elegant polished furniture, oil paintings chiefly of seascapes, and big vases filled with flowers. She was introduced to the plump woman in black, who was Mrs Perret the housekeeper and who went on to talk volubly to Mrs Jelain, partly in English and partly in a strange sort of

French. In the end Mrs Jelain raised a hand to check the flow.

'*Ça suffit,* Perret. Later will do. Miss Lorimer will want to go to her room and refresh herself before breakfast. Is the girl here?'

From somewhere in the ruck of servants the housekeeper produced a tiny thin creature in maid's uniform that was too big for her. She made clumsy bobs, first to Mrs Jelain and then to Sarnia.

'This is Marie, mam'selle,' the housekeeper said. 'She is to be your maid. She knows little English, but if you speak slowly she will take your purpose. Come to me if you have any complaint of her.'

Mrs Perret led the way upstairs, with Marie bringing up the rear. There was a wide landing on the first floor, with more flowers in a Chinese vase and doors leading off on either side. At the end of the landing, the housekeeper opened a door on the right.

'I trust you will be comfortable here, mam'selle.'

The room was three times the size of the one she had occupied at Red Lion Square. The floor was well carpeted, the walls recently papered in crimson, and the bed had a counterpane of red silk. On a marble wash-stand hot water steamed in a ewer beside a large porcelain basin patterned with roses. There were two high windows, one of them open: the muslin stirred in the faintest of breezes, bringing in the smell of summer and also the smell of the sea.

Sarnia went to the window and looked out. Beneath was a walled flagged area set with urns in which shrubs grew; below that several terraces of lawn grass, bordered with flowers, down to a hedge that appeared to hide the kitchen garden. A long way down she saw a tall granite wall, which presumably marked the border of the Jelain land.

And out and down, much further down, the silver and blue sea, stretching to an horizon broken by the prettily irregular shapes of the offshore islands. She tried to recall the names she had been told, but could not. It did not matter: there would be time enough to learn them.

A little cough behind her reminded her of Marie, who had

stayed when the housekeeper went downstairs. She turned to look at her. What a child she was – she could scarcely be more than twelve. And how was she to communicate with a girl who, it was already apparent, knew almost no English? But still … a maid of her own – and a room with such a view! These were luxuries indeed.

After breakfast Mrs Jelain insisted that Sarnia should retire for the morning. Sarnia protested that she was not fatigued, that she had slept enough during the crossing, but Mrs Jelain would have none of it. They had friends calling that evening, and Sarnia must be at her best. She added, smiling:

'Not that you would not look delightfully pretty under any circumstances, my dear, but you do need the rest. I am going to bed myself, and have ordered luncheon to be held back.'

Sarnia went to her room but did not undress. She did not feel at all tired and thought that later she would slip out and explore the garden. Meanwhile she would lie down for a while on top of the bed. She stretched out and listened to the sounds that came through the open window. Birds calling – thrushes, blackbirds, a chattering finch – and a man's voice in distant song: perhaps a gardener. The creak of a wheel, the thudding of an axe on wood. Noises dulled and made drowsy by the somnolent warmth of the day. And something behind them? The faintest of murmurs of the surrounding sea – or was she imagining it? She strained her ears to catch it, told herself that she would get up and go to the window to see how far off were the waves … and came sharply to an awareness of Marie's thin white face peering down into hers. The girl prattled meaninglessly in her native tongue, the *patois*. Sarnia understood nothing of it until the girl pointed to the watch on her breast. It was half past one, and she was being called for luncheon!

She saw the garden in the afternoon in Mrs Jelain's company. It was excellently tended, and she enthused over the flowers and plants which were magnificent in both size and colour. A fuchsia bush, hung with huge bells of scarlet and purple, was more than the height of a man. She said:

'It is scarcely believable that it should grow so big.'

'That is the work of our Guernsey soil and our Guernsey sun. But I am prouder of the verbena.'

It was more a tree than a bush, close on twenty feet in height. They went on to camellias almost as tall, and an enormous twisted fig tree, speckled with tiny green fruits.

Sarnia said: 'I perceive why you are so proud of your island. There is good reason for it.'

'Indeed, there is! But not my island, *chérie* – it is yours as well. You have a birthright to claim. Come, let us go up into the conservatory. There is a vine there of equal age with you: I recall it was put in in the very year of your birth. It is a Black Homburg, and bears magnificently. You would not believe how many pounds we took from it last autumn.'

As they climbed granite steps to the higher level, Sarnia thought about that year of 1832. The Jelains seemed even more amiable here than they had been in London, and she had an impulse to question Mrs Jelain further about the events, until recently not even guessed at, which were still a mystery to her. There must be so much which Mrs Jelain could tell her.

But she still hesitated. For all the kindness the Jelains had shown there remained an obscure sense of disloyalty at the prospect of discussing her mother with one of them. She was telling herself that this was silly – that she ought to know about the past and if the tale proved in any way critical of her mother she could refuse to listen – when their walk was interrupted. A figure waved from the terrace above, and Edmund came down to join them.

His mother, smiling, said: 'You could have waited, since we are going up. I am proposing to show Sarnia the conservatory.'

The looks she directed to her son, Sarnia noticed, were different from those with which she favoured Mr Jelain. Both had indulgence in them, but to Edmund she showed much greater warmth, and enormous pride. Speaking, she put a hand on his arm.

'The exercise will do me good. I meant to have joined you earlier, but I had to take Chevalier to be shod.' He explained to Sarnia: 'One of my horses, and spirited. The farrier is nervous of him and so I cannot send him with a groom – I must be at hand to quieten him.'

'What an absurdity,' Mrs Jelain said, '– a farrier frightened of horses!'

Edmund laughed. 'Absurd, indeed, but he shoes well. And Chevalier in a mettlesome mood can alarm more than poor old Ozanne.'

'That is true.' Mrs Jelain said to Sarnia : 'The man who had him sold him to Edmund because he could not cope with him. I was against the purchase: I have only one son, and he has only one neck. But he is very difficult to move from a course he has embarked on.'

'He had been ill-used,' Edmund said. 'He only wanted a determined mind and a firm hand. Once mastered he was amenable enough, and I enjoyed the mastering.'

He spoke with satisfaction and also, Sarnia guessed, with justification. She had briefly felt the strength of his hands and she was sure he had a determined mind. They were good qualities in a man.

The people who came in the evening were friends of the senior Jelains, and of their generation. Sarnia realized she was being shown off, and felt some embarrassment but more amusement. This, and the close examination she received, was simply part of the curiosity and intimacy which one might expect in the narrow circle of intercourse of a small island like this.

The special character of the life here also featured in the conversation she had with Advocate Martell, the Jelains' family attorney, a thin stooping man with heavy gold spectacles and a drawling but precise voice. Superficially, he said, Guernsey was very like England in its ways, as was natural when one considered the interflow of trade and visitors between island and mainland. But beneath that apparent likeness, the island had its own character and identity, not easily apprehended by a stranger.

'Much lies beneath the surface,' he said. 'Like our wine cellars.'

'Wine cellars?'

'You must get Mr Jelain to show you his. They extend a very long way under that pleasant lawn outside. And that is a part of what I mean about the hidden differences between Guernsey and England. Because the cellars of St Peter Port – *les caves* – derive from our wild and adventurous past. During the wars with the French, privateering was a favourite occupation of the Guernseymen. Many fortunes were made in that business. And when spirits and wines were captured and brought here, they had to build underground vaults to keep them. These proved excellent for the purpose of maturing, and after peace was made with the French wines were still shipped here, this time in trade. Since England maintained a high duty against such commodities, there was a profit to be made from maturing wines here and reshipping them to England.'

Sarnia protested: 'But there would be no advantage, except … You mean, by smuggling?'

He said, smiling: 'Just so. Smuggling brought in probably ten times the money privateering had done. So beneath these charming houses, built in the fashion of Georgian England, there are commonly cellars of a size that on the mainland you would not be likely to find on the premises of anyone but a wine merchant or a duke. And there is many a prosperous and respectable citizen who came by his gold in dubious fashion. Not that anyone would be coarse enough to remind him of it.'

Sarnia wondered if Mr Jelain might be one of those, since his cellars had been spoken of. It was difficult to picture him rolling barrels off a boat by moonlight in some deserted cove, even as a younger man. She could more easily envisage Edmund doing it. But it was quite silly: they were both far too respectable.

They were joined by another man, some years older than the lawyer. He was in his middle sixties, and had sparse white hair above a face that had a curious kind of hollowness, the sharply jutting chin and craggy brow seeming to collapse inwards towards a strangely small nose. In a thin voice, he said:

'Edward, we know it is your custom to monopolize feminine beauty, but I will not permit it tonight.' He took Sarnia's hand. 'I should have needed no introduction to you, my dear young lady. I would know you anywhere for your mother's daughter.'

Sarnia said quickly: 'You knew my mother, sir?'

'Very well. May I introduce myself, Miss Lorimer? Robert Falla, physician. At your service now as I was nineteen years ago, when I brought you into the world.'

V

A FEW DAYS after Sarnia's arrival on the island a ball was held at the Assembly Rooms, to mark the departure of the present garrison. Mrs Jelain had altogether bought her three dresses in London, and the day before the ball insisted that she put them all on in turn, so that she might judge which was likely to produce the best effect.

'After all, this will be your first appearance in society – the Governor will be there, and Colonel Bell, the garrison commander – and we must spare no effort.'

Amused, Sarnia said: 'Does it matter so much, Aunt Jeanne? I am only a visitor here.'

'Do girls not take a ball seriously any longer? We are coming to a sad state, if so.'

'I have not been much used to attending balls. The circumstances of our life …'

'I was joking, my love. I know how much you have sacrificed to the care of your mother.'

'It was no sacrifice.'

'At any rate, not grudged. *That* I perceive. But you are very young and it is right that you should enjoy yourself. And while you are pretty enough not really to need adornment, it is exactly the adornment which is not needed that produces the best effect. Most eyes anyway would turn your way when you go in – I insist that all should.'

So Sarnia paraded in each of the three dresses while Mrs Jelain surveyed her with a critical eye. She said at last: 'They are all delightful, but I *think* the *pou de soie*.'

It was in *gris poussière,* the bodice sprinkled with little rosebuds, very tight at the waist. Mrs Jelain said:

'Grey is a good colour for someone with such fair hair and so fine a complexion. A pale girl would not be able to carry it off, but you have no worries on that score. And some real rosebuds in your hair, I think, and the black mantelet. Black is much the most *comme-il-faut* this season. Let me see you with the mantelet. Walk to the window. Turn. And again. Yes, you handle it very creditably. You have a natural grace.'

She sat back with a sigh of satisfaction.

'There will not be a girl to come near you – make no doubt of it.'

It was true that Sarnia had had relatively small acquaintance with balls and routs. She had affected a little to despise them, probably as a means of easing the deprivation. But Mrs Jelain's enthusiasm could not help but communicate itself to her, and when the carriage came round to the front door she was as eager as anyone could desire and confident, from the latest of a score or more of final inspections in her looking glass, that she was well equipped for the occasion.

The landau took them down the pot-holed hill, and along the broader and better road between town and sea, before turning uphill just short of the church and joining the queue of vehicles waiting to unload their passengers.

The Assembly Rooms were housed in an imposing building of grey granite on the north side of the market square. Uniformed soldiers formed lines about the entrance, serving as a guard of honour and keeping away the common people who pressed close against their backs as the guests arrived. They commented in loud voices, but in the *patois*. She could not understand them but the tone, in her own case at least, seemed admiring.

Mr Jelain presented her to the garrison colonel who, with his lady, was stationed on the landing where the broad sweep of stairs became two, turning back on either side.

He said: 'Welcome to the island, Miss Lorimer. Or welcome back, as I hear is more appropriate. We were in any event sorry to be leaving, but your arrival makes our going a matter of even greater regret. May I have the second quadrille? I ask it now because I know your card will be filled within five minutes of your going in to the ball room.'

In fact it was more like a quarter of an hour before she awarded the last vacancy to one of a pair of officers who solicited her together. She would have preferred the second, who was more handsome, but had to refuse him. The regret over that was tiny; she was enjoying herself too much. Time passed very quickly. She could scarcely believe it when Edmund came to claim her for the supper dance.

'Well done,' he said. 'Apart from officers you have danced with a de Sausmarez, an Andros, a de Havilland and two Careys.'

She was dancing with him now, and finding that he waltzed well. She shook her head.

'I am sure I do not recall their names.'

'Do not let them hear you say so. Their names are the most important things about them.'

'You are unkind. I found them all charming.'

'That is not unkindness. I was being respectful. They would say as much themselves.'

'But you exaggerate. I suppose family ranking must be important in any small community, but I am sure they do not take it as seriously as you suggest.'

He smiled. 'You do not know the island yet. It is not so long that the Jelains have been admitted to occasions such as this. And there are many in the Forties who would turn the clock back if they could.'

'The Forties?'

'The Careys, de Sausmarezs, d'Aurignys and the rest. It is the name they gave themselves because there were, they reckoned, no more than forty families with whom they might condescend to mix. The Jelains belong to the Sixties, whom the Forties see as common pushing people of no background.'

She liked the dry tone in which he spoke; it seemed to indicate good sense and wit. She said, laughing:

'A sad story of division! But who prevailed on them to lower the barriers and let you Sixties in? Were these noble savages converted at last to Christian principles – by Mr Wesley and his evangelicals perhaps?'

'Not Mr Wesley. They find him suitable to preach to their servants, no more than that. No, it was a far more powerful agent.'

'Go on. You interest me.'

'By money, simply.'

'Good heavens! Do you mean that the Sixties have paid for their admission to society?'

'Not payment. But the power of money works everywhere with great effect, does it not? And though, despite what the Roman said, men affect to find a distasteful smell in newly made money, time both deodorizes and sanctifies it. One generation spurns the *nouveau riche*, but the next accepts him – woos him, if he is rich enough.'

Sarnia shook her head. 'You are a cynic.'

'Not at all. A cynic deplores the condition he describes.'

'And you do not? I cannot believe it.'

'I merely observe. I pass no judgement. The way the world goes is the way the world goes. In the interplay of human affairs, many things have power. Family. A man's strength of arm.' His eyes rested on hers. 'Beauty such as yours, my dear Sarnia, has power. But none of these is one tenth as powerful as money. The evidence is undeniable.'

'But I deny it. Money only has power insofar as men permit it to dominate their thoughts. It is possible to be happy with very little. It may also be possible to be happy with much, but I know nothing of that. We are told, at any rate, that the love of money is the root of all evil.'

'You speak warmly, cousin.'

'With conviction, certainly. My mother had very little money, but we were happy together and felt no lack. We had friends, and did not mind what their names were.'

'And do you still have them, now that your mother is dead and you have even less money – so little that you were obliged to take employment?'

It was a charge which pierced her defences, but she said stoutly:

'They are there if I should need them. My life has greatly changed, and I have removed to another part of London.'

'And if it should change once more – if you were to be rich, say – would you not acquire different friends, more suited to your status?'

'I have no thought of being rich.'

'You might become so, despite yourself.'

'Through my father, do you mean? But I would not take money from him, even if he were to offer it.'

'What if that beauty of yours should command a rich man, and so his wealth, by way of marriage?'

'We will not discuss wild improbabilities.'

'You are too modest.'

'It is only that I am amazed you should argue against your own judgement.'

'How so?'

'You have said that the power that can be exercised by good looks, supposing I should have them, is less than one tenth of that which money commands. So although such a one might stand up with me in a dance, and pay nice compliments, his offer of marriage will go to the daughter of someone as rich as himself – or preferably richer.'

Edmund laughed. 'I am no match for your wit.'

He was, she thought, a trifle disconcerted. Whirling her round, he said:

'And I confess myself refuted. I stated a generality, to which there must always be exceptions. Your beauty and charm can exercise a power greater than any fortune. I have no doubt you will have dozens of splendid offers. I trust in your good sense, which is equally conspicuous, to refuse them all.'

'But why should I refuse them, since money is the only thing that matters?'

'Because you say it is not. You cannot argue against your own judgment either. And for my part, I am won over. I will not quibble as to whether your beauty or your argument had the greater force: I accept them both as supreme. Let me take you in to supper: even the rarest beauty is better served by being nourished.'

It was half an hour after supper that Sarnia was approached by a young man she had not previously noticed. She was confident she would have remembered him had she done so, for he was above average in height and had a long handsome face of a distinctive character. He bowed to her.

'Miss Lorimer – for I have inquired your name – I beg leave to introduce myself. Peter d'Aurigny, at your service.'

'I am honoured, sir.'

He was a little dishevelled and his cravat was awry, a little flushed in complexion. That could have come about from the exertions of dancing. It could also, and she judged it more probable, have arisen from drink.

'I am a late arriver in this company,' he said. 'I was detained, on business. Though, to be frank with you, Miss Lorimer, I did not then regard my absence as a loss. In fact I was half minded not to come at all. And that would have been an immense pity; for I should have missed the opportunity of meeting and dancing with the first young lady of true loveliness to grace this company in more weary months than I care to remember.'

His smile was an engaging one which excused his precipitance and even went some way towards making his intoxication supportable. Sarnia said:

'Thank you for the compliment, Mr d'Aurigny. I am glad to have made your acquaintance, too; though I am afraid I shall not have the pleasure of standing up with you.'

'How not?'

She showed him her card. 'Because I am fully engaged.'

He took the card from her and studied it for a moment in silence. Then he said:

'The next is a mazurka. That will do capitally.'

She said, trying to be patient: 'But you see I am engaged for it. I believe my partner is approaching now.'

'Ah, yes. Ogier. He dances abominably.' As the other reached them, he said: 'I am afraid there has been some confusion, Ogier. Always likely to happen with these damn' cards and the press of people. Miss Lorimer is engaged to me for this dance.'

Ogier looked uncertain. He was not a very prepossessing young man, having a slack posture and a lumpy white face. As between the two, Sarnia's preference was decidedly for the newcomer. But she said, smiling, to Ogier:

'It is Mr d'Aurigny who is in error, Mr Ogier. It is your name which is written down for the next dance, not his.'

D'Aurigny shook his head. 'One does not live one's life by little white cards.'

He produced a pencil from his pocket and scored heavily through Ogier's name, scrawling his own above it. 'There,' he said, handing back the card, 'we have the record straight.'

'I am *afraid* …'

D'Aurigny addressed himself to Ogier.

'One of these infernal mix-ups, as I said. A pity, but there it is. Good evening to you.'

He spoke with casual arrogance, the confidence of a man who has no scrap of doubt that he will have his own way. Ogier's corresponding indecision persisted for no more than a moment or two; then he bowed quickly to Sarnia and walked off. Sarnia called after him: 'Mr Ogier …', but he gave no sign of hearing.

'An abominable dancer, as I say,' d'Aurigny said. 'I lay no claim to excellence myself, but I promise you I am doing you a favour by exchanging for him.'

She stared at him, feeling her face go white.

'You do me no favours of any kind, sir. There is only one you can do, which is to grant me freedom from your company. I beg that you will do so without delay.'

'You have spirit as well as beauty, Miss Lorimer,' he said admiringly. 'But I assure you that quite apart from his dancing Ogier is a detestable fellow. It astonishes me that he should have presumed to engage you – even that he should have demeaned this assembly with his presence.'

She remembered what Edmund had said about the attitude such families as the d'Aurignys had to the rest of island society. The present incident clearly reflected it. She was not sure whether she was angrier with d'Aurigny for his insolence or with the wretched Ogier for submitting to it. Turning away, she said:

'If I am not to be permitted to dance with a partner of my choice, I am most certainly not to be forced into accepting one whose conduct I find discourteous and hateful. Goodbye, sir.'

'I will not accept that dismissal. If I have offended you, Miss Lorimer, I humbly beg pardon. It was no part of my intention.'

She remained silent, her head averted. D'Aurigny went on: 'You are with the Jelains, I believe? Shall I plead with Mrs Jelain to soften your obduracy?'

His tone was not sneering, but her resentment provided the sneer. To a d'Aurigny the Jelains were to be classed with the Ogiers, as people whose presence depended on the whims of their superiors. Mrs Jelain was presumed to be flattered by the thought that such as he would deign to notice her visiting cousin. She said in a low, intense voice:

'Go away.'

The fiddles struck up. He put out his hand towards her; to take hers, she thought, and pull her by force into the dance. The notion of such a contact, of the arrogance from which it stemmed, was unbearable. Turning back to him she saw the beginnings of a smile on his face, before her hand came up and slapped him ringingly on the cheek.

The sound seemed to echo through the room. The fiddles faltered, then continued, but eyes turned from all round in their direction. D'Aurigny stood stock still. His hand was extended, holding the card; and she realized she had been mistaken over his intention. He had not been trying to draw her into the dance, but returning the card.

They stared at each other while others stared at them. His face, too, was white. He said, in a low voice but clearly: 'I beg pardon, Miss Lorimer.'

Then he turned and made through the press of people towards the door.

VI

Edmund said: 'It will be the talk of the island by tomorrow. It must be so already. A d'Aurigny slapped in the Assembly Rooms! There has been nothing like it in living memory.'

They had returned from the ball and were in the parlour of the Jelains' house. Mrs Jelain and Sarnia were drinking chocolate, the two men toddies.

'He is wild, that one,' Mrs Jelain said. 'The younger son.' She nodded significantly to her husband. 'And you recall the history. But I would not have believed he would insult a lady in public.'

'It was my fault partly,' Sarnia said.

Mrs Jelain looked at her. 'How so?'

She explained how she had misread his intention. Mrs Jelain regarded her with, she felt, some unease.

'But he was drunk?'

'I would not say so. He had taken drink, clearly.' They waited for her to go on. 'I could not bear his manner to Mr Ogier: it was unpardonably rude.'

Mrs Jelain pulled a face. 'The Ogiers are distantly related to us, but it is not a connection that we maintain. And Stephen Ogier is not of good character. He is not at all well liked.'

'The fact that a man is not well liked is surely no justification for treating him with insolence?' Mrs Jelain shrugged in what might have been agreement. 'And the insolence extended to me. What possible right could he have to score out a name on my card, and put his own down?'

'That is the crux of it, Mother,' Edmund said. 'He was impudent to Sarnia, and she was right to punish him for it.'

'Of course, I agree.' Mrs Jelain sipped her chocolate. 'It is just a pity it was so public.'

'I do not see it,' Edmund said. There was a note of satisfaction in his voice. 'And he walked away, accepting the rebuke. Everyone could see he was at fault. There it is, and there's an end of it.'

Mr Jelain clutched his rummer, more than half asleep, while Mrs Jelain and Edmund discussed the incident. Mrs Jelain, Sarnia was sure, earnestly wished it had not taken place. The d'Aurignys were not just of the Forties, but possibly the chief family of that elite. She did not care for the thought of offending them, however great the justification. Sarnia felt a growing remorse over her own conduct. The man was unpleasant and had been rude; but she had been rash. She said:

'I am sorry if my part in this has been a cause of embarrassment to you, Aunt Jeanne. After all your kindness, it is the last thing I would wish. If there is anything I can do to make amends …'

Edmund interrupted her. 'What you did was needed, cousin – required, in fact. You slapped him, and he richly deserved it.' It was more than satisfaction – exultance almost. 'It is past time the d'Aurignys were brought down a peg.'

Mrs Jelain too said: 'My dear Sarnia, you must not for a moment think I mean to be critical of you! There can be no question of that. He is a quite irresponsible young man, and you did no more than was proper.'

She crossed the room and took Sarnia's hands.

'But you are tired, and want your rest. We ought all of us to be in bed.'

Sarnia was sitting in the garden with Mrs Jelain the following afternoon, on the lawn of the top terrace, when Mrs Perret brought out Peter d'Aurigny's card. Mrs Jelain was flustered by the news of his call. She said to Sarnia:

'My dear, I suppose you will see him … or will you? If you are deeply offended – there is no obligation, of course … It is a decent

gesture on his part – though no more than one would require …
but if you feel …'

Sarnia said: 'Of course I will see him, Aunt Jeanne.'

She did not go in but received him in the garden. He carried a vast bouquet of pink roses.

'I am grateful for your indulgence, Miss Lorimer, in allowing me to offer a more formal apology.'

'It is no indulgence.'

'Will you accept these few flowers?'

'Why, thank you.'

'And my heartfelt assurance of regret for my conduct.'

'Of course.'

'My behaviour was boorish and unworthy; your – your reproof justified. Entirely justified.'

She had thought she would soften towards him when he made his apology; and perhaps admit her own error in misreading his movement towards her on the dance floor. But the stiffness of his speech, the absence of any real contrition in his tone, changed her disposition. When he said his behaviour had been unworthy, her mind supplied 'of a d'Aurigny', and saw in the confession a further boast. When he hesitated before 'reproof', she fancied an implied criticism of herself – a hint that her own action had been unladylike.

She said quietly: 'There is no need to discuss it, I fancy, Mr d'Aurigny. As far as I am concerned, the incident is closed. I am grateful to you for calling. Now, if you will excuse me, I believe Mrs Jelain wishes to see me.'

D'Aurigny bowed. 'I will not detain you, Miss Lorimer. I hope I have the opportunity of meeting you again, under happier circumstances.'

She nodded her acknowledgement. 'So do I, sir. Good day to you.'

This ended the business, she thought, but that evening, while she was dressing before dinner, Mrs Perret knocked at her door. She was panting from the haste with which she had climbed the stairs.

'I would have sent Marie, mam'selle, but you would never understand her. Mrs Jelain is anxious you should join her in the drawing room as soon as possible. The General has called.'

'The General?'

Mrs Perret looked surprised that elucidation should be called for.

'General d'Aurigny. Mrs Jelain begs you to attend on them without delay.'

There was no mistaking the urgency of the message. Sarnia made reasonable haste with her toilette and went down. In the drawing room, Mrs Jelain said:

'Ah, this is Miss Lorimer, General – our Sarnia. My dear, General d'Aurigny has done us the honour of calling.'

It was fairly clear that this was the first occasion on which the General had paid such attention to the Jelain house, and that she was somewhat overwhelmed by it. Sarnia looked at the General with interest.

He was in his late sixties or early seventies, as tall as his son but not otherwise resembling him. His features were coarser and rougher, the nose large and wide-pored, ears outstanding from his head. In fact his face gave an impression not so much of ugliness as indiscipline, as though the parts did not belong to the whole. But there was certainly no indication of indiscipline in his bearing. He carried himself with military authority, and wore a suit of good grey cloth, impeccably styled.

Having been introduced to her, he said abruptly:

'I understand my son Peter has called on you, Miss Lorimer?'

'Yes, sir.'

'And humbly begged your pardon, I trust?'

'Very handsomely.'

'Good. But I did not wish to leave it there. I have given him a roasting, I can tell you. A man who goes into company the worse for drink, blots not only his own reputation but his family's. And then to offer rudeness to a young lady – one newly come to the island, moreover – it is not easily pardonable. If you have condescended to do so, he is lucky beyond his deserts.'

She decided she liked him better than his son: much better. From the intonation he gave to 'family' she guessed he was equally conscious of its standing – most probably more so since he was its head – but she acquitted him of his son's cold arrogance. And she felt he had been genuinely distressed on her account; there was an honest indignation in his voice.

She said: 'It was nothing, sir, and I regret …'

He raised a hand. 'Miss Lorimer, it is not for you to express regrets, and I will not listen to any. You cuffed a drunken puppy and I applaud you for it, while bitterly sorry for the occasion. It marks your return to this island most unhappily. I can only hope that the consideration and respect which you will deservedly obtain from others may make up somewhat for my son's bad conduct.'

'The kindness I have had in Guernsey would make up for anything.'

'That is well said. I am glad to hear it. Let us hope that in time you will forget this unhappy beginning.'

She smiled. 'It is forgotten already, sir. But I shall not have all that much time.'

'How so?'

'I am only here for a few weeks, on holiday. But I know I shall enjoy them a great deal.'

The General looked surprised. 'I understood you had come to live in the island. I see I have been misinformed, and regret it. But regret more that our chances of making your acquaintance should be so much reduced. One may be assured my son's bad behaviour plays no part in this?'

Sarnia shook her head. 'None indeed.'

The General addressed himself to Mrs Jelain.

'You must bring her to the Manoir, ma'am, during her sojourn. I depend on you for it.'

'We shall be honoured, General.'

'On the contrary, ma'am. And now I trust you will excuse me. My housekeeper plagues me if I'm late for supper.' He shook his white head. 'I am not the man I was.'

VII

As a girl Sarnia had occasionally ridden a pony, hired from a livery stable at Maida Vale, but it was a recreation she had given up during the years of her mother's illness. The Jelains kept half a dozen horses and Edmund selected one for her use, a chestnut mare of nine or ten years, amiable rather than spirited. On the morning following the visit from the d'Aurignys he took her out, mounted himself on his black gelding, Chevalier.

Their way led uphill through the nearer outskirts of the town. They reached the College, loud with the cries of black-suited boys at their mid-morning break, and went on along a broader thoroughfare lined with gentlemen's houses. There had been rain in the night – Sarnia had wakened to hear it drumming against her window pane and the wind whistling up from the sea – but the day was fair for the moment. The muddy gutters on the sides of the road steamed in the sun's rays, and the wind had dropped to a pleasant breeze. Clouds scudded across blue sky, coming from over the brow of the hill up which the horses presently laboured.

Pointing upwards, Edmund said:

'We have not done with the rain, with the wind in that quarter. I cannot guarantee you will not get a wetting.'

'I do not mind.' She breathed in fresh air: the sea lay far behind and below them but she fancied it still had the sharp tang of salt in it. 'I enjoy rain. One would not want continual sunshine.'

'Would you not? Are you not troubled by the thought of riding home in wet clothes?'

'Not providing one can change out of them directly, and put on fresh linen.'

He laughed. 'You are most practical! But unless we go deep

into the country we are unlikely to suffer too bad a drenching. There is usually a cottage in reach, and the country people are always happy to provide shelter for the traveller.'

'I can believe that. It is a friendly island.'

'Any place would be friendly to a guest such as yourself. But we do take some pride in the reputation.'

The road passed over the brow of the hill between two large houses, and ran fairly steeply down the other side. The houses here were smaller and gave way to a tangle of cottages with open country beyond. But before that Edmund directed them along a lane to the left. Almost at once they were surrounded by fields, both cultivated and pasture. She saw sheep, and chocolate-and-cream cows contentedly grazing.

'The cows are tethered,' she observed. 'Are they a wild breed that would otherwise break through fences and stray?'

'There is nothing wild about our Guernsey cattle. It is an economy the farmers practise. The cow crops the area of grass in which it is tethered right down to the roots, and then the farmer's wife, or one of his children, moves it to another patch. It means more cattle can be fed to the acre than is usual in England; and so our farmers, though their holdings may be small, are better off than most.'

They rode for a time in silence. She said, after a while:

'Edmund – you are acquainted with my father?'

His horse snorted, bucking at some real or fancied hazard, and he was forced to rein him in. Patting his neck, he said: 'Your father? Yes, I know him. But it is some while since I saw him. Few people have done in recent years. He lives a recluse's life.'

'And is in poor health?'

'Yes.'

'As you know, I was unaware of his existence even, until your mother visited me. She said she came as his ambassador. I recollect I asked her why my father had not written, once my Aunt Maria had told him of my whereabouts, if he wished to communicate with me. Your mother said he had no fluency in writing.'

'That is true. He can write his own name – well enough to sign bonds, at least. And he could probably write a few simple sentences, but it would be a heavy labour.'

'He could have *spoken* a letter, for someone else to put on paper.'

'I doubt if he would trust another to set down his business for him. He has a suspicious nature.'

'Is writing to a daughter lost for eighteen years *business*?'

Edmund laughed. 'To him, everything is!'

'Your mother also said he would hesitate to approach me through being unsure of my response.'

'That also fits. A suspicious man is a wary man. And he has pride. He would not like to expose himself to the possibility of a rebuff.'

They crossed a stream at the foot of a hill, fast running but so narrow that their horses need not wet their hooves. The path turned left, uphill again, passing a quarry with the quarryman's cottage sitting beside the same small brook. Children in shabby clothes stood outside: the girls curtseyed to them and a bigger boy pulled at his forelock. Edmund said with approval:

'Le Page teaches his children manners. Not all the labouring classes are so scrupulous.'

Sarnia said: 'Your mother has not spoken of my father since.'

'Has she not? But did you not make it plain the subject was distasteful to you – that loyalty to your mother's memory made it so?'

'I suppose I did. But still ... Do you think he knows that I have come here?'

Edmund's horse shied again. 'Whoah! Your father, you mean? He may do. I think it probable. He sees few people, but news travels fast on this island.'

'Yet no word has come from him.'

'Do you wish to make his acquaintance?'

She said emphatically: 'I do not.'

'Then so much the better.'

'But if he sent your mother to me ...'

'Did she say quite that? I would doubt it. She herself was curious about this long-lost relation and, being in London for the Exhibition, decided to seek you out. In the ordinary way it would have been no more than that: the satisfying of a natural inquisitiveness. It is a trait that ranks high in our island character. Then, having met you, your charm and beauty provided a second purpose – to bring you back here with her on holiday. Whether or not the first was justified, I entirely approve the second.'

Sarnia supposed this could have been the explanation: the claim to have come from her father a harmless deceit. Though, surely, unnecessary also?

The track they were following had climbed another hill and descended into the dip beyond. Here trees stood thick on either side, their branches rustling and twisting in the breeze, replacing sunlight with sombre shade. At the side of the lane a stone cattle trough, fed from a trickling fountain overhead, splashed in overflow. Edmund took his horse there.

'Chevalier is always thirsty – one would think he ate nothing but salted oats. Do you like it here?'

She nodded, looking along the pretty lane whose grassy borders were dotted with bright flowers.

'Providing the wolves do not come on us out of the wood, of course.'

She looked at him quickly. 'Wolves?'

'Have you not heard of the Guernsey wolves? The largest in the world, and the most savage.'

She half believed him, till he laughed.

'I must not tease you! No wolves, no wild beasts of any kind. None harmful, anyway. Only rabbits and hedgehogs and the like. No foxes, so our gentry have nothing to hunt. No poisonous snakes. Not even a toad to alarm a maiden, though they have them in Jersey. You will find this a sadly tame place, all in all.'

'I am glad of it. I have never thought romantic savageness a thing to desire.'

'Nor I,' Edmund said. 'We see eye to eye on that. Neither

savageness nor privation. It is time we turned homewards if we are not to be late for luncheon.'

An invitation to a dance the following evening was waiting when she got back, and another was brought that afternoon for the evening of Thursday, three days hence. They were both at private houses – with a dozen couples at one and half as many again at the second – and she enjoyed them more than the glittering ball at the Assembly Rooms. The informality was greater, providing more chance to talk with people of her own age. She had a feeling that, quite apart from the novelty of a stranger, a particular interest was shown in her; and guessed this was due to the incident involving Peter d'Aurigny. Edmund said it was famous by now.

She did not encounter d'Aurigny again, and was glad of that, but at the dance given by the Andros family she met his elder brother. He was about thirty and looked even older. He had more of the General's looks than Peter but quite lacked the General's fire. He talked of London: the people, places, occasions were all quite foreign and meaningless to her but he ground on boringly until her hostess came to rescue her.

Fortunately there were pleasanter and younger men. There were no officers – the 54th had recently gone and the 72nd not yet come into society – but others she found entertaining. Particularly one, John Brustin, dark and very handsome, with a cool mocking voice and a talent for witty gossip. He danced three times with her and tended to monopolize her in between, not at all to her displeasure.

Edmund put an end to this, detaching her from Brustin in a somewhat pointed fashion. He said:

'I cannot abide that fellow. He talks a great deal and says nothing worth listening to.'

She said, smiling: 'Do you think so? He was telling me of a game he proposed to make up, with a board and counters, about social life here. He would call it Guernsey Snakes and Ladders. Some of the directions were very amusing.'

'The Brustins are not what they were. They counted at one time but no longer do so. That is why he falls back on mockery.'

She allowed that there could be reason in what Edmund said: she had herself detected a flavour of bitterness in the other man's raillery. But she suspected there might be a personal aspect as well, arising from the pleasure she had shown she took in Brustin's company. That did not displease her, either.

As they danced, he said : 'You are having a tremendous success. They will call this Sarnia's summer.'

'It is a remarkable island,' she said, 'for flattery. In three weeks I shall have returned to London, and in four you will all have forgotten me completely.'

He looked closely at her. 'Not so. And perhaps we shall not so easily let you go. We Guernsey people are tenacious of our good fortune.'

A couple of days later they went riding again. It was a day like the first, fair but with an unsettled prospect, and the rain this time materialized in a sudden downpour. There was no cottage nearby, but Edmund pointed out a building at the far side of a field and they galloped towards it.

It was a hay barn of simple construction: four stout posts supported a sloping roof, and though the west end was planked against the prevailing wind the remaining sides were open. Sarnia took cover while Edmund tethered their horses. Returning he asked:

'Are you very wet?'

'Not very. And, as I said, I do not mind it.'

'You added: provided you can change into dry linen directly. But you may have some time to wait for that, by the look of the sky.'

The heavy shower had come unexpectedly, out of a sky that had a fair measure of cloud but did not seem particularly threatening. Within a short time, though, the outlook had changed. Only in the east were there fugitive patches of blue; overhead and out to the western horizon the sky was a sombre black-bruised grey, and the shower had turned into steady teeming rain.

The hay was packed high under the barn's roof and Edmund busied himself, drawing enough out to form a seat. Sarnia sat down when he had done, aware of the fragrance of the hay and the smells of growing things, sharpened by the rain. There had been no such freshness in London.

Edmund seated himself beside her. 'You face is very wet.' He drew a handkerchief from his sleeve. 'Let me dry that, at least.'

She did not look at him as his hand gently rubbed her skin with the linen. The action had a quality of intimacy that was made greater by their isolation, the lowering sky and pounding rain – even, she thought, by the scent of country life that surrounded them. He said:

'Do you still have kind words for the island, with the sun vanished, and the landscape dull and ugly instead of bright?'

'I do not think it ugly.'

'No. I do not believe you do. But after all, you are an islander. There is something in your blood which responds to it.'

She was silent. Sometimes his fingers rather than the kerchief, touched her face, a brushing soft in itself but with strength behind it. She kept her face averted and at last, kerchief and pretence abandoned, his fingers touched her fully, moving from cheek to chin to throat. She tried to pull away but his hand took her face and turned it, not roughly but with firmness, so that their eyes met. She stared into the dark, heavy-browed face.

'Sarnia,' he said, 'there is something I must say. You may think me impetuous, but I cannot help it.'

'No, cousin …'

The denial, she realized, could apply either to his last sentence or to what she knew would follow. Which had she meant herself? She was not quite sure. She tried again to draw away, but he held her.

'Before you came, I was curious about this long-lost pretty cousin my mother wrote of. Then, when I met you, curiosity became admiration – not just for your looks and agreeable ways, but for your nature. I have a deep regard for character in a woman. This was what I felt on that first day, but by the next my feelings were altering again. You cannot have been insensible of it. I greatly admire you, dear Sarnia, but I love you more.'

Her mind went back to a sunnier day and far different surroundings: the gardens of Lincoln's Inn. She saw Michael's face and felt a swift pang of guilt – she had still not written the letter she had promised him. And though she had not forgotten him, she had not, with all the distractions surrounding her, had him very much in mind.

To her silence, Edmund said:

'Perhaps I should not have approached you so precipitately, but I could not continue to hide my feelings. And there is so little time. In just a few weeks you are supposed to return to London. At least tell me you will not do that. There is nothing for you there, and everything here. This is your island as it is mine. And I love you dearly.'

His hand released her at last, but she did not turn away. The face before her was so much more real than the recollected image of Michael. She had told Michael, when he proposed to her, that there was no one she liked as well. She felt that was still true. In part she liked her swarthy cousin, in part was uneasy of him; and she had never been uneasy of Michael. But she was also aware of something different from liking and, it might be, more powerful: a response, uncertain still, to the strength of this man's will. And there was another thing, a kind of feeling of inevitability, as though she half glimpsed her future and knew that Edmund was destined to play a part in it. A very important part. She felt herself tremble, and did not know whether it was with anticipation or fear.

'Do you have no answer for me?' Edmund asked. 'At least tell me I have not offended you.'

He did not sound as though he believed he could have offended her. Was the feeling of inevitability no more than that – a reflection of his confidence? No man, she resolved again, should take her for granted: she would be mistress of her destiny. Yet she could not be angry with him.

She said: 'Of course not.'

'That is all I ask, for now. You need time to consider my proposal. For you understand, do you not, that this is what it is – that it is my dearest wish that you should accept me in marriage? But I will not press you. I will come to you another time for your answer.'

He was as good as his word and, as the rain streamed down, went on to talk of other things, as though the previous scene had never taken place. Sarnia was a little surprised but on the whole impressed. It showed a consideration for her, she thought, since they were trapped here; and a control of his emotions that was surely admirable.

The rain stopped and they jogged homewards across sodden fields. He pressed her hand when helping her to dismount, but said nothing. But the gaze he fixed on her had meaning in it.

VIII

That evening Sarnia sat down and penned a letter to Michael. She began it with a flurry of apologies and excuses, making her life on Guernsey even more hectic than it had been, and her need to fall in with the Jelains' plans more pressing. With that, though, her inspiration dwindled. It was difficult, if not impossible, to describe her present activities fully without making them seem a continual round of diversions and pleasure – pleasure from which Michael, sitting on his stool in Magpye Alley, was all too obviously excluded.

There was also a constraint arising from Edmund's declaration. Obviously she would not write of it to Michael – it could only give him needless anxiety and pain – but it cast a shadow over the recounting of the rest of her intercourse. All the sentences she tried to frame sounded wrong. She tried to imagine sitting with Michael in the chophouse, in their accustomed ease of conversation. But the scene, and he himself, seemed so very distant.

In the end she fell back on description of the physical features of her new surroundings, writing of the harbour, the other islands, the sea-girt Castle Cornet, the town with its gardens lined by poplars, and the fields and pretty lanes behind it. Even here she had to check her pen from an expression of too great enthusiasm.

He had asked three things of her: to write, not to forget him, and to return at the month's end – and she had promised all three. But she had let almost a week go by before writing, her recollection of him was less strong than he would have wished … and she was already under pressure to extend her stay. Michael had imagined a father seeking to hold on to a rediscovered daughter. The reality was, from his point of view, far worse: not a father but an intended lover.

In the end the letter, on reading it through, struck her as horribly insipid and dull. But she had somehow managed to fill four pages, and she had given him an address to which he could reply.

What she must also do, she decided as she sealed up the envelope, was to ensure that there was no further delay: if the letter failed to catch the following morning's mail packet to Southampton it must wait two days for the next. The mail, she had learned, was collected from the Post Office in the Commercial Arcade at eight o'clock. If she consulted Mrs Jelain she would be told to give the letter to a servant to take there. Instead, she resolved she would get up early and slip out herself: it was no more than fifteen minutes' walk and a pleasant exercise providing the weather was not unpleasant.

And to deliver the letter to the Post Office personally somehow eased her guilt at the delay in writing it. At least she would take no chances over its transmission.

The morning was fair and bright, with a slash of golden sunlight coming in through the window. Her watch told her it was half past seven. She had slept more soundly than she intended, but there was time still. She washed and dressed quickly, and went downstairs. The family were not yet stirring. She heard the sounds of the servants below stairs, but left the house without encountering anyone.

She walked briskly through the narrow streets, thankful that the sun and wind had repaired the damage of yesterday's rain: except for occasional muddy patches the roads were quite dry. Working people were abroad – it was like being back in London after the leisurely life of Les Colombelles – and several gave her friendly greeting, in English or *patois*.

She found the harbour very busy. It was a half tide and rising, and several sizeable ships were loading from the quay. The sea, which had been rough for some days, looked much quieter. The sun stood over the long plateau of Sark and the clouds were high and unthreatening. Mrs Jelain had talked of a picnic as soon as the weather settled. The prospect looked more promising.

67

She turned right near the arch of Cow Lane with its trickling stream and crossed the High Street towards the Commercial Arcade. This was an area of smart shops. The man who built it, according to Edmund, had bankrupted himself in the process, but now it was very prosperous. He had had no head for money, Edmund had explained, and without that a man was lost, whatever his capabilities as a builder.

A pillar-box stood beside the Post Office, but to make certain of the letter's proper transmission and not being sure of the accuracy of her watch, which gave the time as wanting a few minutes to eight, she went down the little passage and rapped, as the instruction suggested, at the closed ticket window. Nothing happened. She let some time go by and rapped again, with the same result. She rapped a third time, more loudly.

While listening for activity on the other side of the window she heard a sound from a different direction, and looked to see someone coming in from the Arcade. She first identified the figure, in the dim light of the passage, merely as a man; then started as she recognized him. It was Peter d'Aurigny.

He appeared to discover her at the same moment. He touched his hat without speaking and came up to the window. He gave the shutter a thunderous bang with his fist, which resulted immediately in the sound of movement on the other side, and very soon after the lifting of the shutter. From unpromisingly sour features the clerk produced an ingratiating grin.

'Mr d'Aurigny, sir – what can I do for you?'

'This lady has priority. Serve her first.'

Sarnia produced her letter. The clerk looked from it to the clock on the wall of his office.

'You will need an extra stamp for late posting on that one, miss.'

She started to fumble in her purse but d'Aurigny intervened. He said sharply:

'It is less than two minutes past eight now, and if your usual practice is any guide this lady has been waiting a good five minutes to attract your attention. Put the halfpenny stamp on the envelope yourself, if in fact it is needed.'

The clerk took the letter from her without a word, while d'Aurigny watched with satisfaction. Sarnia was obliged to thank him for his assistance, and had the impression that this satisfied him even more. Turning away she imagined his eyes on her back as she hurried down the passage.

In the open air of the Arcade she permitted herself a small snort of indignation. It was horrid to have had to express gratitude, even of a formal kind, to this odious man. On each one of their encounters his behaviour and manner had angered her, and in a way this last was the most infuriating of the three. The assistance he had forced on her had clearly been as much to demonstrate his own authority as anything else. And from the look in the clerk's subservient but surly eye she suspected it might in the practical sense have been no help at all. There was nothing to stop the man holding the letter back from the late collection without her being any the wiser.

Exercise, she hoped, might abate her choler. Turning from the Arcade she went up the High Street. It seemed very like a street in an English town, but she quickly discovered differences. In the smaller shops there were signs in French and prices in francs, and on many sides she heard the incomprehensible chatter of the *patois*. And while the steep winding cobbled street was quaintly pretty in its general aspect, she found that as far as cleanliness was concerned it was much inferior to the streets of London. Her petticoats would be badly stained; she would need to change her linen on returning to Les Colombelles.

The High Street forked, one road going down in the general direction of the sea while the other went upwards. She chose that one: it looked cleaner than the first and the shops seemed more attractive. But the way was even steeper and she was glad to pause where it broadened out at the top. There were larger buildings here. To her left stood the impressive edifice, in the island's familiar grey granite, which she knew to be the Royal Court House. She went to take a closer look as three men in lawyer's robes came down the main steps. One of them detached himself and approached her.

'Miss Lorimer.'

She could not immediately put a name to him; she had made so many acquaintances in the past days. While she hesitated, he said:

'Edward Martell, mam'selle, at your service.'

She knew him now – the Jelains' family attorney who had talked about the island's privateering and smuggling past – and apologized for her remissness. He waved that aside, and went on to express surprise that she should be abroad so early. She explained that she had merely slipped out to post a letter.

'Have you breakfasted?' She shook her head. 'Then I insist that you take some refreshment in my chambers. It is no more than ten steps from where we stand.'

She protested that she could not accept – it was bound to inconvenience him. He denied that firmly: he was in need of coffee himself, and it would not take his clerk a minute to bring *croissants* from the pastry shop. She must try the Guernsey *croissants*, which were at least the equal of the French.

Her objections were overridden and she went with him to the row of squat buildings facing the Court House, and to a dark room, musty with law books, which was his office. His boy brought the refreshment he had promised her, and he chatted, chiefly about the island. He spoke of the wars with the French and the long period during which they had held Castle Cornet, scarcely half a mile off St Peter Port; and then of the cult of witchcraft which persisted in the country parishes. Houses were still built with stone toadstools in their gardens and flat stones projecting from corners under the roofs – for witches to rest on when they were tired of flying!

Sarnia suddenly realized how long she had been there, and looked for her gloves. She thanked Mr Martell, but also apologized for taking up time which must be valuable.

He shook his head. 'I have nothing before court, which does

not open until ten. And in any case I have wanted to make your closer acquaintance, Miss Lorimer, since I expect we shall see each other in the way of business in future.'

She said, surprised: 'I do not conceive how that can be.'

'Forgive me.' He smiled. 'I was not touting. But since I have handled your father's affairs for more than twenty years, I thought …'

'My father of course has affairs in the island. But I have none. Has not Mrs Jelain explained to you? Through their kindness I am here, on holiday, but I return to London in a few weeks.'

'I was thinking of your inheritance.'

'If my father were minded to leave me any legacy, I cannot think he would not have communicated with me – he must know by now that I am staying here. Not that it makes a difference. I do not wish to see him, nor to seek anything from him.'

'Nor does it make a difference what your relations with your father are, as far as your inheritance is concerned. It is yours by right.'

Sarnia said: 'I do not understand.'

'As I have said, we have our customs and beliefs which are not the same as those of England. Laws, also. In England a man may strip his wife and children of all that would ordinarily fall to them from his estate: not so in Guernsey. A man domiciled here can make no will of realty; his heirs must inherit his land. In your father's case that does not amount to much, merely the few vergees on which Beauregard stands.'

'Vergees?'

Mr Martell smiled again. 'I still forget how unfamiliar our usages are to you. A vergee is a measure of land, about two-fifths of an acre. As I say, your father's land holding is small. His fortune is in bonds and business interests and specie. But here, too, the island's laws protect a man's family from dereliction or malice. Anyone having a wife and children can only dispose of a third of his estate by will – a third must go to the widow and another third to be divided among the surviving children. Should his wife have predeceased him, the children, or child, must get half of his possessions on his death. Did you not know of this?'

'No. I cannot believe it now.'

'You will find it is true. And while my professional duty prevents me telling you the precise extent of your inheritance, it is no secret that your father is a very wealthy man; and therefore that you are a substantial heiress.'

She was in confusion. Was he jesting with her? She could not believe that, either, and his next remarks dispelled any doubt.

'I can see I have astonished you, Miss Lorimer. But not unpleasantly, I trust. You need not seek any rapprochement with your father, nor depend on the amiability of his disposition towards you: when he dies a half of his estate will be yours. I am glad to have been the one who has brought you this news.'

She still could not take it in. Her mind shied from the subject, turning to another that for all the bitterness that invested it was sweeter.

'My mother, Mr Martell – do you know why she fled the island?'

He hesitated. 'There was discord between her and your father. Deep discord. In my profession one encounters many marriages, unfortunately, where there is more disharmony than harmony. But not many women have the courage your mother had, to abandon security for the sake of freedom. And with a child in her arms.'

'What caused the discord?'

'How can one tell? You know the tale of Beauty and the Beast. Not that I would call your father a beast, but he was and is a man of rough nature and manners. Your mother was truly a beauty. The Beast wooed and won her, then could not hold her. There was a change in him, during their marriage – a change for the better – but perhaps it did not go deep enough. Certainly when she left him he reverted to old ways, old surliness. Yet his despair was new. Whatever she may have suffered from their separation, I think he suffered more.'

When Sarnia found Mrs Jelain after her return to the house, she had first to withstand a volubility of surprise that she should have gone out on an errand the servants could have performed and concern that she should have done so without first breaking her fast. She managed to tell her that Mr Martell had given her refreshment, and to prevent Mrs Jelain ringing for a maid to bring her a proper breakfast. She said:

'Please, Aunt Jeanne. I am really not hungry. And I would like to talk to you. Mr Martell told me something which surprised and disturbed me.'

'I am sorry to hear that. What did he say?'

'That I am bound to inherit half my father's fortune, whatever his wishes may be.'

Mrs Jelain smiled. 'Though it surprised you, I should not have thought there was any disturbance in the news; or, if there were, it would be a pleasant one.'

'You must have known this. Why did you not tell me?'

'In London, do you mean? We wanted to win you into coming back with us. It did not seem that speaking of it would further that project. It could even have hindered it.'

That might be true. Sarnia said:

'But after I had accepted your invitation?'

'There was still no haste. We felt that your sojourn in the island might induce in you a desire to see your father. But that it was better to wait for the notion to arise of itself than to press it on you. That was why we have not spoken of him to you.'

'He must know I am here.' Mrs Jelain shrugged. 'But he has made no attempt to communicate with me.'

She sighed. 'He is a strange man, no doubt of that.'

Sarnia stared out of the window. The westerly wind was filling the sky with cloud overhead, but to the east the sea was blue and sunlit, the other islands and the distant coast of France all sharp and bright.

She said: 'I must see him, Aunt Jeanne.'

'*Chérie,* I am glad you feel so.'

'That is, if it is possible. Do you think he will be willing to receive me?'

'I hope so.' Mrs Jelain smiled. 'I am confident of it.'

IX

For two or three miles from the outskirts of the town the road was reasonably good, though very dusty. Then, just past a pretty church backed by an apple orchard, they took a minor road to the right. It was in much poorer condition, and the coach jolted its way up a hill and then between level fields enclosed by low granite walls. Sarnia saw a ploughman, and heard his distant cry to his labouring horse, but in general this was a deserted silent countryside.

Abruptly the landau turned left into what was little better than a cart-track and so narrow that any encounter with another vehicle must mean a difficult tracking back by one or the other. The track led steeply downhill, and the stone walls and fields gave way to trees that arched to form a leafy roof above them, so that they rocked down into a dim green world in which the faces of Mrs Jelain and Edmund were deeply shadowed.

The tunnel ended where the valley bottomed out, and the coach halted under open sky. On one side of the thoroughfare a stream gurgled, contained in a stone conduit; on the other the screen of trees divided to show a gate with a farmhouse beyond. It was low lying, built of pink and grey granite, pretty to the eye.

Sarnia said to Mrs Jelain: 'Is this my father's house? I had thought …'

Edmund had spoken of her father letting the estate run to seed, not through lack of money but for want of interest. This place was clearly well kept, its lattice windows freshly painted. And the gate was quite new.

It was Edmund who answered. 'No, this is our farm, and I have a message for the manager. If you will excuse me, I promise not to keep you waiting long.'

A man came from the house to open the gate for him. Mrs Jelain said:

'It is only a small detour from the way to your father's house. He would have had to ride over tomorrow morning otherwise.'

Soft in the distance, Sarnia heard the monotonous cry of a cuckoo. There were other birds twittering nearer, and the low of cattle. These sounds, after the wide silence of the fields, were comforting. There was a flower garden in front of the farmhouse, and the faint buzzing of bees underlined the rest. The sun came out and lit up the coloured stones. Half a dozen hollyhocks rose almost level, it seemed, with the low slate roof.

She said impulsively: 'What a lovely place! I should like to see it more closely.'

Mrs Jelain smiled. 'And you shall, *chérie,* I promise you. But it must be when we have more time.'

Edmund returned very shortly to the carriage, accompanied by the farm manager, Mr Bourgaize. He was a small wiry man of about fifty, and carried a stick which he slapped against his gaiters while he talked. He talked and smiled a great deal, and in the end Edmund was obliged to cut him short so that they could resume their journey. He waved his stick and grinned as the landau, the coachman's whip cracking over the backs of the straining horses, took the road again, this time uphill.

Although trees were still plentifully in evidence, this part of the lane afforded a view of the valley to their right which Sarnia studied with interest. The whole aspect had a charm which related to the smallness and deepness of the valley. Toy cows stood on a green shoulder above a hill of bracken; the sky seemed to press down. The farmhouse, below and behind them now, fitted perfectly into the picture. It was almost as though it were imprisoned, part of a toy world. Though how pretty a prison!

The lane joined again onto a wider road, and they drove through a broader flatter valley which at last brought them once more in sight of the sea. But this was the western coast; it had no town or harbour, only a series of scalloped bays, yellow sanded, divided from each other by promontories of jagged rocks. The farmhouse in the valley had offered a reminiscence of a rural English scene, but here was wildness. Clouds had covered the sun again, and the sea was grey to a grey horizon, touched here and there with a cold white. Following the inland stillness, a stiff breeze, salt-laden, blew in at the windows, disordering Sarnia's hair despite the protection her bonnet afforded. On it were carried the shrieking moans of seagulls, hungry and demanding, angry-sounding in comparison with the peaceful cries of land birds.

They were travelling south. Ahead of them she could see the island's south-westerly tip, rocky and desolate, its chief feature the ruins of a round fort.

'We are arrived,' Edmund said.

She looked, with surprise and some disquiet, at bare fields, fishermen's cottages huddled by the shore far below them, the distant prospect of bleak land and bleaker sea. She was about to question him when the coachman cracked his whip and shouted, and the landau lurched to the left. She saw crumbling stucco pillars, felt the carriage jolt violently as a wheel went into a pothole, and stared ahead to see, hidden up to this moment by the lie of the land, the outline of her father's house.

They drove uphill along what had clearly at one time been an ornamental drive, lined with two rows of elm. But the trees had fared badly, from disease and salt air and the gales of winter beating up against this coast. At least half had fallen and those remaining were in sorry shape, grotesque and broken.

Their condition presaged that of the house itself. From a distance it was impressive; built like Les Colombelles in the Regency style, but larger and, since it stood on the brow of a hill, commanding the skyline. There were eight big windows on the ground floor, far more smaller ones on the two floors above: an arrogant defiance of the window tax. But many of the windows showed not glass but the blankness of boards, roughly nailed on their insides. The house, like the pillars below, had been faced with stucco, but the stucco was pitted by wind and weather and in several places had fallen off, exposing grey granite beneath. Twin flights of steps came together to form a balustraded terrace before the front door, but here too dilapidation and lack of repair were evident; and above the door the big semicircular fanlighting was cracked and had panes missing.

As the coachman helped them from the carriage, Mrs Jelain said:

'We warned you that it has not been kept up. But the structure is sound enough. The surface may be crumbling, but there is good granite behind it.'

Edmund was about to get hold of a rusted iron bell-pull when the door was creakingly opened and a man stood before them. He was big but had a little face, its shape strangely child-like, rounded, though he was well into his middle years. He wore a shabby footman's uniform of green, and a sorry-looking wig whose curls fell lankly about his neck. The bow with which he greeted them was awkward; such, Sarnia thought, as a poorly tutored child might give. She looked at his face again. A child's. yes, and a sly unwholesome child. Instinctively she disliked him.

But he addressed them civilly in English, welcoming them on his master's behalf to Beauregard. Mrs Jelain asked as he ushered them in:

'How is Mr Jelain in health today?'

The curls jiggled as he shook his head.

'Not well, ma'am, though better than he was first thing this morning. He had a bad night.'

'Is he well enough to see us?'

'Aye, indeed. I have told him of your coming.' He grimaced a smile at Sarnia. 'May I say, mam'selle, how glad I am to see you return to this house, where I last saw you in your cradle? I am Roger Troutaud. I beg to offer you my humble duty.'

She thanked him, conscious of his stare, and of her distaste for his person. She was glad when Edmund engaged him in conversation, and she could look around. Like the house itself, the hall was impressive in size, with a central staircase of dark oak leading to the upper floors. The furniture, too, was of good quality – for the most part of rosewood, but she noticed a mahogany china cabinet in the French style, its curving belly inlaid with enamels depicting a hunting scene. In the upper half, though, two squares of glass were missing and the green and gold of the Sevres china inside were dimmed with dust. Dust lay thick on every shelf and ledge, and spider's webs drooped from the oil paintings on the walls. Although the atmosphere was dank, there was a buzz of flies, and a strong fishy smell. The floor, of parquet with carpets that may have been good but now were shabby, worn, soiled, had been swept, but she suspected it had been done for this occasion and hastily. There was more dust in the corners.

As Troutaud led them through the house she caught a glimpse through an open door of a high-ceilinged drawing room, with more dusty furniture, a fireplace of pink marble and a huge gilt mirror over it. They were escorted to the rear of the house and along a corridor to an unpainted door where Troutaud knocked for admission.

It was a little room, originally the cook's sitting-room she guessed, since she had glimpsed a cluttered kitchen next door, and barely furnished. There were a few chairs, a plain wooden table, a square mirror on the wall, an old chest-of-drawers with the top drawer open to reveal a mess of litter. Apart from a couple of small rugs on the stone-flagged floor, what little comfort there was came from a fire smouldering miserably behind the bars of a tiny grate. A man sat in a round-backed wooden armchair drawn up close to it. He fixed his eyes on Sarnia as she stood in the doorway, and she looked back uncertainly. This was her father.

Even seated it was clear that he was a big man, taller than Troutaud and broad of shoulder, though age had thinned him. In some respect his face resembled that of Mr Jelain – the beaky nose was familiar – but the general effect was very different. Most immediately, of course, in the fact that where Mr Jelain's face was so ruddy, this one was entirely pallid. But there was a difference that was even more marked than that; where Mr Jelain had an aspect of coarseness, her father's features, even in decay, had fineness in them. The lines of bone under the white skin showed how handsome he must have been in his youth. When Mr Martell had spoken of Beauty and the Beast, she had seen her father in that role, as a powerful ugly man. She had been plainly wrong to do so.

But though not ugly, powerful certainly. The power was still there, in the grey eyes that stared from beneath the white brows. He started to get up from the chair, unsteadily, and she said quickly:

'Pray, sir, do not rise!'

'I will do so.' His voice. though weak, brooked no opposition. 'I am, as I have been told, uncouth and ignorant, but I know enough to stand for a lady, and will do while I have the strength.'

His accent resembled Mr Jelain's. but here too there was less of lowness, a kind of rough distinction. He stood, swaying a little, and she went towards him in case he should fall. He had ragged slippers on his feet, old patched trousers, a grey shirt torn at the neck, and a green cloak of woollen material thrown across his shoulders. She saw him shiver.

'So this is Sarnia. Or am I to say Miss Lorimer?'

She said: 'As you please, sir.'

The deep-set eyes studied her. 'Miss Lorimer let it be. There is no intimacy between you and me, except our relationship in blood. And though your name may be Jelain by law, I would not hold you to it.'

She was silent, and he went on:

'You are handsome, child. You greatly resemble your mother. At any rate in looks. Do you think you take after her in character?'

Sarnia said steadily: 'I would not claim that, though I would hope for it. I know no person of judgement who ever found fault with her character.'

He looked past her to where Mrs Jelain and Edmund stood in the doorway.

'Since you have come to visit me, Miss Lorimer, there are words that should pass between us. Few, indeed, for I fancy we have little to say to one another. But I would have those few spoken in privacy.' The Jelains hesitated, exchanging glances. 'Unless, Miss Lorimer, you fear being left alone in your father's company?'

She lifted her chin. 'I do not fear it.'

'Take them to the drawing room, Troutaud,' he said. 'Give them some wine.'

He shivered again as the door closed on them. Sarnia said: 'I beg you, sir, to resume your seat.'

'When you have taken yours, Miss Lorimer.'

She obeyed the command and sat down. The repetition of her name and the tone of speaking it were designed to wound, she guessed. Yet perhaps they wounded him the more. She said:

'You do not look well, sir. Is not a doctor in attendance on you?'

He laughed harshly. 'Falla rides over now and then – when he wants a fee. He gives me pills, and I trust they do me no harm. Certainly they do no good.'

'You should have more proper care.'

'A nurse, maybe? I do not suffer women in my house, nor have these eighteen years. Troutaud looks after me well enough. But I do not choose to discuss my health. There is another matter which concerns us, and we can deal briefly with it. You have been apprised that you are in part my heiress?'

'Only recently. I wish …'

'No protestations, if you please. You were told this, and you thought it proper to come and see me. I find no fault with that. I am happy to have seen you, and in return I can give you pleasant tidings. The half of my goods and land should fetch a hundred thousand pounds, or better. Even by English standards, I reckon that is riches.'

'I did not seek such an inheritance, and do not desire it!'

'Not desire a hundred thousand pounds? Well, it may be. It will not affect the outcome. Listen, I will tell you something of my disposition in this. In my youth I was a sea captain, and I took my wealth from the sea, chiefly by way of privateering. I had a good crew, and we found good prizes. The money I made I did not squander, as some have done, but invested wisely. For all that, it seems to me, it has done me little good. Never mind. There is a London charity which aids seamen who have fallen on hard times. The half which the law allows me to will, I have willed to them.'

'I would gladly see you give it all.'

'Would you?' He stared at her. 'Yes, it might be so. Money meant little to her. There is a resemblance in temper, as well as looks. But it does not matter what you or I desire. The laws of this island are all that counts. One half will come to you. There is no need for thanks: I would not take them if you offered them. It is the law I accept. You are my daughter, and will inherit half my goods. I do not know how long you must wait to get them. I make no promises on that account, though from the way Falla wags his ugly head at me the delay should not be too great.'

'You distress me, sir, by talking in this fashion.'

'Do I? You came of your own volition, Miss Lorimer.'

'Because I thought it proper to do so. But not to talk of your wealth, nor any prospect I might have of securing part of it.'

'You have no interest in the eventuality?' He laughed. 'I am sure there are others who have, if you do not! But I will not burden you further with talk nor with my company, neither of which can be pleasing to you. I am glad to have seen you, though I will not thank you for it any more than I require thanks for what may be yours in the future. We are nothing to each other, Miss Lorimer. Nothing. And now I give you good day. Troutaud will see you out, with your friends.'

He rose, indicating the door. Sarnia went there and opened it, but hesitated. She looked at him across the narrow room. His gaze met hers, harsh and unyielding. He inclined his head.

'Goodbye, Miss Lorimer.'

'Goodbye, sir. I wish you better health.'

'You are considerate, child.' There was irony in his voice. 'In that case perhaps you will be good enough to close the door carefully behind you. At my age a man is susceptible to chills and draughts.'

Alone in the passage, Sarnia put a hand against the wall, from need to steady herself. The emotions which she had been suppressing rose in her now. She had expected she might find him hard and cold, but reality far outstripped expectation. She could not help but think of that same harsh bitterness directed against her mother. Anger brought grief. She leaned against the wall for a moment or two, uncontrollably shaking.

When she had mastered herself she walked through the shabby run-down house in search of the others. From behind a closed door she heard voices, and turned the handle. The voices ceased as she entered. Mrs Jelain and Edmund were seated and Troutaud stood before them, in the attitude of a servant.

Mrs Jelain said: '*Chérie* ... has the interview distressed you? Troutaud will pour you a glass of sherry wine.'

Sarnia shook her head. 'Thank you. I do not wish it.'

'It will settle your nerves,' Edmund said.

'No.' She breathed in deeply. 'I should like to leave, if I may.'

Mrs Jelain said: 'Of course, my dear.'

She rose, and Troutaud went to the door, to see them out.

X

A PICNIC had been long proposed by Mrs Jelain, but the fulfilment of the project reserved for a day on which there could be no possibility of bad weather marring the occasion. When Monday evening fell calm and fair and the following morning dawned bright and cloudless, with the barometer in the hall at Les Colombelles rising still, it was agreed that that afternoon should see the scheme carried out. The carriage would take Mrs Jelain and Sarnia, together with the two Misses Le Maitre who lived close by. Mr Jelain would not be able to join them, but Edmund had undertaken to ride over later.

They took the road to St Martin's, a pleasant village on the high ground south of St Peter Port, but shortly before entering it the landau turned to the left. For another half mile or so they drove through fields grazed by the familiar Guernsey cattle, and so came to a spur of higher ground where the carriage halted.

'This is Jerbourg,' Mrs Jelain informed Sarnia. 'There are other pretty spots along the southern cliffs, but this is the nearest, and the journey consequently less fatiguing. We can stroll first at this level, and then go down to the pine wood of Divette. The servants are preparing our picnic there.'

Descending from the carriage, Sarnia stared about her. The island afforded many excellent views, but she could not recall seeing any as beautiful as this. From the grassy plateau on which they stood, one saw the sea on either side, very far below, aquamarine, seemingly without the faintest wrinkle of a wave. To her right, westwards, ran a line of cliffs of rugged awesome grandeur. To the left she looked across falling meadows to the flattened northern extremity of the island.

In front, calm in the calm sea, lay the other Channel Islands, breath-taking in their sunlit splendour. Mrs Jelain, standing at her elbow, asked her if she yet knew them all.

'I think so,' Sarnia said. 'The distant one is Jersey, is it not? And over there, Sark. That little one, Herm, and the other Jethou.'

'You have them almost right. Jethou is the smaller of the two near islands; the other is Herm.'

'I see houses on it. Do many people live there?'

'A few fishermen. And, of course, Mr Fernie, the proprietor. He is a very liberal man. He has recently provided a cottage, rent-free, for a schoolmaster, who not only teaches the children but provides religious services on the Sabbath – on weekday evenings, too, I believe. It is said that the taproom is much less frequented than it was, which is undeniably a blessing. On so small an island, with such little scope for recreation, drunkenness can be a curse.'

Catharine, the younger and prettier of the Le Maitre girls, said:

'This schooling is a good thing, though my papa says it may well be carried too far. The Rector of Torteval has even declared that children should be *compelled* to attend parochial schools. That is far too great an infringement of liberty.'

She was an empty-headed girl, vain of her charms, and Sarnia did not at all care for her. She said:

'Do you think the liberty to remain illiterate is something to be prized?'

'They are as happy in that state as when they have learned to read, papa says. More so, because they are less discontented.'

'But you have declared education a good thing.'

'For those who want it.'

'Can a child know what it is he wants in advance of obtaining it? He must be aware at first only of the hard task of learning.'

The elder Le Maitre girl, Elizabeth, was more pleasant and more sensible. She said:

'I believe papa meant it was a good thing for those who want it for their children. Providing an opportunity for the working classes to have their children taught to read and write and sum must be a benevolence; but that would not be so if children were compelled to be educated, whether the parents wished it or not.'

'I do not see …' Sarnia began. Mrs Jelain interrupted her:

'It is too fine an afternoon for us to trouble ourselves with talk of the parochial schools. Come, *chérie,* and we will show you a still finer view further along the cliff top. And let us put up our parasols, before we are scorched to death.'

They walked for a time on the cliff top, but the sun's heat was very great and it was not long before Mrs Jelain proposed they make their way to the shade of the pine wood. They took a narrow path that ran down, twisting and turning and broken in places by flights of steps, between thickets of scrub and thorn. These caught at one's clothes and had to be disentangled with care. Care also had to be taken in negotiating the uneven and occasionally precipitous ground; altogether the descent was quite tiring.

But they came to the wood at last. The surface was more level here, though still falling towards the sea. And there was the softness and hush of pine needles underfoot, a deep cool shade broken by the golden spears of sunbeams. Apart from their own voices, the only sound was the throaty gurgling of pigeons.

Where a ledge of ground, though still shaded by the trees, offered a view of the sea and the islands, two servants from the house had spread a cloth and set out the picnic basket. Mrs Jelain dismissed them, to return in two hours' time. They disappeared along the path by which the others had just come. Sarnia said:

'Must they walk all the way back to Les Colombelles, and then return?'

'It is more likely,' Mrs Jelain said, 'that their journey will take them no further than the tavern at the top of the hill. It is much pleasanter here, is it not?' She looked at her watch. 'We are in advance of time. It wants half an hour until Edmund should join us. I am going to rest. Elizabeth, you can help Sarnia find some of our Guernsey flowers, and we will press them on our return.'

Sarnia accompanied the Le Maitre girls through the wood, but when they proposed scrambling down to the sea level, she excused herself on the grounds of fatigue. Elizabeth suggested staying with her, but Sarnia prevailed on her to go with her sister.

She found a broad-based pine to lean against, and sat there. She was glad to be free of the Le Maitre girls, and glad also of the opportunity to re-read the letter from Michael which had come by the morning's delivery, shortly before they set out. It was a long one, written in a bold and flowing hand. It was almost too lover-like, with many expressions of the unhappiness which her absence caused him and of his longing for her return.

He chided her, but gently, for the coolness of her own letter and the way in which she withheld her thoughts from him. She told him so little, and he was eager to know everything of her circumstances. She did not mention her father, for instance, although presumably by now she had met him.

The letter ran on other topics for several pages, but towards the end returned to the subject of her father. He knew she must feel a filial duty. It was a natural thing; and so much more so in one like she whose heart was so tender. But he hoped that in observing that duty she would not forget her other friends – in particular one who, though separated from her by sea as well as land, held her constantly and lovingly in mind.

Sarnia put the letter back in its envelope with a feeling of contentment. Better too lover-like than not enough. And it was pleasant that he thought so well of her: it was clear he had come to see her visit as motivated entirely by the proper concern of a daughter. She had a twinge of guilt about that, but was glad it was his opinion. It was his disposition to think well of people, and it stemmed from his own basic kindness which only the occasional visitation of jealousy was likely to disturb. And the thought of that jealousy was not unwelcome. Poor Michael, she thought – I will write to him again, and much sooner, and in warmer fashion.

Meanwhile, agreeable though it was to think of him and of their strolls in the gardens of Lincoln's Inn, it was agreeable also to sit beneath the pines and watch the calm shimmering sea, with the sun throwing a dazzling golden road across it. The wood pigeons still called, and she heard the voices of the Le Maitre girls as they explored rock pools; but faintly, below and out of sight. The gentlest of breezes came coolly on her cheek as she closed her eyes. She felt drowsily peaceful and content.

She started at the light touch of a hand on her brow. Edmund stood before her.

'I have caught you napping.'

She said indignantly: 'I was not asleep, merely resting. I did not hear your approach because the pine needles are so soft.'

'I am glad. So charming a scene, and so delightful to surprise you. Not asleep, then. But dreaming, at least?'

She smiled. 'Perhaps dreaming.'

'Of what?'

'No gentleman would ask. A lady's dreams are secret.'

'I accept the rebuke. But I have no doubt they were as delightful and innocent as the scene. It is a pity to disturb it, but my mother has commanded me to call you to the picnic.' He offered her his hand. 'Come, fair dreamer.'

She watched as he helped the Le Maitre girls up from the lower level. Catharine clung to his arm and contrived, Sarnia noted, to slip and require assistance in which her face pressed close against his chest. She had already observed that Catharine, though an accomplished flirt, had her chief interest in Edmund. She guessed that she was a little concerned about the presence of the London cousin. How much more concerned she would be had she known of what took place in the hay barn!

Not that there was any need for apprehension on her part, Sarnia decided. It was true that she had allowed thoughts of Michael to be driven from her mind by the distractions of her new surroundings; true also that she was far from ready to return any positive answer to the proposal which he had made and would undoubtedly make again. Yet her affections turned much more surely to him than they did to Edmund, or, she thought, ever could. She enjoyed Edmund's company, was not unmoved by the awareness of the power of the attraction she held for this virile, somehow sombre man, but there would be no more to it. On her part at the most a holiday flirtation, whatever his hopes might be. She glanced at him as he spoke to Elizabeth, at the strong swarthy profile. There was a pull there, but a repulsion also. She felt a quick unwarrantable fear of him.

She told herself how silly that was as he supervised the picnic, helping the ladies to dainties. He was more attentive to Sarnia than the other girls.

'You must have some of these sandwiches, cousin, made with Guernsey lobster. And here is a fruit as an accompaniment.'

He offered her a dish of round red fruits with rough wrinkled skins. 'Do you know them?'

'They are tomatoes, are they not? Yes, I enjoy the taste.'

'Papa has some plants in his conservatory,' Catharine said, 'but for decoration merely. He declares they are unwholesome to eat.'

'Then I shall not offer you any,' said Edmund. 'I would not tempt a daughter to transgress against parental wishes. But I will have one myself because I too enjoy the taste. I have heard them called love-apples.'

'No, I will have one,' Catharine said. 'I like to try new things.'

Edmund said gravely: 'You must not eat forbidden fruit.'

'Must I not? I declare I shall. And there was no actual forbidding.' She took a tomato and bit into it. 'They are delicious, Edmund, your love-apples.'

Edmund turned to Sarnia. 'How do you find yours?'

'Excellent.'

'Then I am content.'

There was a shade of emphasis on the first word. From the quick look of annoyance that crossed Catharine's face she guessed she had detected it also. On Mrs Jelain's face, on the other hand, she saw a small smile of approval.

From behind a tree Edmund produced a leather bag, which clinked as he lifted it.

'I thought I should bring Rhine wine for such a day as this. Rudesheimer. I have kept it well wrapped against the heat.'

He unwrapped glasses from a napkin, opened the bottles, and poured the wine. It was cool, fruity, holding a sunshine inside it to match that winking on the blue waters beneath them. He said to her:

'Are you enjoying the picnic, cousin?'

She nodded. 'How could I not be?'

Dr Falla made a social call on them that evening. He complimented Sarnia extravagantly.

'You are more beautiful than when you came,' he told her. 'The bloom is more perfect. It is our Guernsey sun and air which have so wonderfully gilded the lily.'

Sarnia smiled. 'I do not accept the imputation, but I am truly grateful for the air and sun.'

Mr and Mrs Jelain were present, Edmund having an engagement in the town. Mrs Jelain said:

'What news of Beauregard? Were you not to visit there this morning?'

The doctor shook his head. 'Not good, I fear. I found him in bed, which is a bad sign with such a man. He would do anything to stay on his feet.'

Mr Jelain said: 'He was always obstinate. He has lived and will die so.'

'Can he not be prevailed upon,' Mrs Jelain asked, 'to come into the Hospital here? He would be well looked after, and you could attend to him more conveniently than by that long ride out to Torteval.'

'I dare not suggest it. I know the answer I would get, and the oaths that would accompany it. He has sworn he will not budge from his house until he is carried thence for burial, and I do not doubt his determination. I did once venture to recommend that a nurse be brought in to see to him, and he would have bitten my head off for it had he still the strength to bite. He will have no one but Troutaud.'

'Troutaud is a good fellow,' Mr Jelain said.

'But no nurse.'

Sarnia listened to them talk without herself saying anything. She thought of the altogether pleasant day she had spent, beginning with Michael's letter and going on to the picnic at Jerbourg. While she had been seated in the shade of the trees, eating lobster sandwiches and drinking Rhine wine, flattered by Edmund's attentiveness, her father had lain gasping in that gloomy run-down house, his only companion the servant whom, whether or not Mr Jelain thought him a good fellow, she herself disliked and mistrusted.

It was of his choosing, she reminded herself. He could have all the care and companionship that money could provide. As far as she was concerned, had she not done everything duty required? She had visited him, and had been rebuffed. It was he who had said it: 'we are nothing to each other'. She could not persist against that cold rejection – it would be wrong to try to do so.

She had put Michael's letter into the pocket of her evening gown, and now touched it with her fingers. She thought of what he had said, of his estimation of her character. She thought, too, of her mother, who so long ago had fled from her father's harshness. If any justification of the action had been wanting, Sarnia had found it in her own brief encounter with him. But then he had been young and strong. What counsel would her mother have now for her, in regard to an old and feeble, probably a dying man?

Dr Falla went at last, Mr Jelain accompanying him to the door. Mrs Jelain settled herself with her embroidery under the gently hissing gaslight. She said:

'There is "A School for Scandal" at the theatre tomorrow evening. It will not be up to the standards of your London productions, but I think you may enjoy it. Mr Harvey who plays Sir Peter Teazle is vastly amusing; I have seen him do it before. For the rest of the day … We do mean to take you, as you know, to the Silkworm Farm, but that can wait till this spell of weather breaks. If it should be as fine tomorrow I thought maybe you would care to try our sea-bathing. There are machines on both the North and South beaches. I think we might go to the North beach – it is said the South beach is in need of cleaning. I trust you enjoy sea-bathing?'

'Yes, though I have not done a great deal.'

'Let us fix it for tomorrow morning. In the afternoon I have engaged us to take tea with the de Gruchys.'

Sarnia said: 'If you would forgive me, Aunt Jeanne …'

'What is it, *chérie*?'

'I wonder if I might be excused from the engagements you have planned for tomorrow.' Mrs Jelain looked at her in inquiry. 'I think I should like to pay another call on my father, since Dr Falla says he is so poorly.'

Mrs Jelain paused before saying: 'I am glad of it.'

'It may be he will refuse to see me again. But I feel I should make the attempt.'

'You are right to do so. Very right. Your feelings do you credit.'

'In the morning, then …'

'The carriage will be ready for you at whatever time you choose.'

Sarnia shook her head. 'I do not want the carriage. Truly. It is not so far. I can easily ride over.'

'The carriage would be more suitable.' She added indulgently: 'But you modern girls go in for things we should never have dreamt of. Ride over, if you prefer it. I know Edmund will be very happy to accompany you.'

XI

SARNIA FELT SOME UNEASE as they rode along the ruined drive, through the avenue of broken trees, towards the house. Both the size of the building and the extent of its dilapidation were more striking when viewed from horseback than through the windows of the landau. Three or four rabbits whirled away with a flash of white tails over what had once been lawn. It was still for the most part close cropped by their nibblings; but here and there thorn bushes grew, and the crumbling stone wall marking the lawn's upper boundary was thick with grass and weeds.

They had talked little on the journey. Edmund had attempted some conversation but, finding her reticent, had been content to relapse into silence. He was a man, unlike Michael, who had no great need for talking. She supposed that might be a good quality. At any rate she had been glad this morning to be left to her own thoughts.

Yet now, on the point of descending at the entrance to Beauregard, she was touched by fear; and would have been glad of a cheerful voice talking nonsense, or the touch of a friendly hand on her arm. Except to herself she had not confessed her real intention, and having made it she had put it from her rather than dwell on it. Now it must be brought to the testing point, and she did not know if she had the courage.

Edmund tethered the horses to a post near the front door. Sarnia asked Troutaud after her father's condition, and the servant shook his head.

'Not good, Miss Sarnia. A man must have victuals to live, and he will not eat.'

He led the way, upstairs this time, to a chamber on the first floor. Unlike the little room in which she had met her father before, this was broad and high-ceilinged, containing equally impressive furniture: two tall mahogany wardrobes with elaborately carved doors, two matching chests-of-drawers, a washstand with a heavy pink marble top and a circular mirror, fully four feet across, above it. But here too all was dust and decay. The French carpet, twenty feet square, in green patterned with big roses, was soft and springy, but dust rose with every step. The crimson brocade curtains that hung from the tall windows were faded by the suns of two decades of summers; and one of the side-windows had been boarded up against the weather. The heavy papers on the walls, white embossed with a design in gold, had come away in many places, through damp and its own dragging weight, and hung in peeling strips.

The bed was a four-poster, whose mahogany twisted pillars rose ten feet to support a blue silken canopy. The canopy itself, though dirty, was not in too bad a condition, but the hangings were stained and frayed, in one place torn in two. Her father lay on the side away from the window, propped on pillows, in a grey nightshirt and grey cap. She was struck again by the fineness of bone beneath the pale skin, and by the strength and fierceness of the eyes that met hers.

It was he who said weakly: 'I did not look to see you again, Miss Lorimer.'

She went closer to the bed. On the table beside it was a bowl of cold and lumpy gruel: the victuals, presumably, which Troutaud had said he would not eat. She said:

'I heard that you were … less well, sir.'

'And came to inspect the progress towards your inheritance?'

She stared at him but said nothing. He looked past her to where Edmund and Troutaud stood.

'Leave us alone.'

When they had gone and the door was closed, he said:

'I beg pardon for that remark. It was ungenerous, and I dare say untrue. But I do not see the reason for your returning here.

You had paid your respects as a daughter, and had them rudely answered. I have told you: you owe me nothing.'

She had been wondering how she could broach her proposal. A simple prospect the previous evening, it had seemed less easy this morning, more and more difficult as she rode westwards and at last came in sight of the house. His bitter jibe, suggesting she was hoping for his death to claim his wealth, had destroyed her intention completely. She was ready to turn back, glad to accept defeat in an impossible enterprise.

But the apology was disarming. She gathered courage, and said:

'I live in London, sir, as you know. I have two more weeks before I return there. I should like you to accept my services, and my company, for that period.'

On the far side of the bed, by the window, stood an elegant small dressing table with a cheval-glass on it. It was impossible to imagine he could ever have used it. It must have been her mother's, this bed their marriage bed in which she had been born.

'Services?' he asked. 'Company? What is this?'

'It is quite simple. Dr Falla says that you need proper care. It would best be given in the town hospital, but you will not leave your home. In that case you should have a nurse. Since you will have no stranger near, I ask to fill that place.'

He shook his head feebly. 'Impossible.'

'Why so?'

'In the first place because you *are* a stranger, not a daughter. Until a few weeks ago you had lived your entire life knowing nothing of me, and I remember you only as a baby. And the memories to be invoked are bad, on either side. Although not recalling me, you will recall the things your mother said of me.'

'She said nothing. That you were dead – no more.'

He paused. 'Aye, dead to her. I do not know which is the crueller.' He was silent again. 'I perceive that your own intention is kindly; but it would not do.'

Weak though his voice was, he spoke with firmness. His answer brought her relief. She had done what she set out to do, and made the offer. No more was required. She would not have to live in this huge crumbling house, attending this man whom her mother had hated, even for a couple of weeks. And this parting, their last, would be gentler, leaving a taste less bitter.

Sunlight came through the window and flashed from the cheval-glass where her mother, as young perhaps as she was now, had sat and stared at the reflection of a bride. Pain clutched her breast and sickened her. She could see the country outside, the fresh green of grass, and thought of riding there with Edmund, riding away from this mansion of decay. Yet she found herself saying:

'I do not offer this. I ask it of you.'

'To what end?'

'You have said: until a few weeks ago we knew nothing of one another. But I *am* your daughter. By Guernsey law half your estate, without any act of will on your part or request on mine, comes to me on your death. I ask that you permit me to give you this small service as a daughter, late though it is, in return.'

'There is no need.'

'For me, there is.'

He propped himself on an elbow. 'You will get the money, and I do not begrudge it you. But I will have no service from you!'

He spoke fiercely and she was afraid of him again, but would not yield to the fear. She said:

'First I offered, then asked. If you will not respond to either, I must insist. I shall ask for my things to be sent over from Les Colombelles today. Troutaud will find me a bed, and show me what is necessary.'

'I will not have you, I tell you – neither your service nor your company!'

She smiled. 'I will leave you now to rest, sir. But I will return shortly.'

She had expected strong opposition from Edmund, possibly even a Sabine return to the Jelain home tied to his saddlebow. But though he expressed surprise and some doubt, the doubt was fairly soon overcome. He said:

'At least let us send you some servants over.'

Sarnia shook her head. 'He is old, and set in his ways. It is enough that I should impose myself on him against his will, without having his house overrun with strangers. I shall be all right with Troutaud to help me.'

'If you are quite sure ... Will you not return with me now, and come over later in the carriage?'

'No. I prefer not to. But pray make my excuses to your mother. She has got tickets for the theatre tonight, and for the recital of the Bearnais Singers on Friday. Not to speak of engagements with half a dozen people at least. Do you think she will forgive me?'

He smiled. 'Your reason is good – a daughter tending her father. Though even without it she would forgive you anything.'

'I shall miss her, and all of you.'

'I will ride over every day.'

'I do not think you should. My father ...'

'I will not disturb him. I will muffle Chevalier's hooves if need be.'

They smiled together. He pressed her hand before unhitching his horse and mounting. He waved as he reached the stone pillars at the end of the drive. Then he was gone, and she felt quite desolate. The day was as clear and sunny as yesterday had been, but here a stiff breeze, a wind almost, blew up from the sea; enough to make her shiver. She went back into the house and felt the stiller dankness of her surroundings. There was a great stain of damp, she now observed, on the hall ceiling, and a hideous fungus-like growth high up on one of the walls.

She thought of the house from which she had come, with all its brightness and polish and busy servants, its well-tended sunlit gardens, its outlook over the bustling harbour and friendly offshore islands rather than barren rocks and an empty western sea. But it did no good to brood on that. She set off briskly to find the kitchen.

Although her expectations had not been high, she had a further shock when she found it. Like the rest of the house it showed no evidence of having been cleaned even in years, and by reason of its function the squalor was very much greater. The smell alone, of decaying food and general rot, was enough to nauseate her. She pinched her nose against it and looked more closely. By the long shallow sink unwashed pots and pans were stacked, higgledy-piggledy; and there were others on the floor. The dresser shelves were empty of crockery, but plates and cups and saucers, all far from clean, were piled in heaps on the cupboard top. Flies rose in a swarm as she approached and buzzed round her detestably. The air was full of them. That was one of the first things that must be seen to.

The stove was big but filthy, and the fire burning behind the bars of the grate was a heap of dull embers. She saw a door slightly ajar, and went to investigate. Something moved, darting into the shadows, and she put a hand to her breast in panic. A mouse. There were sacks of provisions on the floor, open and spilling their contents: oatmeal, split pease, haricot beans, potatoes. The smell was even worse. She retreated and rested a hand on the kitchen table. It badly needed scrubbing, but seemed the least odious of the surfaces which surrounded her.

She was struck by a wave of despair. Last evening it had all seemed straightforward. She would come to Beauregard, nurse her father into better health, and while doing so persuade him to some more permanent arrangement for his proper care. She had known it would not be easy, and had not minded the prospect of hard work, but she had not imagined it could be so sordid. She had never in her life encountered conditions such as these. In the life she had shared with her mother there had been little money, only one servant and a cleaning woman, but cleanliness had been taken for granted. What confronted her was a pigsty: she could not possibly remain here.

Edmund had gone – the reminder brought a new plunge into misery – but the horse on which she had ridden over was still here. She could ride after him and reach Les Colombelles not long after he did. She could say she had changed her mind. The Jelains would not criticize her for it. Edmund, she realized, being a man, would have had no awareness of the state of this kitchen, and though Mrs Jelain might have done she had not known of Sarnia's intention to stay on at Beauregard.

So there was nothing to keep her here, everything in favour of her abandoning this impossible task. Her father had not asked it – she had overridden his objections. No one could expect her to stay in conditions of such foulness.

She took a step towards the door, then halted. There was only one thing worse than the thought of continuing with the enterprise, and that was the notion of giving it up. She could not ride away, to live with the recollection of her weakness, her failure. That was the absolute impossibility.

Footsteps sounded in the house: Troutaud. She called him, and he came into the kitchen.

'Miss Sarnia?'

'This place ... it is utterly disgusting.'

'I am sorry for that, Miss Sarnia. But I am a poor hand at cleaning. It was not what I was employed for.' He showed a trace of oily indignation. 'I have done what I could to help the master, but it has not been easy.'

'If you cannot do kitchen work, you should have got someone who could.' He shook his small head. 'There must be women in the district. In those fishermen's cottages down by the shore, for instance.'

'There are women, all right. But the master would have none of them. Would not have them, nor pay them. He does not part easily with money. Do you know what he pays me? Twelve pounds a year. I could get twice the sum anywhere else. I've stuck with him from loyalty, though with little enough by way of thanks even.'

Even though she disliked him, she supposed it might be true. She said:

'I should like you to get a woman to come in and clean up this kitchen at once. Will you please do that?'

'And as to paying her?'

'I will be responsible for it.' He stared for a moment before nodding his head. 'And we must have fly papers – a couple of dozen at least. And get word to the sweep that we require him. It would be impossible to cook on such a fire as that. I should guess the flue has not been swept in ten years.'

'Nearer twenty, Miss Sarnia. And it is not only the chimney. He will not buy proper coal, only steam coals. There is no heat in them.'

'Order a ton of the best anthracite.'

'He will not like it.'

'That too will be my responsibility.' He stood there, indecisive. 'The woman, first. See to it right away.'

'I was going to show you to your room.'

'That can wait. Is there milk in the house?'

'In the dairy.' He pointed to a door. 'Through there.'

When he had left she looked around once more. Even after he had got a woman, it would take hours for her to make any impression on this mess; and meanwhile her father was in need of nourishment. It was fortunate that because of their straitened circumstances her mother had not been able to employ a cook; she had done the cooking herself and Sarnia had learned from watching her. But she had never been obliged to cope with chaos and dirt like this.

She would need to make something simple and easily digested: she could scramble eggs, perhaps. There should be eggs in the dairy, as well as milk. She went to open the door, then hesitated; and kicked it sharply with the toe of her shoe, to give any mouse that might be lurking within a chance to remove itself. All the same, she entered with a wary eye.

The dairy was as much in need of cleaning as the kitchen, but not quite so noisome. She found two churns of milk, one fresh and one curdled, and a large basin with two dozen eggs or more.

Sides of bacon and salted pork hung from hooks in the ceiling, and there were several bowls of dripping, one of which, she saw with disgust, was marked by mouse tracks.

The outer door of the dairy led into the back garden. Sarnia opened it, tugging against damp swollen wood, and saw a swirl of movement as something darted into the protection of an overgrown shrubbery. It was a tabby cat, ill-used and nervous; it crouched, watching her with big green eyes. She called 'Puss' to it and got no response, but left the door open when she went back into the dairy. She doubted if, wild as it was, it would venture in, but she would not exclude any possible ally against the mouse plague which clearly held sway here.

She took eggs from a bowl, a scoop of butter from another, milk in the cleanest of the pitchers available. In the kitchen, not without difficulty, she tracked down salt and pepper. She still required a saucepan, and examined several with increasing nausea. In the end she picked the one she thought would clean most easily, discovered a scrubbing brush, and set to work under the tepid flow from the hot water tap. It was an unpleasant and laborious task; time and again she thought she had the pan clean but on taking it to the window found intolerable stains.

At least she had scoured it adequately and could cook the scrambled eggs over the dull glimmer of the fire. She also found a cottage loaf – two days old at least, but that would not matter when it was toasted. She had to hold the slices close to the bars for a long time before they started to brown.

Now all that was needed was a tray. She found one propped against the dresser, but it was even filthier than the saucepan. Wearily she embarked on yet another job of cleansing.

Her father was asleep when she went into the bedroom, but awoke as she crossed the room. He stared at her, blinking.

'Are you still here, Miss Lorimer? I ordered you to go.'

'You must eat, sir. I have brought you food.'

'I want none of it.'

'It will restore your strength.'

He glared at her. 'Do not mock me! My strength is gone. There is nothing left but dying, and it will be better if that is quickly done. For both our sakes.'

'I did not think you were a coward.'

'Coward?'

'To take an easy way. It is not what one expects of one who was once a sea captain.'

'You have a quick tongue. That too brings back memories. But I will not let it provoke me.'

'Then consider, sir, what is due to me. I have braved the morass of your kitchen. I have prepared you eggs and buttered toast, with a mug of milk not more than a day old. Is all my labour to be wasted? Even if you are determined to die rather than live, surely it would be better to die as a gentleman, and reward my efforts by tasting what I have brought. I do not ask more than that.'

She spoke with insincere but resolute cheerfulness. This, like the greasy mouse-ridden kitchen, the begrimed saucepan, was something to be tackled and endured. It had been a precept of her mother's, well exemplified in all she did: what is worth doing must be well done. She smiled at the feeble angry old man, and added coaxingly:

'Try just a mouthful.'

He said in a calmer weaker voice: 'I want nothing.'

'But try, at least.'

She cut a small portion of toast, spooned egg on it, and held it towards him with a fork. His mouth reluctantly opened; he took it and, after a moment, chewed on it. She repeated the offering and went on, feeding the food to him in mouthfuls. She presented the mug of milk to him, and he drank.

At the end he stared at her.

'I do not understand why.'

She smiled. 'Does that matter?'

'Tell me.'

'For my mother's sake, perhaps.'

'She hated me. It was why she left me, and took you with her.'
'But loved you once.'

He was silent. She waited for him to speak. He said at last:

'I am grateful to you. And to her, since she inspired your act. I do not speak of the food, you understand.'

'I understand.'

He put his hand out and she took it.

'I am glad of your company, daughter.'

XII

IN THE LATE AFTERNOON the landau brought Sarnia's trunk, together with Mrs Jelain and Edmund. Plus a third person: little Marie crept out after them and stood staring in bewilderment and alarm at the front of Beauregard.

'Edmund said you would not have servants, but you must have a maid.'

'It is not necessary, Aunt Jeanne. I can perfectly well see to myself. I am accustomed to do so.'

Mrs Jelain brushed the objection aside. 'It would not do for you to be on your own – not do at all. And she is very glad to come.' Sarnia looked at Marie and was given a timid smile. 'I declare she has already formed an attachment to you.'

Troutaud and the coachman carried the trunk into the house. Mrs Jelain said:

'We have brought a hamper as well. I cannot believe this house will be adequately provisioned, from what I understand of your father's way of life.'

'You are truly kind. The place does lack for organization. But I am making a little progress. Come in and let me give you some tea.'

'Willingly.' She embraced Sarnia. '*Chérie*, this is an unexpected thing, and yet so proper a one. But not really unexpected from a girl of your qualities. Your father – what are his feelings?'

They went into the house, Edmund following. She said:

'He accepts me. I would not say more than that.'

'But it is enough,' Mrs Jelain said. 'And to have a father and daughter reconciled, after so long a separation – could anything be more inspiring?'

There was a great difference, Sarnia thought, between the present accommodation and what Mrs Jelain was envisaging, but she would not oppose her enthusiasm. She led the way to the drawing room. Mrs Jelain said:

'You have a fire, I see.'

'Yes. The place is so damp that I had Troutaud light it. We have no supply of good coal yet, but he brought these logs in. Please be seated, Aunt Jeanne, while I prepare tea.'

'You should not perform such tasks yourself.'

Sarnia smiled. 'I am used to them. And Troutaud is occupied with taking up my trunk, and has other duties to attend to. Besides, I have already tasted his tea and would not inflict it either on you or myself.'

'But Marie can see to it.' Mrs Jelain spoke rapidly in *patois* to the girl, who nodded her head. 'Sit down and talk to me. You must be exhausted.'

'I promise you I am not. At least allow me to show Marie where to find things.'

She took Marie into the kitchen and gave her the necessary instructions. She understood much of what was said if one spoke slowly and carefully, and was starting to use a few words of English herself. When Sarnia returned to the drawing room, Mrs Jelain said:

'This fire ... I was wondering if there might not be some risk of the old soot catching. It cannot have been lit in years. Though it seems to be drawing well.'

'We have had the sweep. Troutaud encountered him on his mission to find a charwoman. There was little soot, in fact, but he cleared a couple of bird's nests.'

'You are setting about things with a will.' Sarnia smiled and shrugged. 'But what about you yourself, child? Has Troutaud looked out a room for you? We have brought bed linen, for fear there might be none aired in the house. Marie will make it up for you.'

'I have a bedroom, and Troutaud has lit a fire there as well.' She smiled again. 'I promise you I will look after myself. I have no fondness for damp rooms or unaired linen.'

Mrs Jelain went on talking about nothing of much importance and Sarnia listened and nodded. She was a little surprised at the way in which she had accepted the situation, knowing far more than Edmund could of the labour and difficulties involved. But she was relieved not to have to argue about it. Marie brought them tea, on a tray Sarnia had found which was of good silver but grey-green with tarnish, and cake from Mrs Jelain's hamper.

They did not stay long after that, having to be back for the theatre in the evening. At the door, Mrs Jelain said how sorry she was that Sarnia should miss the play; but there would be plenty of other opportunities for play-going in the future.

Not here, at any rate, Sarnia thought. If she were to spend the rest of her time in Guernsey at Beauregard, as she fully intended, there could be no chance of play-going. It would be different when she had returned to London. She thought of those familiar skies, familiar streets and buildings, of Michael's absurd but pleasant banter, and felt a sharp pang of nostalgia.

When Edmund had handed his mother into the carriage, he spoke to Sarnia.

'Are you sure you will be all right on your own here? And at night?'

'Quite sure. And I shall not be alone. Apart from my father, there is Troutaud, and now Marie.'

'I shall ride out first thing in the morning, to make sure all is well.'

'It is good of you, but not really necessary.'

'We are concerned for you.' He held her hand tight in his. 'This will be a long and dreary evening compared with those to which I have grown accustomed.'

She laughed. 'I am sure it will not! You will be at the play.'

'But you will not be there.'

Sarnia watched the carriage down the drive before returning to the house. She felt better than she had done in the morning; in the security of a task fully accepted and at least partly tackled, the knowledge of her father's tolerance of her presence – not least the presence of Marie. She could admit now the unease she had felt at the thought of the night ahead. It was comforting to know that the little maid was lodged in a room just across the landing, within call.

Meanwhile there was much to be done. Lamps, for instance. Some hours of daylight lay ahead, but there must be provision for the dark. Apart from candles she had observed that cruzies were used for illumination: there was one in the hall, one in the kitchen, one in her father's bedroom. The smell of fish which pervaded the house probably came from the oil in these rather than from ancient cooking.

But in her explorations she had come on a lamp room, and found an abundance of colza lamps, and a cask of colza oil more than half full. She had asked Troutaud why the lamps were not used, and he had shrugged.

'By the master's direction, Miss Sarnia. He is not greatly concerned with what kind of light he has in the house, and fish oil comes much cheaper than colza.'

That was probably true, though it was also true that cruzies needed much less attention and so would be likely to find favour with Troutaud himself. But she was not prepared to tolerate either the dim flickering light or the smell of fish. She told Troutaud to trim and prepare at least half a dozen proper lamps. He did not look pleased, but nodded acceptance.

She now went to check on his progress, and found him engaged in fitting a new wick into a big-bellied brass lamp. The brass badly needed polishing, but would have to do for the present. There was so much that had been neglected and needed seeing to.

He said: 'I had to put in a new wick. The other was past using.'

'You were lucky to find one, since those lamps have been so long out of use.'

He said doubtfully: 'I am not sure how it will burn, come to that. The new wick, that is. It must have been on that shelf for fifteen years.'

'We shall try it, anyway. And you must get new wicks tomorrow, when you go for the flypapers and all the other things. I am making up a large shopping list.' She looked about the room. 'How many lamps have you got ready?'

'This is the third.'

'I think six will be enough for now. Take one up to my room when you have finished. And one to Marie's.'

'You may rely on me, Miss Sarnia.'

His tone was cheerful. The slightly petulant tone in which he had acknowledged her earlier instructions seemed to have vanished since the Jelains' visit. Sarnia had noticed Edmund talking earnestly to him; he had probably said something which had had its effect. She was grateful for this thoughtfulness. Although she had declared it unnecessary, she hoped he *would* ride over early in the morning.

She had looked in several times on her father and found him sleeping; she suspected that he had had a bad night and needed the rest. But this time he was awake. He was looking out of the window, towards the sea, but turned his head as she came in.

'How are you feeling now, Father?'

'Well enough. The carriage I heard – have they been here again from Les Colombelles?'

'Aunt Jeanne and Edmund brought my things. And they brought Marie, who has been my maid, to stay with me here.'

'I do not want any of that lot in this house.'

His voice was weak, but the contempt in it plain. Sarnia said:

'They have been very good to me, all of them.'

'Do you say so?' He stared at her. 'You may think, since I keep such limited company, that I am likely to be ignorant of the natures of my fellow men. But once one has learned the lineaments of a rogue, one needs no further practice. Even after a half century in solitary confinement, one would know one when one saw one.'

She reminded herself that what she had undertaken was a task unlikely to be pleasant in any way. Apart from all other disadvantages, there was that presented by her father's character. A man who had been cruel and bitter in his prime, with a lack of decent human feeling, would scarcely be less so in old age. It was probable indeed that he would be still more narrow and fierce.

She must not mind this. Nor, on the other hand, was she prepared to bow to tyranny. She said firmly:

'Edmund has undertaken to ride over again in the morning, and I have welcomed the offer.'

He was silent for a time, then said: 'He is a handsome enough fellow, I dare say, for those with a taste for dark looks. ' He paused but she said nothing. 'Yet you strike me as a girl accustomed to keeping a level head. Am I right in that?'

'I hope so!'

'Though the levellest of heads is not proof against certain agitations.'

He looked away, and she saw the reflection of his features in the cheval-glass on the dressing table: old, tired, unhappy. When he turned back, he said:

'Is Troutaud serving you well enough?'

'Yes. I have him engaged on lamp cleaning at the present.'

'Lamp cleaning? What need is there for that? We use no lamps but cruzies.'

'While I am here, we shall.'

'A useless expense! And who is to pay for it?'

'I will. Or rather I shall ask the Jelains to lend me money to do so. You have told me, you and Mr Martell, that in due course I am to be rich. So I can borrow on my expectations. I am sure they will not press me for repayment.'

Their eyes met. She was frightened of him again, but she would not let her gaze drop. He said:

'Who is master in this house, miss – you or I?'

'You, sir. But while I am here I shall be your housekeeper, and you must leave the running of domestic affairs to me.'

'And if I will not do so?'

'You have no choice. Though I suppose you could order Troutaud to put me out.'

Once more their gazes locked. At last he said:

'Do what you like.'

She pressed home her advantage. 'There is much that has to be done. I have got a woman in to clean the kitchen, but the house needs cleaning from top to bottom. I shall have to employ others. I have ordered good coals, and am making out a list of other things in which there is a deficiency. I tell you all this, Father, so that there shall be no misunderstanding. '

He turned from her, repeating: 'Do what you like.'

'Are you comfortable? May I make up your bed?' He did not answer. 'I will come to see you again later. Try to sleep meanwhile.'

She turned to leave the room, but he called her back as she reached the door.

'Come here.'

He fumbled inside his night-shirt. There was a thin leather thong about his neck, and he lifted a small purse-like object which was attached to it. He untied the top, and drew from it a bunch of keys. He gave them to Sarnia, with one key extended.

'The chest in the corner yonder.'

It was of oak, very old and battered but stout, bound with iron bands and secured by a padlock.

'I will not have you borrow from them. I will not have you under an obligation. Buy what you want, but use my money.'

She hesitated and he said with weak impatience: 'Have sense, child! It is your own patrimony you will be robbing.'

She took the key and knelt by the chest. The lock was very stiff but at last she succeeded in turning the key in it, and could free the hasp and lift up the lid. There were documents inside, many on parchment, and several leather bags. She lifted one and heard the chink of coins. Undoing the string at the top, she let several sovereigns fall into her palm. Her father was watching her.

'Take what you need, and more when you want it,' he said.

'Thank you.'

'Do not thank me. Leave me in peace, and tend to your housekeeping.'

She awoke in the night. The wind was getting up and she heard it howl up the hill from the sea and rattle the loose frame of her window. That too was something that should be attended to, but there was no great urgency about it. It could be left to whomsoever took her place, to look after her father and keep house for him. It should not be difficult to find someone suitable.

The wind howled again, and the draught through the ill-fitting frame made her night-light flicker. This room, though smaller than her father's, was still large, and full of shadows. She felt the unease of being alone in a strange house, a strange land. Marie, it was true, was close by, but she had proved even more nervous than she was herself: Sarnia had felt obliged to accompany her to her bedroom and bid her goodnight there.

But the uneasiness could not dispel her sense of satisfaction in having got so far. And Edmund would be coming in the morning: there was comfort in that thought. Also, she was tired from all her exertions. The night-light flickered again, and the dark shadows danced, but they did not alarm her. Her eyelids drooped, and she fell asleep.

XIII

THE WEATHER BROKE and a gale roared in from the west. Beauregard, exposed as it was, took the full brunt of the buffeting wind and slashing rain. Sarnia realized that, with nothing done for so long in the way of repair, it spoke well for the original construction that the dilapidation was not worse.

She got on with her task of caring for her father, and bringing the house's interior to the requisite minimum of cleanliness and order. She did not take on servants, feeling this could wait for the more permanent domestic arrangement she hoped to organize, but had three of the local women in daily, together with a boy to help Troutaud and be useful generally.

Troutaud's own attitude was not easy to fathom. He was occasionally surly, but at other times went out of his way to oblige. She liked him no better, but had to admit that he obeyed her instructions willingly enough for the most part. She did not think the cleaning women liked him, either, from their looks behind his back. One of them once tried to engage Sarnia in conversation about him, but she had no more than a sprinkling of English words to help out her *patois*, and could not say what she wanted. In the end she had to content herself with assuming an expression of disapproval.

''E – not good.' She wagged her broad ugly head. 'Not good.'

It was a help that Edmund visited so regularly. There were few mornings that did not see him riding up to the house before ten o'clock, and when business did prevent him at that hour he came in the afternoon. Invariably he brought dainties from Les Colombelles: cakes and pies baked by his mother's cook, fruit and preserves, a lobster, specially cured bacon from the Fauxquets farm. He even brought loaves until Sarnia begged him not to: the baker at Pleinmont had sought her custom, would deliver daily, and had a family of thirteen to raise.

His manner was lover-like, but in a sober, untroubling fashion. She was glad of this, partly because she felt herself too busy for the distractions of dalliance, partly through a shrinking back from the man himself. She was glad of his kindness but in a deeper sense still did not know whether he attracted or repelled her. She realized that his determination, his persistence in attentions, would eventually lead to a point at which this must be resolved, but was glad not to be pressed at the moment. The restraint he showed was a relief.

One of the things he brought from Les Colombelles was a letter from Michael. There was little of restraint in that. She had answered his previous letter on the evening of her decision to spend the rest of her holiday attending to her father. In telling him of this (though without mentioning the question of inheritance), she had touched briefly on the isolation and disrepair of the house, and on her doubt as to how her father would receive her in view of his initial coldness.

The effect on Michael had clearly been to elevate further his already too high opinion of her character. She read his praise of her noble nature with embarrassment, and shook her head almost angrily. Although, undeniably, it was pleasant to have him think so well of her.

She wondered if he did not feel some small satisfaction, also, over her removal from the luxury of Les Colombelles to less agreeable circumstances. He had been jealous of the Jelains for taking her away, and apprehensive of the attractions they and the island might offer. Although in her earlier letter she had played these down, she had probably not reassured him. Her taking so long to write had been an argument for alarm in itself.

In her second letter, seeing the pleasant side of her holiday as over, with only a dreary time ahead, she had written more of London, and said how much she looked forward to her return. Clearly she had been convincing, or he had been ready to be convinced. He wrote very warmly of his own anticipations, and of some of the things they might do together. In the Zoo, for instance, in addition to the hippopotamus, there was now an uran-utan – the first to go on show in Europe. A fascinating beast, it was said, greatly resembling a man. From that he went on to say again how much he missed her and to reiterate, even more warmly, his affection for her.

She read his letter while another gale roared in from the desolate western ocean, and thought how truly nice it would be to be back. She had enjoyed life at Les Colombelles, and the company of the Jelains and their friends, but she did not miss them. Edmund? She still saw Edmund and was not prepared – did not wish – to speculate on the future where he was concerned. Very likely he would forget her, once she had returned to London. If not, he would have to come and seek her out, and then … one would see what one would see.

For that matter her acquaintance with Michael carried a question mark of its own, in that she had still not made him aware of her being an heiress. She turned from that, as she did from the entire business of her father's money. She would not think of it, and need not. Her duties at Beauregard were more than enough to keep her attention fully occupied.

Her first objective, of bringing her father into a better state of health, was already showing unmistakable signs of success. As early as the second day of her stay Dr Falla, calling in the evening, was emphatic over the improvement in him. Taking sherry wine with her in the drawing room, he spoke of the difference he had found.

'One would not think him the same man. To tell the truth, Miss Lorimer, when I last saw you at Les Colombelles, I would have given nothing for his chances of being alive in a fortnight's time, and very little for a week. It was not only his physical condition that made me think so. There comes a time when a man ceases to fight against the weakness that besets him – when the grave seems a more attractive prospect than the continuing struggle to no good end. I was convinced that was your father's state, and I have often noticed that the tougher or more vigorous a man is before he comes to it, the quicker he goes thereafter.'

He sipped his wine and held the glass up to the lamplight.

'Your father has kept a good cellar, at least. Though this too may stem from happier days. I would wager that cask has lain a few years untouched.'

Sarnia nodded. 'So Troutaud tells me.'

'You have done a great deal in so short a time.' Dr Falla gazed around the room. 'Cleanliness, comfort, a fire in the hearth, fresh flowers ... the woman's touch that has been so lacking here. And your father recovered from death's door.'

'I have persuaded him to eat a little – bullied him, rather. That was all.'

Dr Falla scratched his little nose, which his large hairy hands made look smaller still. He said:

'What you have done in the practical sense is important. But less important than the restoration of his will to live. It is your presence, your affection, which has achieved that.'

'My duty.'

'Does it matter what one calls it, if the end is gained? I speak as a physician. A few days ago I despaired of your father; now I am hopeful of him.' He rummaged in his black bag and brought out a bottle. 'A dessertspoon after meals, three times a day. It is not medicine that will bring him back to health, but this may help.'

'I will see that he takes it.'

'I am sure you will.' He smiled. 'Whether it is affection or duty or whatever, it would be of small advantage without strength of purpose, which you plainly have.' He got to his feet. 'I leave my patient in good hands, and must do so with no more delay. It is a long jog back to the town, and the day is darkening.'

'Will you take another glass of sherry before you go?'

He shook his head. 'I have drunk enough already, and it is a powerful wine.' He hesitated, and sat down again. 'But a very good one. And my horse knows the way as well as I do, if not better. Thank you, I will take another glass.'

On the fourth day her father insisted on getting up. He called for Troutaud to help him dress, and came downstairs leaning on his servant's arm. Sarnia watched from the foot of the stairs: he was tottery, and held the banister with his free hand, but he managed well enough. His legs, of course, were weak from lying in bed, but it was certain that his strength was continuing to return. He had eaten almost heartily of the boiled fowl she had prepared for his luncheon, and drunk a glass of claret with it.

He moved from the stairs towards the rear of the house. He was heading, she guessed, for that small room in which she had first met him and which, Troutaud had told her, was the only place downstairs that he would use. She had made no changes there, but had had it cleaned, and the fire that now burned in the grate was a warm and cheerful one.

As he passed through the hall, though, he looked in at the open door of the drawing room. He said, with surprise and what seemed like annoyance:

'What is this? A fire here?'

'Here,' Sarnia said, 'and in other rooms, too. I have had them lit because of the dampness of the house.'

He looked at her but instead of speaking shuffled across the threshold and stood inside the room. His gaze ranged round, taking in not merely the fire but the flowers she had renewed that morning, the gleam on glass and silver, newly polished, the freshly laundered coverings on the chairs. His eyes searched slowly, came back to the fireplace, then rose to view what hung on the wall above it.

He started and his face seemed to turn whiter still. He said in a low voice:

'Who put that there?'

She had found it in a lumber room upstairs, turned to face the wall. There could be no mistaking who it was. Her mother had kept no likenesses of herself when young, but the face Sarnia had known as older, pain-racked, was familiar here in bloom and beauty. It displayed her head and upper body, in a black dress with puffed sleeves, white lace tied with pink ribbon at the neck, and a ruched lace cap with small white flowers edged by green leaves. It had been contrived that her left hand should be shown also, and the rings on her third finger: one a flat band of gold, the other of diamonds and rubies. The gold band Sarnia had seen often enough, and kissed it on her dead hand; the other ring, never.

On her face was an expression that mingled love, and trust, and hope. There were recognizable furnishings behind her: a corner of the gilded mirror that hung in this very drawing room, and the edge of the red curtains, then more deeply crimson. The picture had been painted here, during the brief happiness of her early married days.

Sarnia could not leave the picture where she found it. She had taken it downstairs, dusted it, and fixed it on the wall above the fireplace. There had seemed no harm in doing so: the prospect of her father leaving his bedroom, if he ever did, had seemed remote, and she had Troutaud's word that he never used any room downstairs except his little one by the kitchen. But seeing his shocked thin face she regretted what she had done, and blamed herself. She could have hung the picture in her own room, where there would have been no possible chance of his seeing it.

He said again: 'Who put it there?' He was shaking. 'I demand to know!'

'I did, Father,' Sarnia said. 'I am sorry if it upsets you. I will remove it, if you wish.'

'But there – in the exact spot where it used to hang!' He turned in feeble anger to Troutaud. 'It was you, was it? You put her up to it.'

She answered for the servant. 'He knew nothing of it. I found the painting. And I fixed it there because it seemed the right place. A picture was wanting in that spot.'

Her father went forward into the room, Troutaud closely attending. He sat in the armchair that stood on the right of the fireplace. Sarnia said:

'If you are greatly troubled by it …'

His gaze travelled from her face to the painting, and back. He said to Troutaud, without looking at him:

'Leave us, man. I will call when I want you.' When the door had closed behind him, he said: 'And you. Sit you down.'

Sarnia took the armchair facing the one in which her father sat. Outside the wind roared up from the sea and the day, for all that it was June, was raw; but here the fire crackled warmly, heaped high with coals. He would take no chill from being up. His eyes were closed. He opened them, and said abruptly:

'I took that painting down the day she left me.' He paused. She did not speak, and he went on:

'I was minded to smash it, and burn the fragments. I almost did, but drew back at the last. She had wounded me deeply, beyond endurance it seemed, and I hated her as much as I had once loved her. But I could not destroy her likeness, and I think I hated her the more for that.'

She tried to see him as he had been in the vigour of his middle years, a raging savage man, to hate him for the hate he had felt and shown then. But although she saw her mother's worn and sadder features clearly prefigured in the painting, this identification was less easy. He looked so old and ill. Yet she would not pity his white hairs.

He asked: 'She never spoke of me?'

'As I told you, she said only that my father was dead.'

'But did not speak of me, even as one dead? And you – you did not ask?'

'No. Even as a child, I guessed it would be painful to her. From the pain of her loss, I thought.'

He said bitterly: 'That loss, that abandoning, was the only thing that gave her joy.'

'I think the painting tells a different story.'

He was silent for a long time. The fire shook itself with a small roar, and coals tumbled into the hearth. She knelt, restoring them with shovel and tongs. Her father said:

'I can see her, bent just so ... There is resemblance in your face, but more sometimes in your movements, your gestures. Do you miss her greatly?'

'Very greatly. I try not to let my mind dwell on that. She would not have wished it.'

'You are mindful of her wishes. Now you tend me, as a daughter. Would she have wished that, think you?'

'I did not think so once, but now I do.'

He was silent again, then said: 'I did not ask you for the service, but am glad of it. And would like to talk to you of her, but will not if you do not wish it.'

'I will listen.'

He put his hands together and leaned towards the fire. 'She was much younger than I when we met. I was, as would seem to you, already an old man – long past my fortieth year. I had spent a quarter of a century at sea, and made my fortune there. I was happy in the life, rough and rootless as it was, and had no thought of any other; until I met her.

'I had made my fortune, as I say, and people knew of it. A man with money is generally welcomed in society, even though he be a sailor, lacking breeding and still showing the coarseness of his origins. For my part such circles, and the antics of the men and women who inhabited them, amused me. I learned to dance, well enough to stand up at a ball, and to bow in something like the right fashion, and to listen to nonsense with no more than an inward smile of contempt. For the rest, my tailor saw that I was turned out to accord with the fashion.

'These people amused me, and I despised them. Then I met your mother. I was struck by her beauty first. You have grown into a beauty yourself, but though you resemble her somewhat, you do not come up to her. Does this offend you?'

She smiled. 'It does not offend me.'

'I watched her, and paid attention to her, but at first I did not court her. I think maybe her beauty discouraged me a little. With such perfection on the surface, what could lie beneath that would not be a disappointment? But as I watched and listened, I found no disappointment. Her sense, her wit, matched her beauty and surpassed it. I realized that I had discovered perfection in a woman, or as near perfection as made no matter. Then I wanted her, and was determined to have her.'

His voice strengthened as he said it; and for a moment she glimpsed him as he might have been.

'I wooed her,' he said. 'I was vigorous in that as in all my enterprises. I expected to win, but could not believe my fortune when I did. Even though her portion was small, she had suitors in plenty. But she chose me, and I married her in Bristol and brought her here to Guernsey as my bride.

'That was when I discovered a use for the money I had amassed. I determined she should not lack for anything she wanted, either of necessity or luxury. I built this house for her, and furnished it with no regard to cost. She asked me if I had chosen this site, looking out over the western sea, through yearning for that life which I had given up because of her. Not so, I told her. I had chosen it so that each day I might be reminded how much greater a good I had gained than anything the sea had given, or could give me.

'We were happy here – I certainly, and she too, as I thought. She grew big with child, and you were born. Our happiness continued and extended. The small thing that had happened did not affect it – had no part in it.'

He stared for some moments at the painting, as though still seeking an answer to an old question. Then he turned to Sarnia again.

'You are young, a maiden, and my daughter. There are things ordinarily not fit for converse between us. And yet they must be spoken, or the story cannot be told. The nature of a man is not like that of a woman – less tranquil, rougher, especially in its passions. Although I had taken no wife before I met her, I had lived like a sailor, not a monk. Does this shock you, child?'

She coloured, but said: 'It does not shock me.'

'I met your mother, and my desire was only for her. She had a maid when we married; called Marie like your maid, but like her in no other way. Your mother had taken her into service when her mother died and she was left an orphan. You will not have met them, but there are females who pursue men out of desire, as men do women, and this was such a one. I saw her little looks and smiles and recognized them well enough, but they did not touch me. Why should a man drink brackish water, when he has good wine?'

He stared deep into the fire.

'In the ordinary way she could have no power over me. But the time came when your mother was heavy with carrying you. She tempted me again then, one night when I had taken liquor, and that time succeeded. That one time only. I was disgusted with myself and with her, and avoided her thereafter. But it did not seem to me to touch that which there was between your mother and me. How could anything so base have power over something good and noble?

'You were born, and we rejoiced over it together. Some months later, you were left in the charge of that same maid, Marie, when your mother was out visiting, your own nursemaid being ill. She returned to find the girl drunk and you uncared for, unprotected. She had known her weaknesses and pardoned them, but she could not pardon this. The girl was dismissed and, being dismissed, took revenge in telling her what had passed between herself and me.

'Your mother charged me with it. I do not know if she quite believed the story. I could have denied it, as the calumny of a vengeful girl. But I found it hard to lie to her, who was so honest. And although I had been ashamed of my conduct, it did not seem so great a thing. I thought she would forgive my weakness. So I confessed my sin.

'She took it very ill. To her it was no trivial matter, as I had seen it, but an unpardonable betrayal. Women see things differently from men. She turned against me – showed me a cold silent face, removed herself from my bed. I had drunk brackish water out of thirst, when for a time wine was denied me; and now must thirst again.

'Maybe had I been patient, wooed her once more, all might still have been well. I have thought so since. But I was not a patient nor a subtle man. Her coldness enraged me. She was my wife, and I had a husband's rights. I used them and her anger turned to bitter loathing. The more she turned from me, the more I sought her out, and the greater grew her bitterness. I believed I would master her in the end, as I had mastered men who had defied my authority at sea. But instead one day, with no warning, she left this house and left the island, taking you with her.'

Sarnia was overwhelmed by the horror of it – of a woman, her mother, thus tortured by a man's harsh despotism. She was not so much shocked by his reference to the marriage bed as by the fact that he could speak of his own brutish tyranny in this fashion. He deplored its failure and her flight, but did he begin to understand what she must have felt, what misery she had suffered? She did not think so.

'I thought she would come back,' her father said. 'I did not seek after her because of that, and because of pride. It was not a fitting thing for a man to hunt a straying wife. Weeks passed, months, and I realized she had gone for ever. I thought of taking to the sea again, of resuming that life from which she had seduced me. I was in my prime still. I looked out at the sea and thought that there would be a means of forgetting my pain. But when I went in to St Peter Port to negotiate for a vessel, and stepped on the deck of one, I knew it would not do. She had taken the heart out of me, and left me less than half a man. So I came back to this house, and stayed here with my wretchedness.'

He looked at Sarnia. 'That was when I hated her most, finding myself so crippled. I nursed that hatred through the long lonely years.'

She met his look with detestation, hating him for the hate of which he spoke. But he did not seem to notice it. He said:

'Then news was brought to me of her death, and there was the bitterness of knowing she had escaped me forever, the still greater bitterness of knowing that I lived on, in a world through which she moved no longer. You came, child, and I would have hated you in her place. But you returned good for my evil. There is no more hatred. I love her again, as I loved her when the world was young. The painting surprised me, and I was angry, but not with her nor you. I was angry with those I thought were using you.'

He paused. 'You said she would have wished you to tend me. Do you truly believe so?'

She wanted to cry 'No!', to turn away from him, to leave this house in which her mother had suffered, and where this man's hatred had smouldered for so long. But she could not do it. Reluctantly, against volition almost, she spoke.

'Yes, I believe so.'

XIV

After a last wild night of furious battering, the gales died away and the weather settled into a calm. Next morning when Sarnia rose she looked from her window to see the familiar prospect, of waves beating in on a rocky shore, replaced by a dazzling whiteness. The landscape immediately below the house was clear, though at this hour still in the shadow of the hill on which Beauregard stood. Less than a hundred yards away, though, the mist began, and extended as far as the eye could see. It had two aspects – the nearer grey, the second white with the sun's refulgence.

Edmund rode over as usual that morning. He found Sarnia in the kitchen, giving instructions to the cleaning women. He took over the task, speaking their *patois*, and she thankfully relinquished it. Afterwards he said:

'There, that is enough. You must have a break from these domestic duties before they exhaust you. Go up and change into your habit, while I see to the saddling of your horse.'

He had spoken the previous day of their riding together. It would be low tide in the morning and they could ride along the beach to Pleinmont. She protested:

'But we cannot, with such a mist.'

'It is not so dense when one is in it as it appears from here. Go and change.'

She allowed herself to be commanded. When she came down he had the horse saddled and ready at the door. Now the mist was white in its entirety, and there was sunlight on the field across which its upper boundary lay. They rode downhill and into the cloud.

It was, as he said, less dense than it appeared. This was a grey shifting world, but one could see for a dozen paces, sometimes, as the mist swirled and thinned, for much further. It was strange, and in a fashion, exciting. Their voices echoed weirdly and other sounds were distorted: the creak of a cart wheel, a dog's mournful howling, running water, the lofty shriek of a gull – all, divorced from their invisible sources, came as though for the first time to the ear, pristine and startling.

They reached the shore and rode southwards over the grey sand, firm and damp from the sea's lavation. He gave news of the town, and asked about her father's health. Very greatly improved, she told him. He came down each day in the afternoon – had wanted to rise and dress this morning, too, but she had forbidden it.

'You have a great influence over him.'

She ignored that. 'I am glad he is so much better. It means that I can leave him with a good conscience, when I return to London.'

She thought there might be some objection to that, a renewed persuasion that she should stay longer on the island. But he said nothing. She glanced to see his head turned, attentive to something on their right.

'Do you hear?' he asked.

She heard voices in the distance, though unintelligible. But that way lay the sea. She said:

'Fishermen? Do they fish in such a mist as this? And on so rocky a coast?'

'Come. Let me show you.'

He turned his horse down the beach and she followed. She heard the lap of waves, and the voices louder and nearer. Then shadowy figures – of men and, she saw with surprise, a horse and cart. Remembering what Advocate Martell had told her she asked, with something of alarm:

'Are they smugglers?'

Edmund laughed. 'There are no smugglers nowadays, and anyway the smuggling was all onto English shores! They are merely gathering *vraic*.'

'*Vraic?*'

'Sea-weed, in English. It is a custom here. Twice a year men go out to cut the weed from the rocks to which it clings. Do you see those scythes they carry?'

'But to what purpose?'

'That which is cut at the end of winter is laid on the growing crops, as a manure. We have an old saying: *"point de vraic, point de hautgard"*. No sea-weed, no corn-yard, that means. But the present cutting will chiefly be for next winter's fuel.'

'Fuel? Can one burn sea-weed?'

'After it has been laid out and dried in the sun, it will burn. It does not give a very cheerful warmth, but it provides heat; and it costs nothing apart from the labour of gathering and spreading. The common people rarely use coal except on feast days.'

They dismounted and walked further down the beach, Edmund leading the horses, to observe the scene more closely. The rocks on which the weed grew were far out at this point, he explained, and only exposed at low tide. They saw two carts in addition to the first. Figures moved, insubstantial in the mist. While some men cut the weed loose, others forked it up. It made a pretty scene, and he told her that the labour would be followed by feasting; after they had gathered in the *vraic* they drank cider and ate sweet vraicking cakes, and generally made merry.

The task was completed while they watched. The carts, piled high with weed, were driven up the beach, the men following. They vanished into the mist, although voices could still be heard, and the crunch of cart wheels in the sand.

Sarnia turned to Edmund, expecting him to help her remount her horse. He did not move, but stared at her. She was conscious of the intensity of his regard, and also of their isolation.

She put out a hand to take the horse's rein, but he did not give it to her. Instead he let both reins drop against the horses' flanks. He moved towards her then, and his hands grasped her shoulders.

She stared at him. The dark face bent towards her, very slowly it seemed and yet, although she wished it, she could not withdraw her own. The hands squeezed her shoulders, and it was as though they squeezed her heart. The lips came down and fastened hard on hers.

She did not know what she felt, except that it was an emotion utterly strange. There were oppositions in it: urges both to yielding and to flight. His embrace seemed to fulfil her but at the same time touched off a panic fear. She felt her heart's wild beating against his chest. The voices were growing fainter. She heard the waves lapping against the rocks, and her own shuddering breath. She wanted desperately to free herself, but could not break the spell.

Until the lips that were pressed against hers parted, and she felt the intrusion of his tongue. Even that shock had things other than repulsion in it, but it restored her will. She broke from him in a quick movement, and stood gasping. He made as though to renew the embrace, and she stepped back. Their eyes met, and she knew he read in hers the finality of refusal.

He said: 'I'm sorry. It was an impulse. I do not regret that, but the yielding to it. Sarnia, will you forgive me?'

'Of course.' She shook her head, to clear its dizziness. 'It does not matter.'

She took her horse's rein and Edmund helped her into the saddle. His manner was correct. She thought his hand lingered for a brief instant in its grasp of her foot, but could not be sure she was not deceiving herself. She still felt shaken and confused. They rode in silence up the beach, following the path the *vraic*-gatherers had taken.

Her only concern now was to get back to Beauregard. They found the slipway, built of granite setts, which marked the limit of the beach, and clattered over it. Boats were drawn up there, and a fisherman smoked a pipe on an upturned dinghy. He was wearing the blue woollen garment which took its name from the island – a guernsey – and he called a greeting, to which Edmund casually replied. A peaceful reassuring scene, but her heart was thumping still. She set her horse towards the lane that led uphill.

They came quite suddenly out of grey mist into sunshine, and the sight of the house. She felt relief, a quietening of the pulse, but they still rode in silence. It was she who broke it as they came to the house, exclaiming at the sight of a horse, dapple-grey with a conspicuous white streak along its muzzle, which stood tethered outside.

'A visitor? Who can it be, I wonder?'

Edmund shrugged indifferently and, slipping from Chevalier, helped her to dismount. She went through into the hall as he led the horses away, and found Troutaud.

She asked him: 'Who is it that has called?'

The small face gave a small smile, with knowingness in it.

'Why, it is Advocate Martell, Miss Sarnia. He is with the master now.'

Sarnia changed out of her riding habit and washed, using cold water from the jug rather than summon Marie to bring hot. Her mind ran on what had happened on the beach, trying to comprehend her own behaviour. She had not imagined she possessed such a weakness of the senses, nor such a desire to indulge them. It was the mist, she told herself, the feeling of isolation that had been at fault. She must take care that no similar situation should occur.

Because she knew, very surely, that she did not want anything like that to happen again; and not only from mistrust of her own powers of resistance, or fear of the terrible consequences that might ensue. Even while she had responded to the pressure of his lips, the warm strength of his body against her own, she had also hated them. More than anything she had loathed the dreadful sense of helplessness, the essential weakness of her desire as it surrendered to the mastery of his. No, there must not be another occasion like today's. She shook her head: she would see to it there was not.

She was still thinking of this as she went downstairs. She was wearing soft slipper shoes which made little sound, and she saw

Edmund without his being aware of her. At once she halted on the stair, embarrassed by her thoughts and by the prospect of confronting him. Then she realized he was in converse with someone hidden from her by the angle of the hall. His voice was low and confidential: she could not catch the words.

Was he talking to Advocate Martell, she wondered? But at that moment the door of her father's bedroom opened behind her, and she heard Mr Martell's voice bidding him goodbye. Edmund clearly heard it too, and, breaking off his conversation, went through to the rear of the house. As he did the person with whom he had been speaking came the other way and into view, and she saw that it was Troutaud.

She waited on the stairs to greet Mr Martell and ask him to take wine. As they went into the morning room, she asked:

'How did you find my father?'

'Astonishingly well, and in good spirits. I was surprised when he sent word that he had some business for me. I had feared my business affairs with him were over, from the reports I had. But he looked better than he has done for years.' He smiled. 'And this is a business I am very happy to perform.'

He looked as though he might be ready to talk of it, but she was not curious. She was thinking, as she brought the sherry decanter to Mr Martell and poured him a glass, of Edmund. There had seemed to be a kind of intimacy, unlooked for in relation to a servant, in the conversation she had chanced on. And the question of the horse was puzzling also. With so unique a marking it must be familiar to Edmund, who anyway knew the horses of every acquaintance the family had. Yet when she had speculated as to who the visitor might be, he had merely shrugged, as though in ignorance.

But these, she told herself as Mr Martell raised his glass to her and she smiled in return, were absurd fancies. The incident on the beach had perhaps disturbed Edmund as much as it had troubled her: that could well account for his behaviour over the horse. And the talk with Troutaud? No more, probably, than an exhortation to take good care of her in his own absence. He had amply demonstrated his concern and fondness for her. She felt the beginning of a blush and turned away from Mr Martell's view. His fondness all too amply!

Her father came down to luncheon, and in the afternoon asked if she would walk with him. They went out by way of the conservatory, which was large but uncared for, with many panes broken and others missing. He pointed with his stick, of polished ash with a silver handle top.

'That was a good vine, but the frost killed it three winters ago. Or four? I grew oranges here once, and was minded to plant bananas.'

The door into the garden leaned ajar, but would not budge when he pushed it. Sarnia put her own hand to it and it shifted, grating on stone. They came onto a small terrace, arboured on one side, low-walled at the front, which looked across the garden. But the wall was weathered and broken, the arbour riotous, the garden beyond a desolation.

'She liked to sit here,' he said, 'on hot summer days, shaded from the sun. It was a pretty spot, then.'

Sarnia made no answer and they walked down into the garden. There were paths, though greatly overgrown. They passed a vast tangle of rose-bushes, with pink blossoms crowning the mound of green, poised unmoving in the windless air. Her father said abruptly:

'You saw Martell?'

'Yes.'

'Did he tell you what brought him here?'

She shook her head. 'No.'

'There is no secret about it. I called him out to instruct him in drawing up a new will.'

Sarnia was silent. She sensed what might be coming but did not know what to say. The old man looked at her, and she met his eyes.

'As you have been told, a half of my estate will pass to you by law. The remaining half I am free to dispose of. I am leaving that to you, also.'

She felt a heaviness, a reluctance even to think.

'There is no need.'

'Not as far as you are concerned, maybe, but I have a need. Do not argue with me, child.'

The path, with weeds growing up between its stones, ran through what had once been lawn but was now rank grass – did the rabbits not nibble here, she wondered? – to a rustic summerhouse. She had put up her parasol on leaving the house, but the heat struck up from the ground. Her mind seemed stifled by it.

She said: 'Father.'

'Yes?'

'I have been here a week. In another week I shall leave – this house and the island – to return to London. I am determined on it.'

'As you wish. You are welcome to come or go, as you choose. I will make no pleas, and use no threats. It is no condition of the legacy that you stay with me.'

'Before I go, I wish to find someone who will take my place and look after you.'

He looked at her. 'I will not oppose that, either. I understand that it is your need, as mine is to make my arrangements with Martell.'

She was moved by the depth and strength of his resignation. They reached the summerhouse and he sat down, heavily, on the bench outside. There was a quick movement and the tabby cat darted out and away through the grass. Was it he, she wondered, who kept the rabbits out of the garden? He had learned to take titbits from her hand, but was wild still.

She looked at the profile of her father, as he gazed back towards the house. He was far stronger than he had been, but an old man. There was no cure for that, but one.

She thought of her mother's unhappiness and his part in it, but whereas it had moved her to anger and disgust, she felt now more of sadness for a faraway grief. Two people had contended here, and the one she loved had lost, had been humiliated and defeated. And yet, in another sense, had won; because she had had the courage to run away, and had left him empty, yearning for what he could never have again, facing a future without joy or hope.

She said: 'I am going to London. But I shall come back to visit you.'

'I am very glad to hear it. Install your housekeeper, then.' He looked over the garden's wildness towards the house. 'Some renewal of this place is long overdue. And perhaps I am not too feeble to oversee it.'

She smiled. 'I am sure you are not.'

He put a bony hand on hers. 'I spoke to you once, concerning Edmund Jelain. Do you remember?'

'Yes.'

'He visits every day.'

'It is a kindness for which I am grateful.'

'Kindness, to court a pretty girl?' She did not answer that. 'For it is courting, is it not? Has he put the question to you yet?'

She hesitated, and he went on: 'No matter. If he has not he soon will – we both know it. When he does – what answer will you give him?'

His eyes watched her. She said, in this moment knowing it for certainty:

'I shall tell him no.'

'You are sure of that ?'

'Quite sure.'

He said with relief: 'I had not thought you could give yourself to a villain, but it is good to be assured of it.'

She took away her hand and said sharply: 'But I will not listen to him being called a villain. He has been good to me, as they all have.'

'Their goodness, as you call it, has had a purpose. What is their aim, do you think, but that their son should marry you – for the money which you will inherit on my death?'

'That is absurd. The Jelains are rich themselves.'

He laughed, an old man's croaking.

'Rich? Rich in show, maybe! It is true he had money in the past. Would Jeanne have married such a dreary dog without it? But it has trickled through his fingers in bad investments and waste. He sent to me a year ago, looking for a loan. I had his affairs looked into then. The man has been living from bond to bond, and he will get no more. By Christmas he will be in *désastre*.'

'*Désastre?*'

'A bankrupt. His creditors are already snapping at his heels.'

'Then why could you not give him a loan? He is your cousin.'

'And I am mean and hard, a tightfist? There is some truth in it. But I have helped him in the past, and it has done neither of us any good. My legacy to you includes half a dozen of his notes of hand, which you may tear up when you get them. You would be as well to do so, for they are worthless.'

She was silent, trying to reconcile this with the kindness and generosity the Jelains had shown her. It could not be true; yet why should her father lie?

'I have seen through the manoeuvre from the start,' he said. 'Your aunt wrote to me when your mother died. I did not answer it. The letter opened up a wound I thought had healed. But somehow they found out about it. I do not know how, unless your aunt wrote to them also.'

She said involuntarily: 'Troutaud.'

'Troutaud?'

'I have seen him in close converse' – she hesitated – 'with Mrs Jelain, on that first day I came to this house.'

'It might be so. He could have seen the letter. They would have promised him money. No more than promises, but they have some skill in peddling them, and much experience.'

He seemed indifferent. She said:

'It does not trouble you – to think your man might have so betrayed your confidence?'

He smiled grimly. 'My expectations of human beings have for a long time been low, and were never high. Yes, that will be it. So they took that trip to London with the purpose of finding you and bringing you back for that son of theirs. There would be the hope also of reconciling us two. They would be content with getting their hands on half my estate, but only if they could not see a way to getting the whole.'

She was confused. If it were true that the Jelains were in desperate need of money ... But she could not believe them to have been capable of such deceit. It was his cynicism that put that gloss upon their generosity; a cynicism made worse by loneliness and old age.

He looked at her, nodding. 'But I'll warrant you're a match for them. They will not fool you so easily. And the reconciliation between us, which they sought, does them little good, since it gives me more will to live. Shall we walk back to the house, daughter? I fancy it is almost time for tea.'

Martell returned that evening with the new will and it was signed, with Troutaud and Martell himself as witnesses. Her father drank sherry with the advocate in good spirits and declared, when Martell had left, that he had a keen appetite for supper.

He had spoken that morning of his desire for a broth of mussels. Troutaud had obtained them of a Pleinmont fisherman in the afternoon, and Sarnia had prepared the dish as a first course. Troutaud brought them in to where they sat at opposite ends of the long table in the dining room. Her father spooned up his mussels, and said with satisfaction:

'Excellent! Though it is the gravy which makes the difference. You have a heavy hand with the brandy, daughter.'

She had put the brandy into his, since Troutaud said he liked it, reserving her own without liquor. But she thought she had been sparing with it. He continued to eat, with every sign of enjoyment. Probably it would seem strong to him, after his illness.

His appetite was indeed good. He had cutlets afterwards, and some Burgundy wine.

'It is a long time since I dined so well,' he said. 'I do not think the housekeeper you find me will procure meals as good. Good night, then. I will see you at breakfast in the morning. And downstairs. I have had enough of lying abed.'

He kissed her cheek, and took his candle and went upstairs.

A fresh storm arose in the night, with the sound of distant thunder and the wind howling up from the sea. She thought at first it was the wind which had awakened her, and lay there listening. But it came again and was a human cry – a cry of agony.

She lit a candle from her night-light and went quickly to her father's room. He was not in his bed but on the floor, groaning. The groans turned to a terrible retching. He had vomited already; the bed and his nightshirt were stained with it.

She held his head till the fit subsided, and wiped his face. He gasped for water, and she found the glass he had by his bed, but empty. She ran to the landing and called for Marie, who came trembling. She told her to get water and to fetch Troutaud; then returned to tend her father.

Troutaud, when he came, looked gloomily at him.

'It must be on account of those mussels,' he said.

'I had them also, and am not ill.'

He shook his head. 'One bad one is enough.'

'Ride over and get Dr Falla. Hurry. Tell him how ill my father is. Beg him to come at once.'

He glanced towards the window, where the storm was raging outside. She said sharply:

'Go now. Every moment matters.'

Marie re-made the bed and she settled him in it and sat close by, holding a bowl for the continuing bouts of sickness. The night dragged on, the storm gradually easing, and she listened anxiously for the sound of hooves. It was a long way to St Peter Port, and a long way back. The dawn light started to grow in the sky, and as it did his groaning grew less. The worst was over, she thought. When he was quiet at last she thought that he was sleeping and pulled the sheet up over his exposed shoulder, very carefully so as not to wake him.

It was some moments before the extremity of his stillness troubled her, and she put a hand up to his mouth, and found no breath.

XV

'DRINK THIS,' Dr Falla commanded.

Sarnia was in her bed, having been carried to her room by Troutaud, on the doctor's instructions. The two men had arrived at Beauregard to find her weeping uncontrollably beside the body of her father, with Marie frightened and helpless nearby. She was not weeping now, but her mind worked a dreadful treadmill of horror and guilt. She had prepared the dish of mussels, and Troutaud had been right, surely, in suggesting that this had brought on the fatal sickness.

'It was my doing.' She stared at the doctor as he bent over her. 'It is I who have killed him ...'

He held the glass to her lips, and with his other hand behind her head coaxed her to drink. The draught had a sweet syrupy taste. She closed her eyes.

'What am I to do? Oh God, what am I to do?'

'Rest,' Dr Falla said. 'You are exhausted, both in body and mind. Only rest.'

How could she rest? The doctor left her, with Marie in attendance, and she tossed and turned feverishly. She could not rest. But her mind clouded; and she woke up with the sunshine of afternoon flooding in at her window, and Mrs Jelain in Marie's place at her bedside. She was confused and had no recollection of the night. Sitting up, she cried:

'Aunt Jeanne! Why are you here? And why ...?'

Memory returned, gripping her with pain and shock. Mrs Jelain said:

'It is all right, *chérie*. You must not fret.'

'He is dead! And through my fault ...'

'No. You must not think so. He asked for the dish of mussels, and there is nothing wrong with them in the ordinary way. One could give them to a baby without fear. There must have been one among them that was bad. And he, being an old man and weakened by his illness ... it is not anyone's fault.'

She clasped her arms round her body, rocking herself.

'Why did I not refuse him? I knew he had been ill. How could I have committed such folly?'

'I will not have you blame yourself. It is something there could be no reckoning with. And he would have been dead, anyway, if you had not come to tend him: Dr Falla swears to it. You gave him some happiness before his end. It was more than he could have looked for.'

The other woman's compassion brought on a storm of weeping. Mrs Jelain held her head against her while she sobbed. When the fit wore itself out at last, she said:

'Now, *chérie,* we must get you dressed for the journey.'

'A journey?'

She thought in her confusion that the return journey to England was meant, and felt a new surge of guilt. They must hold her responsible for his death, to want to pack her off so quickly. But Mrs Jelain said:

'To Les Colombelles. The carriage is waiting.'

'No.' She shook her head feebly. 'There are things here that I must do.'

'Troutaud can see to all that needs doing at this moment, under Edmund's instruction. It is you that needs care. So terrible a thing – to be left all night with a dying man – no wonder it has disabled you.' She pressed her hand. 'I will send Marie to help you dress.'

Her thoughts lacked order and direction, and there was relief in accepting another's will. Marie helped her to dress, in silence but with little looks of sympathy. She went down to join Mrs Jelain, but looked first in her father's room. His body had been laid out, and rested on a board beneath the sheet. His hands were folded across his breast, and there were pennies on his eyes. Although the lines of his face were hard, the bone sharp beneath the white skin, his expression was peaceful. She thought of her mother lying so, in the room in Paddington. The story was ended. For both of them there was peace.

As the landau jolted its way eastwards she was silent, and Mrs Jelain did not seek to engage her in conversation. The journey seemed an interminable one, but at last they came to the town, and so to Les Colombelles. She must go to bed at once, Mrs Jelain insisted, and once more she felt too weak to refuse. Mrs Jelain was anxious also that she should take some nourishment, but that she could not do. A bowl of soup was brought to her in bed, but she was quite unable to touch it.

Dr Falla came in the evening. The shock had been very great, he declared, the injury to her nerves considerable. He gave her more of the soothing potion, and she drifted into troubled sleep.

For the next two days she remained in bed. She slept on and off, but not restfully. She was troubled by nightmares, and more than once awoke crying out, living again the horror of her father's death. She was fevered and had heavy bouts of sweating. Her mind remained dizzy and confused.

On the following morning she rose and washed and dressed, though with a frequent need for pauses to regain her strength. She went downstairs, holding on to the banister, and saw Mrs Perret in the hall. A moment later, Mrs Jelain appeared from the garden.

'My dear Sarnia! You must go back to your bed. You are not yet fit to be about.'

She shook her head. 'I shall be all right, Aunt Jeanne. I am feeling much better.'

'But one must not take chances. Let me take you back to your room, I beg you.'

'No. I am determined to stay up. There will be my father's funeral to attend. When is it to be?'

'Do not worry about that. It is all over.'

'Over?' She stared in disbelief. 'But when?'

'The burial was yesterday afternoon. Mr Jelain and Edmund attended it.'

'But why so soon? And why was I not told?'

'It is not our custom to keep burials waiting long, in summer especially. As to your not being told, Dr Falla was against it, as something which might distress you unduly. A wreath was sent in your name, and I am told it was much admired. The inscription ran: "From his loving and sorrowing daughter." '

She said wretchedly: 'I ought to have been told. It is quite wrong that it was kept from me.'

'You have been very ill, you know. One must take a doctor's advice in such matters.' She put her hand on Sarnia's arm. 'Now let me see you to your bed. Marie will undress you.'

The hand was suddenly unwelcome, and Sarnia shook it off.

'I insist on staying up!'

Mrs Jelain smiled easily. 'Then stay up, my dear. But at least do not exert yourself. Come, we will make you comfortable on the parlour sofa, and you will have breakfast on a tray. If you wish to restore your strength, you must eat.'

She did feel hungry, for the first time since that hideous night. She said:

'I must see his grave.'

'And so you shall.' Mrs Jelain took her arm, and this time she allowed it. 'But you do not have the vigour for such an undertaking yet. Even to step outdoors would tax you sadly. Eat and rest, and when you are feeling more yourself, Edmund will show you your father's resting place.'

The graveyard was not far from the house, less than ten minutes on foot, but the Jelains insisted on the carriage. Sarnia was still too weak to walk out, Mrs Jelain declared, and Edmund supported the argument. In fact, Sarnia was not sorry to acquiesce. Although she had ceased taking Dr Falla's potion, a lethargy clung to her mind and her limbs felt weak. She was grateful for the help of Edmund's arm as he led her from the landau to the graveyard.

It stood on high ground, on the side of a hill. A granite wall surrounded it but there was a spot from which one could look down over the town, to the harbour and the sea. The day was unsettled, a little chill, and a wind carried seagulls in long shrieking arcs overhead. Despite the protecting walls, it ruffled the wreaths heaped above the low mound of earth. The flowers were fading, and rain had smudged the writing on the cards. There were more of both than she had expected, and she spoke of that to Edmund.

He said: 'We honour the dead, regardless of their disposition or popularity in life. It is an island tradition. The church was packed with people.'

'I should have been there.'

'No. Dr Falla was right. And in fact it is uncommon for members of your sex to attend funerals. That is another island custom. Our women mourn behind closed doors.'

The wreath sent in her name was enormous in size, made up of the huge Guernsey lilies. There had been nothing so splendid at her mother's burial. She knelt by the grave, and prayed. She thought of Michael. He, being a Roman, would have prayed for the souls of the dead, but she could not. They were at peace. She prayed for the strength to believe it utterly.

When she rose, Edmund led her to a seat that looked out over the wall. He was gentle but firm: she must rest. He held her hand and talked of things that had no relation to death or to her father – concerning the harbour, the town, the life of the island. She was thankful for this consideration. She felt her dull depression lift a little, and said with feeling:

'I cannot tell you how truly appreciative I am of all your kindness.'

'It has been very little. And no trouble could be too great in view of the esteem in which we all hold you. In which I especially do.'

There had been a difference of tone in his voice which silenced her. She wanted him to return to talking about casual things; the thought of anything else was intolerable. When he pressed her hand she tried to draw it away, but he held it firmly.

'My dear Sarnia, I have asked you before, and I beg you now to give me an acceptance. I offer you my heart, and all I have. Will you not be my wife?'

'I do not ...' She felt confused again, and all her weakness flooding back. 'I could not – not at this time – could not entertain such thoughts. My father ...'

'I understand your scruples, but you must put them aside. Your father is dead, and you are alone. You need protection, a strong arm to help you. Let me provide it.'

She tried to think clearly. This was nonsense, she wanted to say. The father who had just died had not existed for her until a few weeks ago. She had been on her own, after her mother's death, amid the far greater perils of London, with no protecting male. What difference was there now?

Yet there was one. Then she had been an ordinary girl, orphaned without money, someone who must make her own way in the world, and count herself lucky to be employed as a bank clerk. This second death left an heiress. It was not the girl who needed guarding, but her fortune.

Was it possible that what her father had said of the Jelains, the afternoon before he died, had been simple truth, that everything had been planned with this in view: the acquisition of her father's wealth to shore up their own crumbling finances? If Edmund married her, he would control her money. She still could not believe it, but here Edmund was, making a second declaration only a few feet from the flowers heaped on her father's grave. Surely, on any consideration, it was improper for him to press her at such a time?

She heard her father's voice: 'I'll warrant you're a match for them. They will not fool you so easily.'

She said, gathering her resolution: 'I am grateful – indebted – for this, as for everything else. But I could not even consider such a thing yet. When I have returned to London, and my emotions are more settled ....'

'You must not think of going back to London.' He spoke with great firmness. 'There is no need for it. It is not as though you have connections there. Only an employment, and it is unthinkable now that you should return to that. Why, you do not even have a place to live.'

She had spoken to him of the Wilkinsons, and mentioned Mr Wilkinson's refusal to keep her room in Red Lion Square.

'I can easily find somewhere,' she said. 'An hotel. And I have friends in London.'

'Do you not have friends here? Relations, also. All your interests lie in the island. You must be aware of the change which has occurred in your life. London belongs to the past. Guernsey represents your future.'

'I will come back to the island. Make no doubt of that. But I shall hold to my purpose of returning to England first. I shall go within a few days.'

She saw his brow contract, and thought he would pursue the argument, perhaps angrily. But after a moment his face cleared, and he said:

'We will talk of it another time, cousin. I must see you home. You are fatigued, and still nervous from the shock.'

Later she applied to Mrs Jelain: would it be possible for someone to procure a ticket for her passage back to England, on Friday's mail packet, today being Wednesday? Mrs Jelain repeated Edmund's argument: there was no need for her to return to the mainland, and she must not think of it. She was not yet fit to travel, in any case.

'Monday's packet, then. I shall be quite capable of travelling by that time.'

'Are you so eager to leave us, *chérie?*'

'No. Indeed, not. But I have friends in London. I really must return.'

She saw Mrs Jelain's face cloud. She said:

'I am sure your friends will be willing to spare you a little longer.'

'I must go, at least by Monday's packet.'

'We will talk of it with Dr Falla.'

'I promise you, I am quite well already!'

Dr Falla called that evening. Sarnia was glad to see him at first; but his manner proved more earnest than reassuring, his examination prolonged, his tone dubious. The shock, he pronounced, had been greater than she herself had realized. Her nerves were in a sadly weak state. She denied this and when he wagged his ugly head found herself growing shrill in her protest. His manner showed he found this confirmation of his judgement, her voice became still more unsteady, and she found herself collapsing into tears. He patted her, hatefully, on the shoulder.

'A very great shock, as I say. It will do no permanent harm, but you must take time to recover. Have you been taking the medicine I gave you?'

She shook her head. 'It makes me sleepy, dizzy.'

'But it will fortify and restore your nerves. I must insist that you continue with it. I will give you a draught now, and you will see how it soothes your distress.'

She had to accept it from him. The drowsiness came back; she almost lacked strength to undress for bed. She slept heavily, with weird unhappy dreams.

In the morning she felt her senses still numbed, but her resolution had returned. The medicine was brought with her breakfast tray, and afterwards she tipped it out of the window. When Mrs Jelain came to see her, she feigned more tiredness than she felt; she saw the other's eyes take in the empty medicine glass.

'You need rest, *chérie,*' Mrs Jelain said. 'You will be quite well soon, but for the moment you must rest.'

Whatever their motives might be she would get no help from them. They were determined to keep her here, and they had Dr Falla's support. She had made up her mind that she must act on her own initiative. She would wait for a suitable opportunity to leave the house, and herself purchase a ticket for the boat.

She kept her pocket-book in the top drawer of the bedroom

chest, and as soon as she was alone she rose from her bed and went to get it. She would count what money she had, though she was confident there was ample for her return to London. She pulled open the drawer, and looked inside. The pocket-book was not in the corner where she was used to leave it. She searched through the drawer, and the other drawers. There was no sign of it.

She rang for Marie and asked her to fetch Mrs Jelain.

'Is there anything you want, my dear? A book from the circulating library? We will send in for anything you wish.'

Sarnia said: 'My pocket-book, Aunt Jeanne – it is not in the drawer where I left it.'

'Is it not? But perhaps you left it at Beauregard?'

'I am sure I did not. I can remember bringing it.'

'Your mind was so disordered, I doubt if any recollection could be reliable. Edmund will ask Troutaud about it, when he next rides over.'

She knew, with a swift and appalling conviction, that the other woman was lying. She did not at first understand why. Even though they might wish to have Edmund marry her for her fortune they could not surely desire, she thought wildly, to strip her of the few sovereigns she had brought with her. She said:

'It was here. I am sure of it!'

'My dear, do you accuse the servants of theft? Marie, perhaps? It is she who has attended you.'

Understanding came. It was not the money of which they wished to deprive her, but the opportunity of leaving the island. They had foreseen the possibility of her purchasing her own ticket, and were determined to prevent it. Without money, she was helpless.

The tone of Mrs Jelain's remark had been a little indignant. Now, perceiving Sarnia's hesitance, she was sympathetic again.

'I know you would not think of such a thing. Edmund will search for the pocket-book at Beauregard. But it is not of great concern.' She pressed Sarnia's hand. 'You have no need of money while you are with us. Only say what you want, and we shall see that you get it.'

She lacked even the penny for the stamp. Giving the letter to Marie, she asked if she had one and, when she nodded, begged the loan of it. She would pay it back, she said, and Marie nodded again, though it was doubtful if she understood. Sarnia turned to the scant French she remembered, and explained haltingly. She wished her to post the letter, but tell no one. It was a secret. But very important.

'*Tu le comprends?*'
'*Oui, mam'selle.*'
'You will do this for me?'
'I will.' Marie slipped the letter into her dress. 'I will, mam'selle.'

XVI

SARNIA WAS AT BREAKFAST with Mrs Jelain when Mrs Perret announced the caller. It was a little after nine o'clock, and Mr Jelain and Edmund had already breakfasted and left the house. Mrs Jelain said, with surprise:

'A caller? At this hour? Who is it?'

The housekeeper handed her a calling card, which she examined suspiciously.

'Is it Dowling? I cannot read without my spectacles. Look at it for me, Sarnia. We know no one of such a name.'

Her heart pounding, Sarnia said: 'I believe the caller is for me, Aunt Jeanne.'

'For you?'

There was astonishment in her tone but also, Sarnia thought, suspicion. She said:

'At least, I knew a Mr Dowling in London. He also worked in Mr Merton's banking house. It could be he.'

'But did you know he was to visit Guernsey?'

She was glad to be able to be truthful.

'No. I had no notion of it.'

'How very strange.' She looked at the calling card again. 'But it is plain he knows your whereabouts?'

'I have corresponded with him.'

'I see.'

There was a pause while Mrs Perret waited for instructions. What would happen, Sarnia wondered, if Mrs Jelain were to refuse him admission – send the housekeeper to say they were not at home? Surely she dared not? If she did, there must be open defiance: Michael must not be turned away. But Mrs Jelain said at last:

'Show this gentleman into the morning room, Perret. Tell him we shall join him directly.' When the housekeeper had gone, she looked keenly at Sarnia. 'This is an odd occurrence, a very odd occurrence.'

On that, Sarnia was very much inclined to agree. She had written to Michael, saying merely that she had lost her pocket-book, and asking if he could send her money to enable her to pay her passage home: she would repay him on her return to London. She had been hoping for a letter from him by this day's delivery. She had not dreamt of his appearing in person.

She had hoped to have the opportunity of seeing him alone, but it was not to be: Mrs Jelain accompanied her to the morning room. Sarnia was apprehensive of what he might say, knowing his antagonism towards the Jelains; but his manners were good. He apologized for the early hour of his call. He had not wished to disturb anyone, merely to apprise Miss Lorimer of his presence on the island.

Mrs Jelain asked: 'Have you been long in Guernsey, Mr Dowling?'

'A couple of hours, only. I travelled by last night's mail packet.'

'I see.' Her surprise was marked, and meant to be. 'Do you have accommodation?'

'I have taken a room in Garner's Hotel. It is not far from here.'

'No, indeed. Do you plan a long stay?'

'I am not yet sure how long.'

'You are on business, perhaps?'

'No. Merely on pleasure.'

Mrs Jelain smiled, without warmth. 'It is a rare coincidence, is it not, that you should have chosen to come on holiday to the same spot as Miss Lorimer?'

Michael said easily: 'Scarcely a coincidence, ma'am. Miss Lorimer has written in such glowing terms about the island that anyone who read her letters must be tempted to visit it.'

'And yet you did not write to her, to tell her in advance of your intention of coming here?'

'The opportunity was an unexpected one. I am here in advance of any letter I could have written.'

Mrs Jelain continued for some time to quiz Michael, receiving polite but evasive replies. The atmosphere was, on her side, distinctly chill; there was no offer of refreshment, and no suggestion of retiring to leave the two of them alone. Eventually Michael said:

'I must not trespass any further on your time and patience, ma'am.' He bowed to Mrs Jelain, and said directly to Sarnia: 'I hope you will permit me to call on you again, Miss Lorimer, at a more convenient hour. And you can get word to me at any time at Garner's Hotel.'

Sarnia saw Mrs Jelain frown at the last sentence. She said to Michael: 'I will walk with you to the gates.' The frown deepened but she disregarded it. 'It is a fine morning and the air will do me good.'

Mrs Jelain looked as though she would have dearly liked to prevent her, but did not know how to set about it. They left the house and walked along the drive, and she asked urgently:

'*Why* did you come here?'

'In case you needed help.'

'But I asked merely for the loan of money, not for you to come after me!'

'You said you had lost your pocket-book. You were staying with these relations, who entertained you so lavishly in London. If want of money were your only concern, surely you would have applied to them?'

'I did not wish to do so. But …'

'Your letter made me uneasy. You spoke of your longing to be in London again, in a different fashion from before. It was as though you spoke of something from which you were being held back.' He looked at her. 'I was worried on your account, deeply worried.'

Sarnia had already come to regard her earlier anxieties as absurd, and Michael's unexpected appearance only reinforced this. How could the Jelains possibly have kept her from returning to England? Even if there had been some scheme for Edmund to marry her, how could they possibly carry it through if she refused him? It had probably been unnecessary even to apply to Michael for a loan; she could almost certainly have got the money from Advocate Martell as an advance on her expectations under her father's will. She said, managing to laugh:

'You have too powerful an imagination, Michael! This is not some South Sea island, peopled by savages. What could there possibly be to cause concern?'

He said gravely: 'I do not know. But I thought it best to make certain.'

'And you have come so quickly! You could only just have received my letter. How did you manage that? How did you get leave of absence from the bank?'

'Mr Merton granted it. I asked for it in lieu of the holiday I was to have later in the summer. He readily agreed – you know how indulgent he is.'

She said quickly: 'You did not tell him that you were alarmed on my account?'

'I did not speak of you at all. I spoke of an aunt at Southampton who was ill, and needed me.'

She laughed again. 'What a dreadful lie! And even if Mr Merton does not find it out, you will have to confess it to your priest, will you not?' He looked unhappy, and she put a hand on his arm. 'Dear Michael, I am well aware that you have done this through concern for me, and am truly grateful. But you should not have. You have sacrificed your later holiday, and for nothing.'

They had reached the gates. In the lane outside, ragged children played in the mud, and further down a knife grinder cried his services. Michael faced her, and took her hands.

'All that matters is that I am here. I do not regret coming. I have money for you, and will give it to you now, if you wish.' She shook her head. 'But I would rather you permitted me to escort you back to London. Will you do that?'

Probably her fears *had* been illusory, the notion of a conspiracy to capture her father's fortune nonsensical. On a morning like this, with the sun breaking through scudding clouds and the sea blue and sparkling at the foot of the hill, it was impossible to believe otherwise. But she was glad of Michael's hands on hers, glad of the presence of a man who would protect her if need should ever arise, and for whom she was never likely to feel any fear, illusory or not.

She said: 'Yes, I will.'

'By Wednesday's packet?'

That meant the next mail packet, since this was Monday. She said:

'But having come so far, will you not wish to get some advantage of the journey by having a holiday here?'

'I wish only to get you safely back to London.'

She shook her head. 'It would look strange if you returned so soon. The Jelains must think it peculiar.'

'I do not care what the Jelains think.'

'But I care. They are my relations, and have shown me much kindness. No, it would not do. It would give them offence, and for no good reason. After all, now that you are here there is no longer any need for you to be worried about me.'

'Then Friday's packet?'

She hesitated. 'They will still be shocked. I am sure they will regard it as improper for me to undertake such a journey with a male companion.'

'And you will mind it, if they are?'

She looked at him, aware again of the ease she found in his company, of the contrast with that of Edmund.

'No, I shall not mind it.'

Mrs Jelain's reaction to the news was precisely as Sarnia had anticipated. She made no attempt to disguise her disapproval; and hinted that it represented a liberty more appropriate to the lower classes than to a person of breeding. Sarnia understood what was implied and thought how ridiculous it was. Her virtue had been far more seriously threatened in a few minutes on a misty beach with Edmund than it could possibly be during long hours with Michael, sharing the public accommodations of boat and train.

She could scarcely say that, but she did make plain her determination to return with Michael; and Mrs Jelain ceased her objections. When the subject was mentioned during luncheon, Mr Jelain and Edmund appeared to accept it fairly easily. She guessed Mrs Jelain had apprised Edmund of the news in advance, and that they had agreed together that opposition might do more harm than good. When Sarnia was alone with Edmund in the afternoon, he merely expressed his regret that she should be leaving so soon. He relied, he said, on her coming back to Guernsey at an early date. She should wind up her affairs in London, and come next time not to visit but reside – a child of the island returning to her true home.

Sarnia agreed, crossing fingers behind her back, that this might well be so. She was chiefly relieved that things were proceeding so smoothly. There was no mention of Dr Falla, or a possible medical veto on travelling. She felt she had Michael to thank for that – that Mrs Jelain had been impressed by his firmness and strength of character, had seen the folly of contesting her with such an ally in her support, and had counselled Edmund on those lines. Sarnia felt a quick rush of affection for Michael. She still could not contemplate the idea of marriage to anyone, but reflected how much it must reduce one's apprehensions concerning the wedded state to envisage it as shared by a partner so comfortingly strong, and yet so gentle-natured.

The policy of the Jelains in fact seemed to have altered to one of encouraging Michael rather than being cool towards him. He was asked that same night to dinner, and their manner was entirely amiable. In fact he was invited to join Mrs Jelain and Sarnia in an outing the following afternoon. The coach took them to the north of the island, and they were shown the rich flat agricultural land there, the wild moorland of L'Ancresse, and the golden sands that lay beyond. This northern part had been a separate island until quite recently, Mrs Jelain told them; the ditch had been filled in a little over forty years ago. She could remember as a child watching the tide flood up between the two shores.

'The Collases,' she said, ' – that is my family, Sarnia – were from the Vale, which is what the island was called. They lived there for four hundred years, and my father has told me that if one of their daughters were to marry outside – marry into the High Parishes as they called the main island – they thought of her as marrying among savages. They were quite likely to cut her off from intercourse.'

'How large was the Vale island?' Michael asked.

'A little over a mile at its widest point.'

He shook his head. 'It is strange to think of it.'

'This is a strange country, Mr Dowling. You do not yet know how strange.'

She spoke lightly; her whole manner towards him was good-humoured. The initial reservation and suspicion had in any case been no more than natural, in the case of a stranger suddenly appearing and at such an hour. Sarnia was ashamed again of her own suspicions of the Jelains. They would have liked her and Edmund to marry, but there was nothing wrong in that. She had been misled by the prejudice and resentment of an old man, unbalanced by years of loneliness – yes, and miserliness also. He had probably thought that everyone he met was seeking his money.

Next morning, Sarnia and Michael were taken into the town by Edmund and he showed them the sights. Sarnia had already seen them for the most part, so this was clearly for Michael's benefit, which pleased her. They looked in at the Royal Court House and saw the Bailiff and the Jurats trying a case. It was all in French – to do with the ownership of a plot of land, Edmund told them – and they did not stay long. They went down to the High Street, while Edmund pointed things out. He was preparing to lead them into the Town Church, when Michael drew back. He said, with a smile:

'I will wait for you outside. I am a Roman.' Edmund looked at him quizzically, and he went on: 'It is not from prejudice, but simply because I might unwittingly fail in some necessary mark of respect. I prefer not to run the risk of seeming discourtesy.'

Edmund shrugged. 'We will pass the church by, then. Sarnia already knows it. We will go on to the Fish Market. We are very proud of our Fish Market.'

They went after that to the Commercial Arcade, and took coffee in the circulating library where, Edmund pointed out, yesterday's *Times* newspaper was already available: such was the swiftness of modern communications. Sarnia saw him consult his watch, and he did not encourage them to linger. He led them on through the Arcade, and although their progress was casual and unhurried Sarnia had a feeling that the expedition had become more purposeful, that there was some appointment in view.

From the far end of the Arcade granite steps provided an entry to the Market Square. Edmund would want to show Michael the Assembly Rooms, she thought. She was thinking of the night of the ball when she became aware of a man approaching and preparing to address them. It was Peter d'Aurigny.

He was dressed with great elegance, having a satin waistcoat of red silk, embroidered with peacocks, and a grey silk cravat with a pin that sported a large emerald. He bowed to her and nodded to the men, and she thought again how detestable was his arrogance. Edmund introduced Michael to him with a show of deference that disappointed her. And she was enraged by the cool stare with which d'Aurigny took in Michael's appearance. She was aware of this as a summing up and dismissal of him: a London clerk, beneath the consideration of a d'Aurigny.

'Deuce of a row,' he said. 'One can scarcely hear oneself speak. Are you taking your guests up to see the show, Jelain? I have had more than enough of it.'

She had been aware of considerable noise from the direction of the Square. She could hear shouts and laughter. A mummer's show, perhaps, or dancing bears? D'Aurigny, at any rate, disengaged himself, to her relief, and they moved on. She was thinking of the ball again, and hoping Edmund would not speak of the incident with d'Aurigny. With this in mind she did not pay too close attention to what lay ahead, though she realized that the square was full of people. The cries and cheers were louder and she was also aware of a cracking sound, sharp and regular.

Edmund forced a way for them up the Assembly Rooms steps, from where they could see over the heads of the crowd. She looked where he indicated. She saw the cage first, a square wooden affair mounted on a cart in the corner of the square. But the focus of attention was nearer, where stood an iron triangle, as tall as a man, its point towards the ground. A figure, bare from the waist up, was strapped to it and another figure, masked and in black, stood behind him. His arm rose and fell, wielding a whip which cracked in the air as it descended on the thin white back. As it landed, the victim shrieked in pain, and the mob drowned his cry with a roar of satisfaction.

But it was not a man, she saw with horror: it was a boy! He looked no more than eleven or twelve. He writhed with the hurt that was being inflicted on him and she saw his face, small and white and agonized. She looked away, but could not help hearing the sound of the next lash, and the accompanying shriek and cheers.

She felt sick and dizzy. She was aware of little except that someone was supporting her, helping her through the throng and out of the square. It was Michael. He got her into the Arcade, to a point to which the noise came only distantly, before he said:

'Are you all right now?' He spoke to Edmund who was on her other side: 'Perhaps we can find a place where she can sit down?'

She shook her head. 'No. I am all right, truly.' She thought she heard the crack of the whip again behind them. 'I would sooner walk on.'

Edmund said: 'I am sorry you were so distressed.'

His manner was sympathetic, but she thought his voice had something other than sympathy in it: she did not know what. Michael said:

'Would not any lady have been distressed by such a sight?'

Edmund shook his head. 'I had not thought the punishment would start so soon.'

Even if it had not been for d'Aurigny's remark, she would have been sure that he was lying. He had timed their arrival for the whipping. But why? What purpose could he have in exposing her to so brutal a scene? The callousness of doing so was horrifying in itself, apart from the cruelty she had been forced to witness. She could see the small figure strapped to the iron triangle, the falling whip …

'A mere child,' she said, ' – to be punished like that, as though he were a hardened criminal!'

'He is older than he looks,' Edmund said. 'Thirteen, I understand.'

She echoed: 'Thirteen!'

Michael asked: 'And for what crime is such a punishment inflicted?'

'He stole empty bottles from a catering establishment, along with another boy. Ten, I believe.'

'Ten empty bottles? This must be a poor sort of joke.'

'Both boys are known as old offenders, but his record is the worse of the two. The other escaped with a month's imprisonment, twenty days of it in solitary confinement on bread and water. He is younger, also. The Jurats felt that imprisonment was not enough in this one's case, and awarded him fifty lashes as well.'

Sarnia thought of the Jurats as she had seen them only that morning in their robes of office; dignified men, prosperous and well-fed. Fifty lashes for a boy of thirteen, for stealing a few empty bottles … it was beyond all credence.

They had come into the High Street. The sounds from the square had faded behind them, leaving only the ordinary noises of the day: two dogs growling at one another, a child sobbing somewhere but probably over nothing worse than a broken toy, a man with a tray crying muffins. Michael said:

'That fellow in the mask – does he do much business, then?'

'He earns his pay. Before the whipping they are brought through the streets in a cart, following a route long established by custom. It takes almost an hour. He is our hangman, too, though there is less call for his services there.'

'And do you say this is a civilized land?'

Michael's voice shook a little. Edmund said:

'Did you not have a similar procession in England, to the Tyburn gallows?'

'For murderers and highwaymen. And it is nearly a hundred years since it was done. Do you have to retain such relics of barbarism in this peaceful island of yours?'

Michael's tone was even more aggressive than his words. She thought Edmund was bound to be insulted by them, and perhaps angered. But he said calmly:

'It is exactly because we are firm in punishing misdoers, and at an early age, that this island stays peaceful. You will find no highwaymen here, no footpads. When the English have such civil peace as we enjoy, they will be welcome to come and tell us how to run our affairs.'

He smiled. 'But let us leave a subject which I perceive Sarnia finds distasteful. If we go down by this narrow passage we can watch ships unloading on the wharf. Our harbour, as you have seen, is small, but there is a project for constructing one twenty times the size. In Guernsey, we look to the future. Sarnia, permit me to take your arm. The steps are very steep, and could prove treacherous.'

XVII

EDMUND HAD MADE ARRANGEMENTS to take Michael to the Army and Navy Club in the High Street during the afternoon of Thursday, pressing the invitation beyond any possibility of refusal. There were several gentlemen he was anxious that Michael should meet, and also he was determined to engage him in contest at billiards, which Michael had spoken of playing. Michael was clearly reluctant, but had to accept out of courtesy.

Since there could be no question of Sarnia accompanying them to a gentleman's club, Mrs Jelain proposed a different outing for her. She reminded her of the farm in the valley, where they had called on that first journey to Beauregard, and how she had said she would like to see more of the place.

Sarnia demurred. While appreciating the offer, she felt that she would prefer to stay in. There was the packing still to be done for her departure the following morning.

'Marie can see to that.'

'Not without some overseeing. She is a good girl, and willing, but I fear my clothes will be in a sorry jumble if she is left to do it alone.'

'She will not be alone. Perret will make sure everything is in order. She packs for me and has never creased my silks yet.' Her tone was friendly, but brooked no opposition. 'We can be back long before dinner, if you wish to check on her. And you cannot leave the island without seeing something of Les Fauxquets, where your forefathers farmed for generations.'

Michael had been asked again for luncheon, and Sarnia and he had the chance of a few moments alone together afterwards. He said:

'I would give anything not to be going on this jaunt. An assembly of bone-headed military men and sea-dogs. I shall not enjoy it.'

She smiled. 'I am glad, though, that you are being polite. A refusal would have given offence.' He shook his head, discounting this. 'And they are my relations, and have been good to me.'

'I shall be glad to board the packet in the morning.'

'Why, so shall I. And that is all the more reason for accommodating ourselves to them today.'

He pressed her hand. 'Thank God it is not for longer. I cannot tell you how much I look forward to taking you away from here.'

She smiled, and withdrew her hand to put a finger to her lips.

'Ssh. That is Mrs Jelain returning. Enjoy yourself at your billiards.'

As they got into the carriage a sharp gust of wind nearly carried away Sarnia's bonnet, and when they came out onto the Esplanade she saw that large waves were breaking against the sea wall and occasionally spilling over, the tide being full, in high spumes of spray. One such breaker slashed against the landau's window and drenched coachman and horses. Fortunately they had not far to go before they turned inland.

Looking at the swell rolling in, the white caps on the waves out in the Russell, Sarnia said:

'I fear I shall not have so peaceful a crossing on my return as I had when I came here with you.'

'Do not worry over it,' Mrs Jelain said. 'The glass fell quickly and is rising again. It will have blown itself out long before tomorrow.'

The wind followed them as they drove up the hill and down the other side, out of St Peter Port. Its gusts rattled the carriage and at times were so furious as to tilt it precariously to one side. But the sky was largely blue, the sun hot and only briefly obscured by fast moving clouds.

They came at last to the narrow lane leading down into the Fauxquets valley. Almost at once the wind dropped, and when the carriage rolled to a halt in front of the farmhouse, it had almost completely abated. The coachman helped Mrs Jelain and Sarnia to get down, his cap still dripping water from his dowsing on the front, and she exclaimed over the stillness of the air, enlivened by no more than an erratic breeze. Yet up on the crest of the hill she could see trees threshing under the gale's belabouring.

Mrs Jelain said: 'It is the most sheltered spot in the island, I believe. We have often been astonished to go out from here and find storms raging. Ah, there are the Bourgaizes.'

The farm manager greeted them with the same garrulous cheerfulness he had shown before. His wife, who now came out with him, was a large shapeless woman, who said little. She looked dour, but might not, Sarnia felt, have much chance to talk against her husband.

They were taken into the house and to the parlour, which looked out over the flower garden. It was a room of very low ceiling, oak-beamed, but clean and prettily furnished though in simple style. They were served tea in pink lustre cups, and pressed to eat from plates heaped high with food. When she was already quite full, a great dish of strawberries was brought in. Sarnia protested that she could not eat a single berry.

'You will not get berries like this in England, Miss Sarnia,' Bourgaize urged. 'Nor cream to compare with our Guernsey cream. I was in Devon once, and tasted that which they make so much of. I thought it was skim milk they were serving me. You must have a few berries. They are at their best, towards the end of the crop. Next week there will be none worth talking of.'

Laughingly she allowed herself to be persuaded. It was very pleasant to sit here, with the sunlight reaching in through the quarrelled windows and the flowers nodding outside. Mr Bourgaize talked of the farm and the valley, volubly and not uninterestingly.

Later they were taken outside, to be shown the farm, and she met the two Bourgaize daughters: Elizabeth, a girl of sixteen as plain and large-boned and silent as her mother; and a smaller and younger girl, Helene, who seemed more to favour her father. They had a son, also, Bourgaize explained, the eldest child, at present working out in the fields.

Sarnia said: 'I fear we are keeping you yourself from things that need to be done.'

He laughed. 'Not so, Miss Sarnia! I can think of no pleasanter occupation than the present; while as for needs ... we Guernseymen are not like your Norman farmers – nor your English, either, for that matter – to work ourselves to death. We know how to take our ease.'

But the cleanliness and order of the farm, the tidiness of all the equipment, belied his claim to idleness. It was a dairy farm chiefly, he explained, though he grew some wheat and potatoes, and vegetables for the market; and he showed them the shippon, empty since the cattle were out grazing, and the stable. There was a horse in its stall, lamed through picking up a stone, and he took it a sugared crust of bread. He fussed the beast almost as one would a child.

Sarnia had expected that by this time Mrs Jelain would be making some move towards their return; it was long past five o'clock. In the end she herself remarked:

'Ought we not to be getting back soon, Aunt Jeanne? I still have my packing to see to.'

Already there would scarcely be time before dinner. Mrs Jelain said to Bourgaize:

'Will you see how they are progressing with the repair of the landau?'

He left them to go to the coach-house, a square building that adjoined the farmhouse on its west side. Sarnia asked:

'What repair is that?'

'You did not know of it? Ah no, I recall. It would be when you retired to make your toilette after tea that Henry told us.' Henry was the coachman. 'A sprung shaft, or something similar, due to the poor road and the wind's buffeting. He and Bourgaize's man are working on it. They should not be long.'

They were still working, Bourgaize reported, but should be finished soon. Meanwhile he would take them down to see the duckpond. It was a pretty little spot, and there was a meadow beyond in which, in the spring, celandines grew almost as big as sunflowers.

Sarnia began to be restless about the delay, but Mrs Jelain showed no concern. It would be a pity if they were late for dinner, but Mrs Perret would keep it for them. They looked at the ducks and strolled through the meadow before leisurely making their way back to the house. There they learned that the repair had suffered a further setback: it would require another hour before it was completed.

Sarnia said: 'An hour! But in that case we shall not be back before dark.'

'It is turning out more difficult than they bargained for, it seems.' Mr Bourgaize was cheerful about it. 'But at least you are snug here, and we can give you a tolerable supper. Mrs Bourgaize is roasting a goose: I got a good smell from it when I passed the kitchen window. And for refreshment now, I mean to pour you some of our own sloe wine.'

Sarnia said to Mrs Jelain: 'Would it not be better if I were to ride over? I could tell them what was amiss.'

She said: 'I doubt if Bourgaize will have a lady's saddle.'

He shook his head, grinning. 'Do not worry, *chérie*. Everything will be all right.'

But an hour later, Henry made his report: the repair had defeated them. Sarnia asked if they might not risk returning in the carriage as it was – after all it had got them here? The coachman shook his head. It would not go another quarter mile on a bad road.

Mrs Jelain was unperturbed. Bourgaize's son would ride over to Les Colombelles, and arrange for another carriage to come out to fetch them.

'Your trap!' Sarnia said to Bourgaize. She was delighted by the thought: a farmer must have a trap. 'Can we not use it to get us home?'

'Gladly, if it were available. But a neighbour has borrowed it, to deck out for the wedding of a daughter – and every other trap for miles around. You have come on us at a time when we are confined to our house. Fortunately there are several bedrooms we do not often use. My girls will prepare two of them for you. It is a humble place, but I trust you will be comfortable enough.'

'But we are not to stay the night!'

'It is the only thing,' Mrs Jelain said. 'By the time another carriage can get here it will be pitch-black. There will be no moon until after midnight. It would be madness to try to drive back, over such roads as lie between here and the town.'

'But I must be there to catch the morning's packet.'

Mrs Jelain smiled. 'There is no difficulty to that. The carriage will be here as soon as it is light, and Mrs Perret and Marie will have seen properly to your packing, I promise you. Be at ease, my dear. Think only how fortunate we are, being able to spend the night in warm beds, instead of being tumbled in some ditch, with broken limbs maybe.'

She had no choice but to accept the inevitable. Knowing that the Jelains shared none of her anxiety that she should be in time to catch the mail packet – that they would be glad probably to see her miss it – she would have been alarmed, except for the thought of Michael. She was no longer alone and friendless. He would see to it that she caught the boat, if it meant coming over for her himself. The assurance comforted her, and though she had eaten very well at tea she did justice to the excellence of Mrs Bourgaize's goose.

The room Sarnia was given was clean and comfortable, smelling faintly of the apples which she guessed were stored here in the winter. The mattress was tight filled with soft feathers, one or two escaping, and she sank into its embrace and slept soundly.

When she awoke, it was broad daylight. She reached for her watch but, from tiredness and perhaps from the unfamiliarity of her surroundings, she had failed to wind it: it had stopped at a little past three o'clock.

She slipped from bed and ran to the open window. The sun stood above the shoulder of the hill which meant, she guessed, that it must be getting on for eight o'clock. And with the boat due to leave at ten! Where was the carriage that was to have come for them, and why had she not been wakened?

She turned to find her clothes and dress when the sound of hooves drew her back to the window: a solitary rider was coming down the lane. She could not see him for the screen of trees, but was sure it must be Michael, coming to take her away. She leaned out of the window, happy in that thought. Then the rider came out from behind the trees and she saw it was not Michael, but Edmund.

She watched, unsure of herself again, as he dismounted and tied his horse by the gate. He looked towards the house and caught sight of her.

He swept off his hat. 'My dear Sarnia, how pretty you look. Especially in so charming a *déshabillé*.'

She pulled her wrap tighter. 'Where is the coach?'

'Alas, there is no coach.'

'But I am to catch the boat at ten!'

'Alas, again.' He smiled. 'I fear you will not.'

Something was wrong. Half-formed suspicions of the previous evening concerning the repair to the landau – a recollection of a look of shiftiness surprised on the coachman's face – clarified into a realization: that it had been a plot with the object of preventing her return to England on this morning's boat. She was dismayed, then cheered again by the thought of Michael. He knew where she was. He would find her and take her away. Not in time for today's sailing, perhaps, but there was another on Monday. She made a resolution: she would quit the Jelains at once and stay the remaining nights at Michael's hotel.

Edmund had been waiting for her to speak, but she tilted her chin in silence. He said then:

'I bring you a message. From Mr Dowling.'

She said quickly: 'What is it?'

'He most sincerely regrets that it was not possible to see you before he left the island, and sends you his respects and good wishes.'

She looked at him. 'You lie. He has not left the island.'

'True.' He took out his watch and consulted it. 'He will still be in St Peter Port for more than an hour. He leaves with the packet, at ten o'clock.'

She said scornfully: 'A lie, and a poor one. Michael will not go back to England without me. I am quite sure of it.'

Edmund smiled. 'I have deceived you.'

She said, with contempt: 'I knew it!'

'But in a small way only. He gave me no verbal message, but wrote one to you.' He took an envelope from his pocket. 'I have it here.'

XVIII

SARNIA PASSED Mrs Bourgaize at the foot of the stairs. Angry and agitated, she went into the parlour where Edmund awaited her.

'You have hurried in your dressing,' he said, 'and the haste becomes you. You flush most charmingly, cousin.'

She put her hand out. 'I will see that message of which you speak.'

'Of course. I would not keep it from you. Take it, by all means.'

The envelope carried no name or address. It was a trick, she thought; probably some message forged to deceive her. But as she opened out the letter inside she could see it was written in Michael's hand. His way of crossing the 't' was unmistakeable.

It was short and simple.

> Dear Sarnia,
>
> I greatly regret that affairs of business oblige me to leave the island without having the opportunity to bid you farewell in person. I am most grateful for the kindness shown by you and your relations during my brief stay, and extend my sincere good wishes for your future happiness and prosperity.
>
> Very truly yours,
> Michael Dowling.

Sarnia stared at the note. It was in Michael's hand, certainly, but it was not his letter. The form of address alone showed that. In the previous letters she had had from him, the first had been addressed 'My dear Sarnia', the second 'My very dear Sarnia'. And had ended: 'Yours most sincerely, Michael.' Nor was the stilted phrasing his. This was a dictated letter; but how could they have prevailed on him to write it? Horrors ran in her head. Fearful, but for Michael only, she said:

'Where is he? I demand to know!'

'Boarding the packet – where else? He is probably on board already. I fancy he was anxious to make sure he did not miss the sailing.'

'You lie! He is a prisoner somewhere – you have forced him to write this.'

Edmund smiled. 'With rack and thumbscrews, perhaps, or some more ingenious machine peculiar to the island? But the handwriting is steady, is it not? It does not look as though it were the result of torture.'

'I will not believe it. He has not written such a letter of his own volition – he could not. Even if you told him some lie – said I had changed my mind about leaving Guernsey – it would make no difference. He would not accept it.'

'Perhaps not. But I suspect his departure is connected more with his own eagerness to quit the island than to any misapprehension over your desires.'

'Nothing would persuade him to go, and leave me behind.'

'Do you not think so? You have a touching faith in the depth of his affection. I do not doubt that the affection exists, but something might outweigh it in the balance.' He spoke with contempt. 'Fear might.'

'Fear? Of what. With what have you threatened him?'

Edmund said: 'I do not think he was at his ease in the Army & Navy Club yesterday afternoon. There was some talk about the papal aggression. A great deal of anger has been raised by the Romans building a church here. We do not take as kindly to their insolence as they do in Jersey. And the Talbot case is fresh in people's minds. Things were said about the Romans' fondness for getting their hands on the fortunes of heiresses. Your friend did not seem happy over the turn or tone of the discussion.'

She said, with contempt of her own: 'And am I supposed to

believe that idle chatter would cause him to abandon me – when it was our plan to leave the island together this morning, and so be free even of such prattling rancour as that? The notion is quite ridiculous.'

Edmund looked at her in silence. She said:

'You have taken him prisoner, and are holding him somewhere. That too is ridiculous, because eventually you must release him. Even in Guernsey there is a rule of law. And when you do, he will come for me; and if you do not, I myself will raise a hue and cry.'

'I can see I must be frank with you,' Edmund said.

'It is past time you were!'

'Though I would have spared you if I could, Mr Dowling being a favoured friend of yours.'

His manner had no sign of discomposure: satisfaction, rather. She felt a quick coldness at heart, but was determined not to reveal it. She stared at him.

'Say what you have to say.'

'I can more easily show than tell.' He drew from his pocket another envelope, of foolscap length, and brought out a sheet of paper. 'Come, cousin, read while I hold it for you. It is too valuable a document for me to allow it to leave my hands.'

She crossed the room and stood before him. This writing, too, was Michael's. A declaration of some kind. She read the first few lines and felt her eyes swim. Edmund said:

'I am sorry to be the means of introducing you to something so unpleasant, and indecorous; but you have forced me to it.'

She brushed her eyes, and read what was on the sheet of paper.

> 'I, Michael Ambrose Dowling, banker's clerk, of Longmans Street by St George's Fields, London, do hereby voluntarily and without constraint make this confession.
>
> That on the night of June 20th, 1851, being in liquor, I did assault and ravish Madeleine Blunier, chambermaid at Garner's Hotel, Guernsey, after summoning her to attend me in my room.

And that, in consequence of the said Madeleine Blunier accepting my abject and humble apology, and being willing not to press charges against me, I undertake at once to quit the island of Guernsey, and never return thither, on pain of due punishment for my wicked act.

Michael Ambrose Dowling.'

There were signatures of two witnesses appended. One name she did not know, the other was Edmund's.

She attempted to take the paper to look at it more closely, but as she stretched out her hand Edmund withdrew it. A valuable document, he had said, and she took his meaning. But it was still a lie.

'If you believe that is a true account,' she said, 'why did the girl not press charges? Out of kindness to a man who had so dreadfully abused her?'

He smiled. 'Scarcely. But she preferred financial redress to the process of law. She was given money.'

'By Michael?'

'His means would not have been sufficient for her just claims.' He bowed. 'By your humble servant, cousin. You may acquit me of the debt in due course. I did not think you would wish to see him convicted of assault and rape.'

'How could he be? I know he is innocent.'

'Does an innocent man confess his guilt?'

'Tell me what happened – what you say happened.'

'It is really not suitable, to recount to one of your age and sex. But if you must hear it … He had been drinking heavily in the evening. I know, because I drank with him. I walked him back to the hotel, and he retired. It seems he rang for some service, and the Blunier girl answered his bell. Screams were heard. The night porter was called by another guest, and came eventually to find the girl with her clothes torn and disarrayed, she herself weeping and distressed.

'Because it was known that I had accompanied him back, that

he had been a visitor in our house, a messenger was sent after me. I returned, and managed to rescue Mr Dowling from the extremity of his folly. Do I not earn your gratitude for that, sweet Sarnia?'

'You tell me he admitted all this?'

'Not at first. He told some story of the girl coming to his room unasked for, of engaging him in conversation and then ripping open her dress and screaming for help, though none was needed.'

'And why was he not believed? It was no more than the girl's word against his.'

'So he himself declared. But I felt obliged to point out that, whatever my own view as to what had taken place, our Guernsey courts would not be over-eager to take the word of a visiting banker's clerk from England, a Roman at that, against that of a Guernsey girl whose family have a respectable history that runs back for centuries. What reason, after all, could such a girl have to traduce him? His conviction would be certain.'

What reason indeed? Only too plainly that same reason Edmund had given for her agreement not to press charges. It was not for that she had been given money, but for accusing Michael falsely.

The plot was plain now, and its perpetrator stood before her, smiling. They had been determined that Michael should not take her away, but determined also that he should not remain on the island to interfere with their plans for her. And it had been cunningly worked out. A young visiting Englishman, heavily in liquor – Edmund himself had seen to that – who summoned a chambermaid to his room at night ... she saw how magistrates, knowing nothing of Michael's true character, might believe such a story.

'I felt obliged also,' Edmund went on, 'to point out what must follow. Rape is punishable by death. He would make a closer acquaintance with that fellow in the black mask whose work so offended him a few days since. And the Jurats might order a flogging first; it has been known.'

That visit to the Market Place when the boy was being whipped … She had thought it was deliberate, and wondered why he should wish to expose her to such a scene. She saw now that it had not been she for whom it was intended, but Michael. The project had been in hand already, and the sight had been meant to prepare him for its denouement. When Edmund, last night in the hotel, spoke of flogging and the public executioner, his words would evoke a picture with the sharp outlines of recent witnessing.

Yet even so, how could Michael have submitted, signing his name to a lie that irretrievably blackened his character, for the sake of saving his skin? And knowing that by doing so he left her alone and defenceless, in the hands of people who had shown themselves utterly lacking in scruples?

Edmund said: 'He still demurred. A man has his pride, of course, even your Mr Dowling. So I pointed out how others, entirely innocent, might find themselves suffering on account of his obstinacy. There is, as you know and he knew, much feeling against the Romans since Wiseman got his red hat. More here than in most places. Anger that in the first place was directed against him could easily extend towards his fellow religionists. It would be a pity if the mob were to put torches to that handsome new church they have built, especially if the flock were inside doing their God-eating at the time.'

She said in outrage: 'Have you no decency at all?'

'Do you not call it decent to warn a man of the possible consequences of his acts, even if one paints a dark picture in doing so? At any rate, it appeared to clinch matters. He ceased to rant about his innocence, and wrote the confession which you have seen.'

'Which you dictated to him!'

'It had to be in proper form, leaving no possibility that he might return to dispute the matter. The note to you I dictated also. It was not strictly necessary perhaps, but it seemed to tie up a loose end.'

How Edmund must have relished the enforcement of his terms on Michael! And how proud he must be of the ingenuity he had used – first engaging him in drinking, for which he probably had a poor head, surprising him with the girl, and then threatening him – confused by what had happened and muddled with the liquor – with such terrible consequences. Michael must have felt he had no alternative but to submit.

And yet, he ought not to have done so. Had he had the courage with which she had credited him, he would have defied the threats, however dire. She herself would have helped with every means in her power. She could have got word to Mr Merton, and implored his help. He, too, knowing the man, would have disbelieved the charge; and she knew from her own experience that he was a person of firmness as well as liberality. He would have put all his resources into the fight.

The island might have its own laws and customs, and it might well be that a stranger's word would not be readily taken against that of a native inhabitant; but justice could have been fought for, and won. The Queen ruled here as in England, and so the Lords would have been the final judges. Edmund had spoken of the risk to his fellow-religionists as providing a justification for capitulation. Justification, or excuse? She wished she could believe the former. From the tone of his comment, she did not think Edmund believed it.

One thing, at any rate, was certain: he had abandoned her and would not return. If he had not been able to stand out last night, there could be no question of his doing so at any future time – with the damning evidence of the confession in Edmund's possession.

The realization of Michael's weakness was more desolating than the thought of her own position. Yet that was disturbing enough. That the Jelains should have gone to such lengths to remove Michael provided chilling confirmation of their resolve to keep their hold on her. But did they think that by stripping her of her one friend and ally they could induce her to marry Edmund? She supposed there might be some young women, weak in disposition, who could be so isolated and then coerced. But surely they could not believe that this would be true of her!

Nor, even here in Guernsey, could there be any question of forcing a woman to marry against her will. The Church of England was the established church, the Jelains members of it. Did they envisage dragging her, bound and helpless, up the aisle of St Peter Port church, to have the Dean pronounce her married, for all her screams and protests? The absurdity of the picture heartened her.

She fully believed now that her pocket-book had been taken so that she would not have the money to buy a ticket back to England. She had appealed to Michael, and he had failed her. But there were other quarters to which she could appeal – to the lawyer, Martell, or even to Mr Merton. She was confident he would help her.

The sickness she had felt in understanding Michael's defection was ended by the anger which now rose in her. However much she had been disappointed in him, she was not to be either hoodwinked or browbeaten by the Jelains. She said, with a show of indifference:

'So he has gone. It is not of importance. I still mean to return to England, but there is no great urgency about it. For the moment I am prepared to stay at Les Colombelles. At what hour will the landau be ready to convey us there?'

'I am glad you take it lightly.' He was watching her closely. 'But the landau will not convey you to Les Colombelles.'

'Why should it not?'

'I learned something else from Mr Dowling before we parted. We had wondered as to the reason for his visit here. I suggested it might have been in response to a letter from you, and he admitted it.'

That, too. But why seek to keep anything back from a betrayal? Yet she closed her eyes for a moment. Edmund said:

'I explained to him how greatly you had been agitated by your father's death, the circumstances of it. I told him you were in good hands, and would be cared for. He accepted that, or at least said he did. And we must care for you indeed. For your own good, we must prevent you from writing wild letters. This is a protection more easily accomplished in the country than in the town. You must reconcile yourself for a time to this quiet retreat.'

No letters, then; and no chance of a visit to Mr Martell's office. In plain words, she was to be a prisoner here. She felt fear rise again, and fought it down.

She asked him: 'How long a time?' He merely smiled and shrugged. 'Until I consent to be your wife?'

She managed to put scorn into those last words, hoping to discompose him. But he smiled still.

'I truly hope that you will do me that honour, dear Sarnia.'

'I never shall!'

'You said: how long a time? Never is too long. I recommend you not to use that word.'

'I wish to end this interview.' He bowed acknowledgement. 'If I am not to return to Les Colombelles, I presume you will send Marie here to me?'

'You have grown accustomed to the notion of a personal maid, it seems. Already you are vastly changed from the little lady banking clerk my parents discovered in a cheap London lodging house. Well, there is nothing wrong in acquiring a taste for luxury, and when the time is right I trust you will satisfy it in full measure. But the time is not yet; nor would Marie be suitable. Curious about that letter which brought Mr Dowling here hot foot, I took the liberty of interrogating her. As a result, she has been dismissed. It did not seem to me that the execution of secret commissions for our guests came within the scope of the duties for which we were paying her.'

No Marie, either. She would not let him see how this further blow hurt her. She stared at him, full face.

'In that case, sir, I have nothing I wish to say to you.'

'Do you not? But I hope you will have. I am sure of it. And I am in no hurry.'

XIX

In the middle of the morning the landau was brought round to the front of the house. There had been no need of a second carriage, Sarnia thought with dull unhappiness, because the first had not been in need of repair. It had been part of the plan, an excuse for keeping her the night at the farm. And it showed they had not been entirely confident of their plot against Michael succeeding. They had not been sure he would not defy them, and ride like Lochinvar to rescue her, to the west not out of it. A comical notion, indeed, but she did not feel like smiling.

Before going to the landau, Mrs Jelain came to see her, in the room where she had slept and to which, after her talk with Edmund, she had again retired. She showed no change in her appearance of amiability, and said:

'Are you comfortable, *chérie*? Is there anything that you require?'

Sarnia said: 'What answer would you expect to that, ma'am, from one who is a captive?'

'You should not look on it in that light, my dear.'

'In what light, then? Is it not true that by tricks and lies and threats, your son has forced that man who might have helped me to leave the island? And am I not confined here against my will?'

'You have a clever mind, but I fear it is prone to fantasies. I understand that the man you speak of has proved a blackguard, and is lucky to escape the consequences of his villainy. As to your being confined, yes, for a little while, and in your own interests.'

Sarnia said wearily: 'Why must we have this playacting? You are determined I shall marry Edmund, so that he can come into possession of my father's fortune.' She looked at the older woman with defiance. 'And I am determined I will not do so. That is why I am being kept imprisoned here.'

'This is more of your fantasy. It is plain that your father's death has unsettled your mind, even more than we guessed. You will do better here, in this quiet place, than surrounded by the bustle and nervousness of society. I promise you that you will have the sympathy of all those who have made your acquaintance while you have been with us. And they will understand that you are not well enough just now either to make calls or receive them.'

Sarnia understood what was being conveyed to her: that there would be no awkward inquiries. She could believe it to be true. They had probably spread widely the story of her mind being disturbed, as the result of that night spent with her dying father in a lonely house. And the removal to Les Fauxquets had been smoothly engineered and would not occasion comment. There would be pitying whispers over the tea cups – nothing more.

Her only hope, then, was to escape. It was not as though this were some moated castle, with barren hostile country stretching for hundreds of miles around. It was an ordinary farmhouse, in a small, thickly populated island. This valley was as deep country as Guernsey afforded, but it was probably less than five miles from the town of St Peter Port. Once clear, she could walk there in a couple of hours.

Mrs Jelain said: 'If you think later of anything you want, Bourgaize will bring us word. Goodbye, *chérie*.' She did not approach to kiss her, but stood there, smiling. 'You will be restored to your full health soon. I am confident of it.'

Luncheon was brought to her room, but she did not eat it. The younger Bourgaize daughter came to remove the tray, and stared at the untouched plates. She was the one Sarnia had thought might prove talkative, and she attempted to engage her in conversation. But the child only gave her a quick wary look, picked up the tray and left. She had no doubt been forbidden to talk to her – very likely told she was mad.

In the afternoon she tried out the extent of her confinement. The other girl was knitting in the kitchen, whose open door gave her a view of the stairs. She watched Sarnia come down, but said nothing. Sarnia went out into the front garden, and the girl followed at a distance, watching her as she leaned against the gate.

It was a dull grey day of sticky heat. Even after walking so short a distance she felt uncomfortable from it. Running would be decidedly unpleasant. And it would do no good. A sound of hammering came from the rear of the house. If she were to open the gate, hitch up her skirts and run, the alarm would be given; and Mr Bourgaize or his hired man or his son – or perhaps all three – would catch her within minutes.

While she was being watched, she had no hope of getting away. She returned indoors and went upstairs again, and sat on the edge of the bed. Michael would be halfway to Southampton by now, perhaps gazing over the rail at the ship's wake pointing back to Guernsey, and thinking ... thinking what? She knew him well enough to know he would be full of guilts. She shook her head. Let him be so. She had too many troubles of her own to waste time either despising or pitying him.

The front gate, and therefore the way into the lane, were overlooked by the front windows of the house. Even if she managed to dodge the sentinel in the kitchen, there was too great a risk of being seen from one of them. What about the situation at the rear of the farmhouse? She racked her memory for details. The hall turned at right angles into a passage that led to a big larder, hung with hams and sides of bacon. There were two doors out of the larder, one going into the dairy, which jutted out from the main building, but the other giving exit to the open. If she could get through there unseen, the dairy would mask the view from the back windows of the house. And a high hedge of thorn, marking the limit of the kitchen garden, came close to the dairy's far end. It would give her cover to get away from the house and up towards the valley. Once clear, she could surely find her way across country to a thoroughfare, and so to the town.

But first she must get past the watcher in the kitchen. She stole out of the bedroom and went very quietly to the stairs, and part way down. The girl had a view of the lower part of the stairs and a section of the passage, but at this point she could look at her without being seen.

Crouched on the stairs, Sarnia watched her. She was knitting a stocking of an intricate design. Normally she knitted with her eyes fixed on the open door, but when she came to a difficult piece she dropped her eyes to be sure of getting the stitches right.

Counting seconds in her head, Sarnia worked out the length of time in which the girl was not on watch. More than half a minute. She waited and checked again. Half a minute. Long enough, surely, to get down and along the passage. She checked one more time.

When the girl's eyes dropped again, Sarnia was ready. She had taken off her shoes and, holding them in one hand, moved quickly down the stairs. A stair creaked, but the girl did not look up. She reached the hall and sidled along the passage. She had not been seen.

She crept through the larder, empty apart from a ginger cat that blinked at her with yellow eyes. Through the window she saw the yard outside was empty also. She put on her shoes, opened the door, and looked out. A few hens scratched in the dust; there was nothing else. She hurried along by the wall, keeping very close and dodging beneath the sill of a window as she passed it. Where the building ended she hesitated, gazing around. A figure was ploughing or harrowing high up on the slope of the facing hill, but working in a direction away from the house. A few feet from her was the blackthorn hedge; she gathered up her skirts and ran for it.

Once in its cover she could go more slowly. The hedge was on her left and scrub land rose steeply on her right. A cow moved in silhouette at the top, grazing. The hedge petered out in a few straggling bushes, but not far away a small plantation of elder trees grew along the bottom of the slope. Sarnia darted across and into their green gloom.

She was quite out of sight of the house now. Brambles caught at her dress. Trying not to snag the material as she freed it, she reflected with joy that she was free herself. It would be an hour, probably, before tea was brought up to her room. If she could enlist the aid of someone with means of transportation, she would be in St Peter Port by then!

Beyond the plantation lay open fields, but provided she kept close to the valley's side she would remain out of view from the house. The meadow was marshy, with one of the small streams the islanders called douits running through it. She picked her way, trying to avoid muddy patches. Gnats hummed around her in the humid sunless air, and she felt one sting her cheek. But a few gnat bites, however unsightly the swellings, were trifles set against the thought of freedom.

It was at that moment the shout came. She was startled by it, and even more by the fact that it came not from behind her, from the direction of the house, but from in front. Somewhere up on the hillside. She looked, and saw a figure emerging from a clump of bushes and coming down the slope towards her.

The cry was repeated as she picked up her skirts and ran. She could not make out what was said, even whether it was in English or the *patois*, and did not care. Her only hope was to get clear while he was slipping and sliding down the hill. There was a third shout, answered this time by another from down the valley; he had not been calling to her, she realized, but summoning another to his assistance.

She ran on, gasping, struggling to keep up her dress and give her legs freedom. A patch of swamp lay directly in her path and she splashed through it regardless of the mud. She heard her pursuer splashing after her, and knew he was gaining on her. The swamp dragged at her feet. Above her own panting, she heard his. Then a hand roughly caught her arm. She tried desperately to fling it off, slipped and fell among rank-smelling water weeds, and the man crashed with her. She lay, bedraggled and helpless, and felt the heat of his breath against her averted face. He was in no hurry to rise. She understood, with deep revulsion, that he was seeking to prolong the physical contact.

He got up reluctantly, as someone else approached. This was Mr Bourgaize; the one who had pulled her down was his son, Martin, an oafish overgrown youth of seventeen or so. Mr Bourgaize gave her a hand to get to her feet and she stared at him, trying to get her breath.

'You had better come back, Miss Sarnia,' Bourgaize said. 'You will be worrying people, running off like that.'

The valley, empty except for cows, offered no hope. If she were to scream, it would only mean a filthy hand across her mouth – the youth's grin almost solicited her to do it. The whole business of her attempt to escape had been anticipated and prepared for. The girl in the kitchen had been unimportant. The real watch had been kept by Bourgaize's son, concealed on the hillside.

'Come along now, Miss Sarnia,' Bourgaize said.

He took her arm and she went with him, unresisting, across the meadow towards the farmhouse.

This time a key was turned in the lock after the bedroom door had closed on her. Later, when tea was brought by the younger girl, the son unlocked the door and stood by as the tray was carried in. Sarnia asked:

'May I please have water, to wash myself?'

She was filthy with caked mud, from her fall in the swamp. The girl looked at her, saying nothing, and the door was once more locked. Sarnia waited, but no one came. The tea cooled in its pot, and the grey day gradually drifted into a greyer dusk.

She heard hoofbeats in the lane and went to the window. Edmund, she guessed, but it was not he. The figure that dismounted and walked, stiffly from riding, to the front door, was Dr Falla.

He had gone out of view before she could open the window to call. She rushed to the bedroom door and banged her fist against it. They would make some pretext to send him away without seeing her … She screamed his name through the locked door.

'Dr Falla! Help me! I am here … Help me, Dr Falla!'

She heard a murmur of voices downstairs, and cried out again. Footsteps mounted the stairs, and in a moment the key was turned. The doctor entered, a smile on his craggy face.

'My dear child, how are you?'

She wept with relief. Between sobs she tried to tell him what had happened, but incoherently. Bourgaize stood in the doorway.

'You perceive how disordered she is, doctor.' He shook his head. 'A terrible thing to see, in one so young.'

They were trying to make out she was mad, but a doctor could not be deceived. She clutched his arm, weeping and shaking, and implored him to get her away, to take her to a place of safety.

'Ran away, she did,' Bourgaize said, 'though we told her she was to await your coming. Through the brambles and swamp. And wouldn't wash herself when we got her back. Like a wild thing, she was – we were hard put to hold her.'

'A lie,' she gasped. 'They would not give me water.'

She saw her reflection in the dressing table mirror: filthy dirty, her dress torn and dishevelled. Behind her the image of Bourgaize gravely shook his head. But surely Dr Falla would know the truth. She dropped to her knees before him.

'Help me, I beg you. There is no one else who will, no one I can trust.'

He patted her on the head. 'Do not fret yourself, child. I will help you.'

She tried to stammer out thanks. He turned from her and she watched him rest his black bag on the wash-stand. He opened it, and took out a phial whose shape and colour were familiar. It was the medicine she had been given after her father's death, the draught which made her sleep and dizzied her mind. She shrank away.

'No. I will not drink that.'

'It is for your good,' Dr Falla said. 'It will calm your nerves. In the morning you will feel better.'

He believed Bourgaize's story – believed that her senses were disordered. She got to her feet and backed off.

'I will not drink it! You cannot make me do so.'

'My dear, you must do as I tell you. I am your doctor.'

'No. No!'

He looked away from her. 'Bourgaize, I shall need your help. Call up your son, as well.'

When they had gone she lay exhausted on top of the bed.

She had struggled but they had mastered her. Bourgaize's son seized the opportunity to take gross liberties with her person; her breasts were sore from his grasping fingers. And it had availed her nothing. They had forced her down and Bourgaize had blocked her nose so that she must open her mouth to breathe, the draught had been poured down her throat and her mouth then held until, choking, she swallowed it. Much of the liquor had spilled – the bed was damp from it and the air reeked with its cloying sweetness – but more had found its way down her throat. She felt sick, but already too she felt drowsy.

The twilight darkened and, confused and half asleep, she heard footsteps on the stair again. They would be bringing supper, she thought, and determined she would eat nothing. Nausea, in any case, had banished her hunger, even after a day without food. But it was not the girl who came in with a tray, but Bourgaize and his son. The son carried a lamp, the father a bag of tools and a number of iron bars.

They ignored her and went to the window. The door was open behind them, and she had a moment's wild hope of escaping through it. But they would catch her before she was halfway down the stairs. She would gain nothing, except more grasping and fumbling. And she felt anyway so weak, so lacking in any kind of strength.

She watched dully as they went about their work. One by one the bars were set in place across the window, and iron cleats laid over their ends and secured with six inch nails. The hammering and rasp of metal made her head ache.

They finished at last, Bourgaize tried the bars, tugging hard to satisfy himself they would not budge. He picked up his tools and turned towards the door. The son, carrying the lamp, made her flesh crawl with his look. At the door, Bourgaize paused.

'Good night, Miss Sarnia.' His voice was as light and merry as when he showed her and Mrs Jelain round the farm. 'Sleep well.'

The door closed, and the key turned in the lock.

XX

SARNIA AWOKE to the ordinary sounds of farm life – hens clucking, a dog's piercing bark, the distant clatter of geese and still more distant bray of a donkey. Her mind was hazy from sleep and the effects of the drug, and she lay for a moment or two with no clear realization of where she was or what had happened. Then, seeing the bars across the window, she recalled it all, and buried her face in the pillow.

Soon afterwards there was a knock and Helene brought in a breakfast tray. Through the open door, Sarnia glimpsed the figure of Martin Bourgaize on the landing, peering in. He grinned as she pulled the sheet up over her bosom.

When the girl put down the tray, Sarnia asked again for water to wash herself, and soap and towels. They had wanted Dr Falla to find her in the wretched state which had resulted from her attempt to escape, but they could have no reason for wanting to keep her still in dirt. The girl did not speak, but nodded and went away.

The tray held a pot of tea, bread with butter and jam, and a dish of fried bacon and eggs. The smell of this latter made her realize how hungry she was. Nor was there any point in weakening herself by continuing to fast. Whatever lay ahead, she would need her full strength. Yet the thought of eating in her present filthy condition was deeply repugnant. She waited, then hammered at the door and called through. She could hear people downstairs, but no one came.

The bacon and eggs were getting cold. In the end she overcame her distaste and ate them. She felt better for doing so. They could not keep her imprisoned forever: all she needed was the resolution to stick it out.

The carriage brought Mrs Jelain and Edmund an hour or two later. She had tied her hair as best she could, having no comb or brush, and rubbed the caked mud from her face with a corner of the sheet, but she was very conscious of her dirtiness. She burst out to Mrs Jelain:

'Madam, I have asked for water to wash myself, and none has been brought. Cold water will do if there is no hot, but I must have the means to cleanse myself. It is monstrous that I should not be allowed to do so.'

'It will be seen to, I promise you,' Mrs Jelain said. 'Some confusion with the girls, no doubt – they are not of the brightest. But tell me, *chérie*, how are you today? Did Dr Falla's medicine enable you to sleep? I am sure it did.'

'I should prefer to make my toilette first, and converse afterwards.'

Mrs Jelain smiled. 'Why, child, you must not mind us! We are your family. And although I was anxious to find out how you were, I cannot stay long. Dr Falla visited us last evening, after he had seen you.'

She was indignant still, but curiosity kept her silent. Mrs Jelain went on:

'He spoke of your condition. It is not uncommon, he says, in those of a nervous disposition, when there has been such a shock as that which was caused by your father's death.'

'My disposition is not a nervous one!'

Ignoring her, Mrs Jelain said: 'It produces melancholia, and a form of derangement of the mind. This must be closely watched. There is a risk of violence, both to the melancholic and to others.

'In the ordinary way he would be obliged to order confinement, until the illness was relieved, in the place provided for such unhappy wretches – the asylum for lunatics at Câtel. It is not a pleasant place, I fear, and the appearance and behaviour of its inmates would be likely to shock a person of sensitivity. Fortunately in your case, since we have this farmhouse remote from the town where you can be looked after, he is prepared to agree that you should stay here.'

'I demand to be allowed to see another doctor.'

Mrs Jelain shook her head. 'You are not in circumstances where you can make demands. You must understand that. Nor would it serve you if you could. Dr Falla has been in practice in the island for forty years. No other physician would dispute his judgement.'

This was the story they would need to put about to anyone inquiring of her whereabouts. It was clever enough. With any other form of sickness there might be offers to visit, but with this there could be none.

'You cannot keep me here,' she said.

Mrs Jelain looked at her. 'Conditions such as this, Dr Falla says, may last a long time. For years, even.'

'And if I were to agree to marry Edmund?'

She paused. 'They can also end quickly. A change of circumstance – a happy event – such a thing might produce a rapid cure.'

She tried to shake off the despair which settled again. She whispered:

'Why do you keep up this pretence? You know what it is you seek, and know I know it.'

'Try not to distress yourself, *chérie*.'

'Do you say that my marriage to Edmund is not your object?'

Edmund said: 'I am happy to say it is mine.'

She stared at him. 'Do you offer marriage to – a lunatic?'

'No. To my dear and beautiful cousin, whose mind has been upset by shock, but who can readily be restored to health and happiness.'

She turned her head away in silence. Edmund said:

'We might go, for the *lune de miel,* to the Italian Lakes. Or perhaps to Switzerland, where they have railways that climb to the snowy peaks of mountains. Would you not like that?'

Sarnia looked at Mrs Jelain. 'Will you see to it, ma'am, that water and towels are sent to me?'

'Not "ma'am", child. Aunt Jeanne. I will speak to Bourgaize about it.'

She kept her word. After they had gone, the elder Bourgaize girl brought a large jug of hot water, soap and clean towels; and also fresh underlinen and a dress which Mrs Jelain had fetched from Les Colombelles. Sarnia washed and put on clean apparel. She felt much better, but within half an hour Bourgaize came, with his son.

'Your medicine, Miss Sarnia.'

'No!'

'It has to be taken morning and evening, by the doctor's command. It is late today because Martin had to ride into the town for it.'

'I cannot bear it.' She appealed to him. 'It disorders my mind.'

'Dr Falla has prescribed it, and he knows best.'

'Leave it, then. I will take it directly.'

'We have orders to see that you drink it. Come, Miss Sarnia, do not put us to the trouble and yourself to the indignity of forcing you to it.'

The son moved, shifting his feet. She saw the big hands, roughened and grime-creased from working in the fields, the mouth whose heavy lips parted in a half-grin, the small bright eyes. She said wretchedly:

'I will drink it.'

Bourgaize gave it her in a spoon and watched her swallow. The sweetness nauseated her. He said:

'That is better, Miss Sarnia. It will do you good.'

The hours passed slowly, and at first in the misery of despair. It had penetrated to her at last how completely she was within the power of the Jelains. They could restrain her here indefinitely, with a doctor's approval, and even with his aid. For the medicine which Dr Falla had ordered she should take, to soothe what he said was her nervousness, would contribute to the overcoming of her resistance. In fogging her mind, it also sapped her will: she could detect its effect already. In the end the confusion would be too great for any rational thought. In the end, she would give in.

And then? The marriage, which was the object of their coercion and contrivance – and through it Edmund's control of her father's money? She sat up, recalling, despite her drugged state, the crux of what was involved. A marriage. No doubt they would choose a private ceremony, without guests, giving out that the condition of her health prevented anything public. They would have their own men for witnesses – Bourgaize for one, perhaps. But they must also have a clergyman, to make the union legal. And if she then, at the moment of his officiating, refused consent, they could not carry it through.

She tried, through the haze of her drugged thoughts, to think of what the Jelains might do – of the worst they could achieve. Perhaps declare her mad, and have Dr Falla commit her to the lunatic asylum of which Mrs Jelain had spoken. But whatever horrors might surround her there, it was better surely than this present helpless confinement. She would at least be free of them. And surely also she could convince the doctors at the asylum, eventually if not at once, of her sanity?

This, she was convinced, was the plan she must adopt. Docility, acceptance – only at the last moment, with a clergyman present as independent witness, protest. She felt hope stirring again. She wished Edmund might come back, and planned what she would say to him. And yet it was probably better to have it wait a little. Her agreement should not seem too easily won.

The day faded into night. Morning came, with more medicine to take. She slept on and off during the day. In the evening she asked Helene, who brought her supper, if Mr Jelain had not been to the farm that day, and was answered with a shake of the head.

The next day too she saw no one but the Bourgaize girls, and Mr Bourgaize and his son making sure she drank down the drug. She felt, even in her stupefied state, the growing oppression of loneliness and boredom. Once she heard hoofbeats in the lane, and rushed to the window to look out. It was only Martin, returning from an errand.

Edmund came at last as dusk was falling. As he stood in the doorway she felt a wave of loathing. But she looked steadily at him, showing nothing.

He said: 'Good evening, cousin. How are you today?'

'As well as can be expected.'

'You look more rested.'

'Do I?' She paused. 'I have been considering … all this.'

'I am glad. It is an advantage of being thrown onto one's own company that one has time to think, and perhaps one thinks more clearly.'

'If I were to accept the proposal of marriage you have made me …' He was watching her closely. 'I should not have to stay with you? I would have leave to go, if I wished, once I was your wife? To England?'

'I should regret such a thing, of course, but I should not attempt to detain you, if that was what you wanted.'

'You would have the money, and that would suffice you? I am glad you are honest about it.'

She was not able to keep contempt out of her voice. He said:

'This money you speak of – it should have come to our family as of right. Apart from you we were his closest, his only kin. And without us you would not have had it – would never have known of it. He left unanswered the letter that was written by your aunt when your mother died. He wished no part of you. We discovered it through Troutaud, and my parents brought you here, where you might learn of your patrimony. It was we who took you to Beauregard, and paved the way for his willing the other half of his fortune to you also. All that you stand to inherit, you owe to us.'

He spoke with a kind of passion. Loathing him still, she understood him better. Avarice, by his reckoning, was no sin but a virtue. Almost any monstrosity could be justified by money, and what they regarded as their claim to it. Seeking to communicate with him in his own terms, she said:

'Would I be given an allowance?'

'Indeed. A very handsome one. You have my word on it.'

It was astonishing he should think that after all that had happened such a pledge could deceive her. But she must seem to be deceived.

'In that case, I agree. I did not seek this fortune, and it is not worth the price of my liberty. If you still wish it, I will marry you.'

'I am delighted.' He smiled. 'I knew you were a girl of sense, cousin.'

'May I be released now from this imprisonment?'

'At the earliest opportunity, I promise you. The two things will come together.'

She had not really thought there could be any other answer. She said:

'Banns can be dispensed with if you obtain a special licence of the bishop.'

'It shall be done. Tomorrow's packet will take me to England on just that errand. It is not far from Southampton to Winchester – less than half an hour by the railway. I can complete the business and be back here on Tuesday morning.'

'The sooner the better. I cannot bear this confinement.'

His look was amiable. 'When we have married – you will wish to leave directly?'

'Yes.'

'But, for the sake of appearances, you will permit me to accompany you to England?' She nodded. 'It can be put out that we are departing on an extensive honeymoon. When I return alone … it should not be difficult to make up a story. There is a family history of broken marriage ties, is there not?'

'You may say of me whatever you wish. I am not concerned for my reputation in this island.'

'We shall not blacken your character. It will not be necessary. And after all, you will be my wife, though in name only. Yes, sorry as I shall be to part from you, I am inclined to think an early departure from Guernsey is wise. It reduces the risk under which you lie.'

There was something in his voice which disturbed her, an unctuous note. She said sharply:

'Risk? What risk?'

'Concerning your father's death.'

'How, concerning? I do not understand you.'

'If there should be gossip, perhaps an investigation, you will not be here, and no one can force you to answer.'

'To answer what?' She felt her head spinning. 'What gossip?'

He spoke slowly, watching her. 'It was a sudden death, and unexpected in view of his previous recovery. Falla set down the cause as food poisoning, from the mussel broth. Family doctors are not given to entertaining ugly suspicions in such cases, and the conclusion was reasonable. But there might have been another cause. Arsenical poisoning, for instance.'

'Poisoning?' He must be mad, she thought. 'You are not suggesting that I murdered my father with poison?'

'I am saying only what others might say – people with more suspicious minds than Dr Falla. It is known your father made a new will, the very day he died, and that in it he left everything to you. It may also be known that you purchased a large quantity of fly papers during the previous week, and arsenic can readily be obtained from them. The two things put together might well cause tongues to wag.'

'But it is absurd!' She put her hands to her head. 'And so easily proved false. I would not wish my father's body disinterred, but it could be done, and a post-mortem examination held. It would show there was no arsenic in him.'

'Would it do so? You are quite sure of that?'

'Of course, I am sure!'

He had a strange look on his face. He could not – *could not* – have himself suspected her of such a dreadful thing? Then why that menace, why the questions in a tone of voice that implied the answer must be hideous – that poison would be found?

Her head swam with faintness. She fell more than sat on the edge of the bed. She was aware of Edmund coming towards her, of his hands on her shoulders.

'Why, cousin, do you feel unwell?'

His voice was not mocking, but carried a note of triumph that was worse. She shook herself free.

'You killed him,' she said.

She still could not believe it but, looking at him as she spoke and seeing no change in expression on the dark heavy face, knew it was true.

'You thought he might warn me against you – as he did. And then protect me from you. You could have lost the money which you had been planning to get through me. And the change in the will made the stakes twice as high. You resolved to waste no time, but kill him then. God in Heaven! I knew you to be wicked, but not so vile as that.'

He said calmly: 'You are unhinged, cousin. It is what one must expect, with your illness. It was you who made that broth. I was not at Beauregard that night, nor any of my family.'

'Troutaud!'

She had cooked the food, but it was he who had brought in the dishes from the kitchen. He could have put poison in her father's dish – nothing would have been easier. She remembered her father's jest about the amount of brandy in the sauce. She had not poured so much in, but Troutaud might have done, to mask the bitterness of arsenic.

Edmund said: 'Do you charge Troutaud with such a crime? But if poison were found, who would believe him to have been responsible? He was your father's man-servant of long standing, and stood to gain little by his death. A hundred pounds, I think it was, whereas what comes to you is more than a thousand times that sum. And Troutaud is a Guernseyman. I do not think you would get far – a stranger from England – in levelling such an accusation.'

'You paid him for it!'

He smiled. 'That, too, you would find hard to prove. He has had no money from me.'

'But will – after you have got your hands on it.'

He shrugged, not bothering to answer. His confidence was frightening, and she could not but think with reason. She was a stranger, as he had said; and she already knew how insular, how suspicious of outsiders, were the people of the island. If poison were found in her father's body – and she no longer doubted that it would be found – she would be the one they held guilty. Those fat sleek Jurats, who had awarded fifty lashes to that child – they would never believe her protestations, even without the evidence of the Jelains, suggesting madness.

Yet why had Edmund told her this? She only had to put the question to know the answer. He too had thought of the possibility of her refusing consent on the very threshold of marriage. She had reckoned with the chance of being despatched to an asylum. He was pointing out what the true risk was. They would not label her lunatic, but murderess. And when she was hanged, the Jelains would have a claim on the estate as nearest kin.

She whispered: 'How could you have done such a thing?' She recalled the night-long agony of her father's death. 'No beast could be so cruel!'

But no beast could have such a lust for money. His avarice, she had thought, justified almost any monstrosity in his eyes. She had been wrong: the justification was entire and absolute.

'It is an unpleasant subject,' Edmund said. His expression was unmoved. 'But let us hope it need not concern us any further. Let us look forward to happier things. Our wedding, at least, if not our life together.'

Every moment the horror was more real, thicker, like cobwebs clinging round her. She shook her head as though to free herself from the web, only to feel it closer.

'After what you have told me,' she said, 'how do you think I could ever become your wife, even in name?'

'I have told you nothing, except of the danger that might threaten you; but need not.'

'Go away.' She turned from him, unable to bear the sight. 'I would die sooner.'

'Do not make rash vows,' he said. 'I was surprised, I confess, that you had come round so soon. But you will have time to reflect and see where your best interest lies. Time enough. Goodbye for now, dear cousin.'

The door opened and closed, but she did not move. The key creaked in the lock. She threw herself along the bed, her heart too shocked and sore even for weeping.

XXI

WHEN Bourgaize brought her the medicine, she appealed to him. He was the Jelains' man, but not surely to the extent of condoning murder? She spoke as quietly and rationally as she could, telling him what she had learned. He listened without interruption, then said:

'Come on now, Miss Sarnia. Drink down your medicine. I have things to do still.'

'But have you not heard what I have told you – that Troutaud poisoned my father, and that they threaten to bring me under suspicion for it?'

He said, in a soothing voice: 'No one, I am sure, would believe it of you. And you have things wrong. Your father died of poisoning, but it was a creature from the sea that poisoned him. You have mistaken Mr Jelain's meaning. Now cease finding cause to blame yourself, and take your potion. You might have bad dreams, otherwise.'

'But he was poisoned with arsenic! And it was done through Mr Jelain's instigation.'

'Dr Falla warned us you might say strange things, your brain being so fevered. You must put these wild imaginings out of your head. I know you cannot help them, but I do not have the time to listen to them. Here, take the spoon, and drink.'

Did he really believe her crazed, or was he also privy to the murder? If so he disguised it well, his tone blending sympathy with the impatience of a busy man. And what difference did it make, she thought miserably? All that mattered was that he would not listen to her. She took the spoon from him, and drank the mixture.

Next morning, Dr Falla visited her. As she saw him ride up on his horse she felt a small rush of eagerness and renewed hope. He as a doctor would know that her father's symptoms could have been the symptoms of arsenical poisoning. Dare he disregard the possibility that what she said was true? Surely he would order a disinterment, and find out.

The hope lasted until he came into her room and greeted her.

'My dear Sarnia, I hope I find you better.'

His voice was warm and hearty, but a doctor's to a patient. Even if she convinced him, and a post-mortem examination were carried out, and arsenic found – how would it serve her? She would be worse off rather than better; if not a maker up of mad tales, a murderess. What better explanation for the sickness of nerves he had diagnosed than guilt, as happened with Lady Macbeth? If the choice should lie between her and Troutaud, he more than anyone would choose her as the criminal.

So she merely answered in a low voice that she felt much better. She asked to be rid of the medicine, and to be allowed back into society: her behaviour, she promised, would be entirely proper if she were. But the pleas were made with small hope of their being granted, and were not. He told her benignly that she must be patient, and trust in him. Time, he said, pulling out his watch, was the great healer.

Edmund said: 'Bourgaize tells me you have kept a good appetite.'

In fact, her appetite was poor, but she had forced herself to eat. She did not answer, and Edmund went on:

'I am not sure this is a good thing. Physical nourishment may nourish the fancies which plague you. I have told Bourgaize so. In future he is to serve you bread and water. I am told it is a specific for obstinacy.'

'And when Dr Falla sees that I am growing thin?'

'He will be regretful, but probably not too much surprised. Aversion from food is not an uncommon trait, in lunatics.' He smiled. 'It might be that you suspected the worthy man of poisoning your food. I gather you have some delusions of that sort. No, I do not think a change in your appearance would be anything to remark, except as an unfortunate sign of deterioration.'

She said in agony: 'What do you want of me?'

'You know what I want, and when your spirit is humbler you will renew that consent which you withdrew. And this time hold to it, knowing what the consequences must otherwise be.'

She could see how it might, in the end, come to that. His confidence, she thought despairingly, was infinite; and why not, since she was so utterly in his power? His eye studied her, critical and appraising.

'Some change in appearance, in fact, might be a good thing. I recall you were distressed when you lacked the means of washing yourself. It might be an advantage to have you go dirty. And this too, in case you have Dr Falla in mind, is a common quirk of mad women.'

'And if in his presence I beg for food, and soap and water?'

'I do not doubt you will get them, though he will probably not stay to see you eat. And that which has been made clean is easily dirtied again. Martin would be willing to lend a hand, I'll warrant.'

She could not repress a shudder of disgust, and saw him mark it. He leaned towards her, smiling.

'And I have other shots in my locker. However strong your resistance, cousin, I promise that eventually I will break it. In your heart you know this is true.'

Few callers came to the house. It was too remote for the ordinary run of peddlers and hawkers: who would be likely to venture down that narrow lane, a tunnel of gloomy green, in search of trade? The few that did call would be familiars of the Bourgaizes; and would have been told the sad tale of the mad Jelain girl who had been placed in their care.

She thought of somehow trying to get another letter off – to Aunt Maria or Mr Merton – and spent a long time considering, insofar as the drug permitted her to think clearly, how it might be done. She had no paper, and she asked Bourgaize if she might have a book to read, thinking she could tear out a page and write on it. Though how, since she had neither pencil nor ink? In blood, perhaps. But she lacked even a means to prick her finger: her pins had been taken from her along with her brush and comb and other toilet articles.

No book was brought. She did not know whether Bourgaize had referred her request to Edmund and it had been refused, or whether the denial was his own. She could no longer doubt the depth of his complicity with Edmund. All that the latter had threatened was punctiliously carried out. The only sustenance she was given was bread, night and morning, and water sometimes at her request. This was brought in a mug, and the mug removed when she had drunk from it, in case she tried to wash herself in the few drops remaining. Yet in all this Bourgaize's manner, and his smile, did not change.

She felt her person become noisome, and this was harder to bear than hunger or thirst. The windows of the room were kept tight shut, nailed so that she could not open them. The weather, following a rainy spell, turned hot again and she sweltered, gasping, through unending afternoons.

The small hopes she had entertained withered and died. Even if a book had been brought, and she had contrived to tear out a page and find a means of writing on it, how could her message have been delivered? No one came into her room, except the Bourgaizes, and Edmund and Dr Falla. And the Bourgaizes were Mr Bourgaize and Martin only: the girls were no longer permitted there.

Shame and disgust were her constant companions, and despair held her each day in closer embrace. She had no hope of release; Edmund must win. Why go on torturing herself, and prolonging this misery?

At first she had rushed to the window at every sound of someone approaching. The impossible might happen, and it could be a rescuer. Or some stranger who would see and take pity on her, perhaps require an investigation of her plight. Even when it was Edmund, it offered some variation to the terrible monotony of loneliness. However much she loathed him, he was a link with the world from which she was quite cut off.

But as the slow days passed, even this flicker of interest went. On a sultry afternoon, at an hour when Edmund might have been expected to come, she heard the clop of hooves, the whinny of a horse, and lay, sweating and lethargic, on her bed. He had wrinkled his nose the last time he visited her, and afterwards she had wept. Her dirtiness and dishevelment were of his doing, but that did not make it any easier to bear. In this, as in everything, he mastered her.

There were no footsteps on the stair, but a drone of voices from below. She listened, through the buzzing of flies and the distant farmyard sounds, and heard a voice which was not one of the Bourgaizes, nor Edmund. She could not make out what was being said, even after she had gone to listen at the door, but was almost sure the voice had a familiar ring. It was not Dr Falla, nor Mr Martell, but someone she had heard before.

The voices moved away down the hall, in the direction of the front door. Sarnia went to the window and looked out. A big grey gelding was tethered by the gate. Farewells were being said at the front door, and she craned her neck to look. A figure came into her field of vision, but only Bourgaize. Then another walked along the path towards the gate, and she recognized him. It was Peter d'Aurigny.

She called to him. 'Mr d'Aurigny! Pray, speak with me.'

He did not check, and she guessed he had not heard her through the closed windows. With her elbow she jabbed in between the bars, and shattered a pane. Glass fell tinkling down the granite wall, and he stopped and looked up at the window. She pushed her head close to the bars.

'Help me, Mr d'Aurigny. I am imprisoned here. Whatever they have told you, I am not mad. For the love of God, help me!'

The arrogant handsome face stared upwards, scrutinizing her. For a moment he said nothing. Then in a gesture of exaggerated formality, he swept off his hat and bowed to her. He called, in a loud clear voice:

'I am sorry, mam'selle, to find you so unwell. I trust it will not be long before you are restored to health, and to the company of society and your friends.'

With that he turned his back, walked the few further steps to his horse, and mounted. Bourgaize opened the gate, and she watched him ride off up the lane.

Sobs filled her throat. The glass which stood on the washstand had originally been taken away, to prevent her even attempting to tidy her hair with her fingers. The previous day it had been returned, and that too must have been with purpose. She stared at her frowzy image, with hair sticking to her temple and otherwise lying lank and ugly. The mirror had been returned for her to see how hideous she had become, to break her spirit further. It showed her now what Peter d'Aurigny had seen, looking up at the window. No beautiful maiden in distress, but a wild and filthy creature. Even had they not told him she was mad, he must have thought so.

She remembered his impudence at the ball, and the way she had answered it. How far a cry from that Sarnia, in her lovely frosted grey gown sprinkled with rosebuds, to the bedraggled wretch on whom he had turned his back! He could only feel contempt for her, as everybody who saw her must. She wept. Tears blurred the image in the glass, but could not shut it out.

Dusk came early that day. The sky had darkened with cloud that only increased the sticky oppressiveness of the heat. And Bourgaize had not yet put new glass in the window but had nailed boards over it instead. She had been left her watch, in the knowledge probably that awareness of time's passing was torment, not advantage, and when, with shadows thickening, she looked at it, she saw that it was not yet eight o'clock.

Her supper of a quarter of a loaf of bread had been brought an hour before. All that lay ahead was the rite of taking Dr Falla's draught, and then the black oblivion of night. She had no night-light now, professedly for fear that she might use it to set fire to the house, and must lie in the dark. From her bed she watched the window's square turn sombre, blending into the shadows of the room. In her mind, fear and misery and self-contempt contended over a field from which all else had vanished.

Even without hope, she thought, she might have still resisted, but pride had gone, too, and without that she was lost. There was nothing left to approve her obstinacy, and so no point in its continuance. The wickedness of the Jelains – their murder of her father, their brutal treatment of herself – no longer mattered. All that mattered was the thought of being free to groom herself. A basin of warm water was worth any loss of spirit, any forfeiture of integrity. When Edmund asked her again, she would consent, and this time mean it.

Even after she had made this resolve, she tossed and turned in restless agony. She wondered if Bourgaize might have forgotten about the medicine, and was desolated by that thought, too. However much she hated it, the thought of a night of sleeplessness, here in the dark, was worse. When she heard footsteps on the stairs at last, she started up almost in thankfulness.

It was Bourgaize, but Edmund was with him. Either she had not heard his arrival in her misery, or he had come the other way, from Beauregard. Bourgaize carried the lamp. She stared at them in its light, sunken-eyed.

'Give her the medicine, Bourgaize,' Edmund said.

She watched him set down the lamp on the small square table by the door, and obediently drank from the spoon he held to her. Edmund said:

'Now leave us.'

As the door closed, he said:

'Bourgaize told me of the breaking of the window. That was foolish of you.'

His voice was grim, but had satisfaction in it. She sat on the edge of the bed, but did not answer.

'That fool d'Aurigny had no right to come prying here, and anyway could not have helped you. But as it is he has seen your condition and is welcome to report it. The look of disgust on his face, Bourgaize tells me, was very eloquent.'

All she wanted to say was yes, she was defeated: that she would accept whatever terms he offered, if only she could have a light left with her and water to wash herself. But he was not at this moment looking for words from her, and she felt too tired and feeble to interpose any.

'I have been over at Beauregard,' he went on. 'The repairs will be costly, but it will be worth it. I shall have a town house as well, but it will make an excellent summer residence.'

He spoke as though everything was settled, her acquiescence certain. As it must be: she had herself acknowledged it. He talked of the improvements he proposed at Beauregard, and she listened in a stupor. This was the house which her father had built for his young bride, in which she had been born, in which their marriage had turned from bright joy to dull despair. As all things did in time: some sooner, some later. Nothing lasted, nothing was worth-while.

He talked then of her father, venting an old spleen. It was he who had gone to him, in that last appeal for money, and been turned down. He looked at her, smiling in the lamp light.

'But I have won, have I not? You dispute it no longer.'

It would be absurd to say anything but yes. What was it her father had said? 'You are a match for them.' It might have been true once, but was true no longer. She was beaten, and nothing remained but to admit her defeat. Yet though she willed surrender, she could not speak the words.

'We shall be married, cousin, is that not so?' He moved closer as she shrank back. 'Say it.'

She stared at him, helpless. With a laugh, he said:

'A touch of defiance left, even now? But there is a final way to prove my power over you.'

Another step brought him beside the bed, and she felt the hardness of his booted leg against her own. She could not get away, could only huddle up against the bed head. His hands grasped hers, and his face came nearer. She saw his eyes and grinning mouth, and screamed.

'That will do you little good. Do you fancy Bourgaize will come to help you? And there is an easy way of stopping your noise.'

His mouth fastened on hers, his teeth bruising her lips. She was silenced and half stifled by the kiss. She remembered those moments on the beach, in the mist, when despite herself she had responded to his strength and maleness. All she felt now was horror, shame, disbelief. He could not purpose such a thing. She was conscious again of her own uncleanliness, enforced by him and fully known by him in this vile intimacy.

It could not be. He meant to frighten her: no more. But in that he had succeeded well enough. She struggled, seeking a way to beg for mercy, but her lips were sealed by the devouring mouth. He pulled her hands up roughly, bringing them together. In prayer? She prayed, at least. Then one of his hands grasped both of hers in an iron grip and the other went to the top of her dress, ripping it down.

XXII

SHE AWOKE AS THE DOOR CREAKED OPEN, and cried out in fear. It was pitch black except for the light of a lamp beyond the doorway, and she could only indistinctly make out the figure who held it. It must be Edmund, she thought, returning to ill-use her further, and she cried:

'For God's sake! I will do whatever you wish, but please do not approach me. I cannot bear it …'

The figure with the lamp stepped through, and a man's voice said:

'Hush. There is nothing that needs alarm you.'

Sarnia struggled up. She saw the face above the lamp, but could not believe it.

'Mr d'Aurigny … But how? – why have they permitted you to visit me?' She stared at him wildly. 'It is another trick. It must be!'

He put the lamp down on the table.

'You are a sound sleeper, not to have heard the noise. Those girls screamed louder than you did. Fortunately no one would hear them, in this remote spot. And if they scream again it will be to even less effect. The cellar has a good thick door, I noticed.'

'The cellar…? I do not understand.'

But his tone, light and easy, was reassuring her. He said: 'I trust I took your meaning correctly this afternoon – that I have not locked up the Bourgaizes to no purpose? It would be a pity if I had come all this way, only to have you send me packing.'

'But you turned from me when I called!'

'With Bourgaize in attendance, I thought it best. I carried no weapon, and while I hope I could see to Bourgaize himself easily enough unarmed, his son and hired man were within call, and I am no Hercules. Then, too, it was broad daylight, scarcely an hour for rescuing a maiden in distress. It seemed better to let him think all was well, and return at a more suitable time.'

She was dazed still. 'What o'clock is it?'

'A little past four, and though there is a moon it is well beclouded. I had a devil of a job finding my way back here. My first thought was to bring about your escape in true romantic style, by means of a ladder set up against your window. But I recalled that the window was barred, and I did not know where Bourgaize kept his ladders. So it seemed simpler to enter the house by breaking a downstairs window, and persuade the inhabitants to accept my untimely call.'

'Persuade – how?'

He tapped his belt, and she saw there was a pistol there.

'It was lucky I chanced on Bourgaize's bedroom first, for I found he keeps a shotgun in it. The scream the girls gave when we got to them would have brought him running with both barrels cocked. And a pistol is not likely to fare well against a shotgun at close range.

'But, Miss Lorimer, though I have them well secured and the chances of another caller at this time are small, I do not think we should remain long here in discussion. Are you ready to leave with me?'

His eyes were on her, and she became conscious again of her condition – her begrimed body, and the stained and bloody bed on which she lay. She said faintly:

'Please … do not look at me.'

He had something in his hand which now he offered her. His voice was gentle, quite unlike the tone of cold arrogance which she associated with him.

'I have brought you a cloak. I will look away while you put it on. There.'

She slipped from the bed, pulling it together again so that he should not see it, and put on the cloak. The movements made her wince with pain, but she tried not to show it. She put shoes on also, and pulled the cloak tight round her. She said:

'I am ready.'

He set her on his saddlebow. He could, he explained, have taken one of Bourgaize's horses for her but did not think it wise, she being unfamiliar with the beast and the night so dark. Nor could the horse be easily hidden later; and if it were found it would provide a pointer to the way they had gone.

She asked: 'Where are you taking me?'

She put the question, but felt no urgency to know the answer. Already she felt safe.

He said: 'To the cottage of a fisherman I know, and can trust.'

'And after that?'

He paused before replying. 'Your relations have played a cunning game. There is an order out, making you a ward of the Royal Court, within their custody. You are not safe anywhere on the island. Once they found you, they could have you taken back.'

'Can you assist me to get to England? I have no money for a ticket, but once I am there I can find means to repay you. I promise it.'

'There is no packet today, this being Thursday. But if there were, it would scarcely help you. It departs at ten. Bourgaize's hired man comes down the valley to start work at seven. Within five minutes he will have freed them, and within half an hour Bourgaize will be hammering at the door of the Jelains' house. There will be constables scrutinizing all who seek passage from St Peter Port.'

'Then how …?'

'You must be prepared for a less comfortable sea journey than the packet provides. I am taking you, as I said, to a fisherman's cottage. I mean to hire his boat. We shall go to Jersey in the first place. Guernsey's writ does not run there. Even if you were discovered, it would not matter. And from St Helier you can take a boat to England.'

They came to the top of the lane and turned right. It was lighter out of the tunnel of trees, with a hint of moonglow in the west and a faint brightening of the horizon to the east. She said:

'But what of you?'

'I shall accompany you. I have nothing to engage me at present, and it is over a year since I saw the mainland.'

'When you return to Guernsey … will you not find yourself in trouble? You say they have got the law on their side, and you have defied it. And broken into the Bourgaizes' house and locked them all up at pistol point. Will they not have you charged with all that?'

He laughed, and she felt the shaking of his body.

'I doubt if they will be so keen to prosecute such a case once you are safe in England. And a Jelain does not lightly take a d'Aurigny to court. Have no fears on my account.'

It was the familiar arrogance, but whereas before it had infuriated her, it gave her confidence now. The horse stumbled, throwing them close together. D'Aurigny stretched a hand round her, to pat the animal's head.

'Easy, boy. If you break a leg here, we are all in trouble.'

They reached the road leading to the village of St Martin with the sky paler in front of them. In one or two cottage windows a lamp's light proclaimed an early riser, but they saw no one. A quarter of a mile further on, he turned the horse's head down another lane, and they headed south. They came, with dawn truly breaking, to a path that led steeply downwards, a stream trickling at its side. In the half light she had a glimpse of the sea, pearly grey, far below them. The descent grew steeper still, and he dismounted. She moved to do the same, but he prevented her.

'Stay. He can take one easily enough. But it is better if I lead him now.'

'Is it far still?'

'Not far. But not an easy way. Come, boy. We shall soon be at our grazing.'

The track, for it was no more, twisted and turned along the hillside. Then quite suddenly they were at a cottage, snuggled deep into a fold of land. There was a light in the window, which must be visible far out at sea. D'Aurigny knocked, and was answered by a woman's voice.

'We are expected,' he said. 'But she would be up in any case. She does not sleep much when her man is on the water.'

She was a small woman, dressed in black, rosy-cheeked and neat in her person. D'Aurigny spoke in the *patois* to her, and she replied, looking at Sarnia with a kindly eye.

He held out his arms, to take her from the horse.

'All is well. She has hot water ready for a bath for you. There is clean linen, and a dress. It will not be in any great style, but it should fit you tolerably. It belonged to her married daughter, who is much of your figure. Then breakfast, and after that a return to bed. We can do nothing more until tonight, and you have sleep to make up.'

She began to cry, helplessly. He held her against his chest.

'It is all right, I tell you. You are safe now.'

When she awoke, in a strange bed, the day was far advanced. She heard the howl of gulls, the heavy ticking of a clock in the room below. The cottage had but three rooms: two bedrooms and a living room which was also a kitchen. She got out of bed, poured water from the jug into the basin on the washstand, and washed herself, luxuriating again in the tingle of water on her flesh, the awareness of her body's cleanness.

The dress which had been put out for her was of pink cotton, well-worn and mended in places but clean. Stays and patched white petticoats had also been provided, but no drawers; probably country women here, as in England, did not wear them. The previous owner of the clothes, she found, had been bigger in the hip and smaller in the bust than she was, but she could get into them.

A heavy tortoiseshell comb with a silver spine lay on the chest-of-drawers, and a small wooden-framed mirror was propped against the wall. She did what she could to arrange her hair, and looked curiously at the comb as she put it down. It was not what she would have expected to find in such a place as this. Then she noticed the initials, cursively chased along the silver: P.L.J.d'A. It was his: he had thought of that, too.

The stairs led from the tiny landing directly into the sitting-room. He was drowsing in a wooden rocking chair, but roused at the sound of her descent and stood up.

He smiled. 'You look a great deal better, Miss Lorimer, if you will permit the observation.'

'Please – Sarnia. I owe you far too much for there to be formality between us.'

He shrugged. 'You owe me very little, and that has already been repaid. I am glad to have been of service. And life can be dull on this small island.'

The remark surprised her a little, but she made no comment. She held the comb out to him.

'I fancy this is yours. Thank you for lending it to me.'

'Keep it, at least until we can get another for you in Jersey.' He looked round the small cramped room. 'Would you like to take the air a little?'

'Is it safe to do so?'

'Quite safe. There are other cottages not far off, but we shall not be within their view.'

He stopped at the door of the cottage all the same, to make a careful survey of the outside, and then guided her up a narrow path. The cottage itself dropped from view, hidden in the fold of the hill, and they were quite alone. Where a blackthorn thicket gave additional protection from any prying eyes, he put down his jacket on the rabbit-cropped grass for her to seat herself.

He sat beside her. Heavy clouds, white at their tops but showing flanks of black, towered in the sky. It was warm even in their shadow; hot when the sun shone from drifting gulfs of blue. Inland, in the enclosed valley of the Fauxquets, it would be humid and sultry, but here a breeze blew, light but refreshing.

She felt more at peace than she could ever remember. Over eighteen hours had passed since she last took the drug, and her mind felt clear, though languid. There was the enormous relief of freedom, the joy of being clean and properly fed. She reminded herself that the freedom was conditional still – that the Jelains would be hunting for her and on the island had the power to apprehend her. But even that reflection did not trouble her much.

They were silent for some time. She felt no need of talking, but still was glad when he spoke. He pointed to the small rock-lined bay beneath them.

'Do you see those fishing boats?' There were three, moving slightly on blue water scored with gold. 'The one lying furthest is Tostevin's, which will take us to Jersey.'

'It is very small.'

She spoke lazily, not critically nor in alarm. Peter d'Aurigny said:

'I warned you there would be no luxury in the voyage.' She shook her head, smiling. 'In fact, it is likely to be unpleasant. The sea looks calm enough now, but Tostevin declares the weather is breaking.'

'I shall not mind if it is rough.'

He looked at her. 'I know: you have been on a pleasure steamer from Yarmouth to Lowestoft, with an east wind blowing.'

She laughed. 'It was from Margate to Brighton, which is much further.'

'These waters can be very wild. We shall need a west wind to get there, but I fear it may be stronger than I should like. At first, Tostevin was for postponing the trip.'

She shrugged. 'I do not care.'

'But his wife has been into the village this morning, and come back with the news. It seems we have stirred a hornet's nest. There is a great hue and cry on. More than I would have expected. They are determined to lay their hands on you again. It is a greater determination than I would expect of such as the Jelains.'

She supposed she ought to be afraid, but was not. They could not touch her now. She said:

'They wanted me to marry Edmund, and so have control of the inheritance from my father.'

'I had guessed as much. They have a great love for money, and lately a great need. And yet ... Sarnia, look at me.'

She obeyed, very willingly. His eyes, she decided, were a deeper grey than any she had seen, his features even more handsome than she had thought, his look not really arrogant but calm and self-assured. He had a snaggle tooth on the right, but like the rest it was strong and white. Their gazes held, and she felt beneath the languor a small bubbling spring of joy.

He said suddenly: 'You are not mad, and never have been.'

She was startled out of her reverie.

'Did you think I was?'

'It was put about. A physician's word carries weight.'

'Then why did you come to rescue me, if you thought I was mad?'

'You were plainly in distress. Mad or not, you were being kept against your will, and I did not regard Jelain, or his grinning ape Bourgaize, as proper custodians. You would be better off, I thought, among friends in England.' He smiled. 'I planned keeping a wary eye on you, in case you turned on me in your madness. I think I can abandon that precaution.'

'You really thought me mad?'

'Unhinged, perhaps, by your father's death. The story was told luridly and in detail – of screams and hair-tearing and smashing crockery. It was all schemed so that you could be kept a prisoner, in the hope that eventually you would agree to marry Edmund Jelain? I still do not follow it. True, they would control your fortune once you were his bride, but you would have to become so first. Even if you said yes in private, how could they be sure you would not say no at the altar?'

'I had such a notion, but he was ready for it.'

'How?'

'Through my father's death.' He looked at her in bewilderment. 'It was not caused by the mussel broth; or not at least through a mussel being bad. Arsenic was taken from fly papers, and put into his dish. Troutaud did it, but it was I that bought the fly papers. They would accuse me, and the Court would take Troutaud's word against mine. It would be thought I poisoned my father, having first persuaded him to change his will in my favour.'

'Are you sure of this?'

'That such a threat was made? Yes. Unless I *am* mad.'

He squeezed her hand in reassurance. 'Now I understand. This is why their need to recover you is so urgent. Knowing you are with me, that you may have told me the story, they are in fear not merely for the loss of a fortune, but for their skins.'

'But is it not true what he said – that being friendless, a foreigner, having as it might seem cause to wish my father dead, it is I who would be judged guilty?'

'It might have been so. But the situation has changed, has it not? You are no longer friendless.' His hand still rested on hers. 'You believe that?'

'I believe it.' Her fingers moved, but to hold his not avoid them. 'Do you mean – I could face them out? Would it be best to do so?'

'First they would get you back.' He shook his head. 'That must not happen. They will be desperate and, having murdered once, might do so again. After all, you are the chief, the only witness against them. But once you are safe in England, it will be possible to look into things more closely.'

She said quickly: 'You will not yourself run into danger? If they are desperate, as you say …'

He grinned. 'Have no fear on my account. The Jelains cannot touch me.'

Because he was a d'Aurigny, he meant. She discovered she did not mind that at all: quite the reverse. His eyes were fixed on her.

'Tell me,' he said. 'If none of this had happened, you would still never have married him. Would you?'

She thought of Edmund and into her imagination, dreadfully real, as though all were happening again, came the scene of the previous evening. Her body was stabbed with physical pain and sickness as her mind was by shame and horror. The sense of freedom, the beauty of this afternoon, the joy in Peter d'Aurigny's company, had all been based on a refusal to think of that ultimate degradation and defeat. She had kept it out of her consciousness because it was unbearable to remember; and now the memory possessed her utterly. She gasped in agony and closed her eyes, but the scene which she blotted out was this soft sunlit one, and not that lamplit hell.

'What is it?' His voice was full of concern. 'Tell me what troubles you.'

'I cannot.' She began to weep. 'Do not ask me.'

His arm embraced her shoulder. 'Never mind. It was an absurd question and does not need an answer. And do not cry, Sarnia. All will be well in the end. I promise you.'

Even in the depth of her misery, she could almost believe him.

XXIII

THE FISHERMAN Tostevin was small in stature like his wife, but spare where she was plump and brown where she was rosy. He wore rope-soled canvas shoes, trousers of blue cotton bleached almost white, and the familiar guernsey with sleeves rolled up to the elbows. Unlike his wife he spoke English as well as the *patois*, in a clipped but lilting brogue.

Before they left the cottage, Mrs Tostevin set a meal before them: a cassoulet of pork and haricots which had simmered all day in the furze oven, with fresh home-baked bread and cider in big earthenware mugs. The cider was strong and raw, and after a mouthful Sarnia asked for water. Peter and the fisherman drank theirs down and passed their mugs to be refilled. He caught her eye, and said:

'Are you recalling that at our first meeting I was in liquor, and you were obliged to reprove me? I have not forgotten it.'

She shook her head. 'I meant no reproof.'

'Nor do you need to. I am a reformed man.' He smiled. 'Or very nearly so. But this will be a rough crossing, as I have warned you, and we shall need something to put heart in us. I have some brandy, if the cider is too sour for your taste.'

She smiled, but shook her head again. Tostevin said:

'Aye, she will be rough. When she does blow up, she will blow hard.' He pulled a face. 'We wanted a wind. But not a storm, eh?'

'We shall be safe enough for Jersey?'

'Cor damme, yes! She will not blow really hard before midnight, and we will be in Jersey long before that. With a good wind and the tide running, we will be tying up in St Helier while it is still light.'

'Do we start soon?'

Tostevin shrugged. 'As soon as you like.'

She realized he had not once said 'Sir' – that altogether he treated Peter more as an equal and friend than as a superior. And Peter did not seem to mind or notice: there was nothing of the d'Aurigny arrogance in his manner here. He said to Tostevin:

'You are the best judge, *mon vieux*. As far as Miss Lorimer and I are concerned, the sooner the better.'

'And now is better than sooner, eh?' He mopped his plate clean with the last of the bread, downed his cider and stood up. 'They were talking, over at the inn. About the young lady. 'Tis said they are crying a reward for news of her.'

'If we are seen going down to the boat …'

'Who will see us, eh?'

'Perhaps other fishermen.'

'If they do, they will say nothing.' He grinned at Sarnia. 'We talk a lot, eh, we Guernseymen. But we know when to keep our mouths shut, as well. And if one did not know, there are plenty would tell him. It is little good having a reward, eh, if you lack teeth in your head to eat your victuals. Come, mam'selle, we will take our leave.'

Tostevin and Peter dragged a small dinghy down from the pebbly beach into the water. Then, as Tostevin fixed oars in the rowlocks, Peter lifted her. She was conscious of masculine strength again, but this time supportive not threatening. They sat side by side in the bows, while Tostevin pushed off and rowed out to the fishing boat.

It was a single-masted lugger, about fifteen feet in length, and of the simplest construction. There was no cabin: it lay open to the skies and the weather. The outside of the hull was painted blue, with the paint flaking away in patches; the inside was varnished wood, smelling strongly of the fish which was its usual cargo. Nets were heaped in the stern, and planks down either side formed rough seats. Assisting her to one, Peter said:

'She is no vessel of luxury, as you see.'

She smiled. The mood of calm exaltation she had known on the hillside had come back.

'I make no complaint.'

He left her to help Tostevin in casting off from the mooring and hoisting sail, and she looked back at the beach and the steep rise beyond. Cliffs stretched away on either side, ruggedly beautiful. It was a lovely island, but her heart felt only joy and relief at leaving it. Could it really be true? Or would figures suddenly appear, crowd into the other dinghies drawn up on the shingle, and row furiously out to drag her back? Although she could visualize the scene, she felt no alarm. The sail unrolled and flapped as Peter loosened a rope. While he was here, she was safe.

Slowly the boat moved out, the sail still slack for want of wind. The beach dropped away, the cliffs extended, the island itself began to take on shape under a sky dark with cloud. She thought, for the first time in days, of Michael.

In the wretchedness of her confinement at the farm she had shunned such recollection, aware that it could only twist the knife further in her wounds. But now, in the haven of happiness to which she had come, she could think of him again – with regret, but without pain. She had liked him, and might have come to love him. He had intelligence, a warm heart, sympathy and understanding. Such things were fine in a man – she thought, with a shudder, of Edmund – but they were not enough. The pressures the Jelains had put on him had been cruel and heavy. Yet if similar pressures had been applied against Peter, would he have yielded to them?

She looked at him as he stood in the stern, his gaze on the retreating coastline. The notion would have been laughable, were it possible to laugh at something so hideous. Because he was a d'Aurigny, and pride of family supported him? But Michael had the support of his religion to give him strength, or so she had thought. Thinking of that she saw how much, without realizing it, she had been affected by the appearance of strength he had shown in that regard – by the forthright assertions of his Roman faith when people talked of the papal aggression.

She had warmed to what she had seen as courage as much as to his amiability. And it had taken courage of a kind to stand up against idle or abusive chatter. He did have that. It was the greater fortitude needed to stand up to Edmund's threats – of disgrace, flogging, possibly death – that was beyond him. And yet, but for the accident of his coming after her to Guernsey – to her aid, she recalled with amazement – his weakness might never have been manifested. And if she herself had not come to Guernsey, if her aunt had never written the letter which brought the Jelains in search of her, she might well have married him, thinking him a man of spirit.

She shook her head in disbelief, but knew it to be true. Just as, without her imprisonment by Edmund and his rescue of her, she might all her life have thought of Peter as a rude and cold man, full of vanity and self-conceit.

'What are you thinking of? Something far away, I'll wager, from the abstraction of your look. The pleasures of London?'

He stood in front of her: the slap of waves, squeak and creak of rope, groaning of the mast had masked the sound of his coming. She looked at him and, feeling a blush colouring her face, quickly looked away.

'Never mind,' he said. 'In a day or two you will be there.' He looked at the sea and sky. 'We are moving better now, with a tide. But we are short of wind still. Though with a sky like that, we should not long be so.'

The boat rolled and lurched on a westerly swell, but though the sky darkened more with thickening cloud, they still lacked wind to fill the sail. Then drops of rain began to fall, a few at first but rapidly increasing to a downpour. Tostevin had provided Sarnia with an oilskin and sou'wester, and she huddled inside them. She had felt a slight nausea at first from the boat's rocking, but it did not turn into a *mal de mer*. She still felt more exhilaration than discomfort.

Suddenly the sail filled with a harsh cracking noise, and at the same time she felt the wind, gusting sharply from the west. Like the rain, once it had come it soon began to show its strength. But it did not trouble her. She watched Peter, outlined against the rocking sky, and wondered about the future. Her speculations were happy ones.

The rain slashed across, almost horizontal to the sea, and the wind howled in the stays. Peter came back to her.

'You are not frightened?'

He held his hand out, and she put hers from under the oilskin to be grasped. In the rain's wetness she felt the warmth of flesh. She looked at him, smiling but not speaking.

'This squall will not blow long,' he said. 'Emile says so.'

'You are soaked through,' she said. 'I have taken the only waterproof.'

He laughed. His shirt, sticking to the skin, showed the ridged muscles of his chest.

'Emile and I are well accustomed to summer storms. I have been caught in them often enough, when he has taken me out lifting lobster pots. We shall dry off before we reach Jersey.'

The squall increased in violence and the boat rolled with it, heaving out of the water and falling back. But, while she knew nothing of ships and the sea, she could tell that this, though small, was a stout vessel, well capable of riding rough waters. None of the islands were visible now; they were isolated in a dark grey heaving waste. That did not trouble her, either.

Tostevin, leaving the tiller to Peter, came grinning to her.

'You are a good sailor, eh, mam'selle? We could make a fisherman of you, I reckon. And the worst of this is over. She will blow herself out soon.'

Within ten minutes or so she could feel the wind dropping and the rain growing thin. Then the rain stopped altogether and the wind, after a few brief parting gusts, subsided. From the lashing violence of a quarter of an hour ago, they had come into an astonishing calm. The boat still rolled in the swell, but the sail hung limp from the mast.

The sky was a dull blackish grey, the air sultry, yet somehow tingling. Tostevin said:

'A flat calm, but she will blow again.'

'Can we be sure of it?' Peter asked.

'The rain told us.'

'Told us what?' He laughed. 'I was not attending closely enough!'

'By coming ahead of the wind. Did you never hear that old saw?

> If the wind before the rain,
> Soon you may make sail again.
> But if the rain before the wind,
> Then your sheets and halyards mind.'

'But how soon?' Tostevin shrugged. 'At least, we have a tide still.'

'Until she turns.'

'How long till that?'

'Two hours, maybe a little longer.'

'Long enough to get us to St Helier?'

'Maybe. Maybe St Aubin. But I look for her to blow again first.'

They were surrounded by the heaving changeless waters. Time crawled by, as featureless, but she no more felt tedium than she had felt fear in the storm. She was content to be where she was – glad, rather. The greyness of the sky thickened into dusk, and Tostevin produced bread, and cheese and a coarse *paté*, out of a box. She munched the food with an appetite. Even if night fell with them still out here, no port in sight, she did not feel it mattered.

Tostevin said at last, peering ahead through the gloom:

'There's Jersey, eh?'

She strained her eyes and saw a blacker line that might be the coast. She asked:

'Does that mean we shall soon be in St Helier?'

Peter shook his head. 'Not soon. There are only barren sands in this part. We must round Corbiere, and beat along the south coast for an anchorage.' He said to Tostevin: 'How long to the turn?'

'Half an hour.'

Peter went forward to the bow. 'And still no wind. How long can such a calm last?'

As though in answer thunder rumbled to the south, and a lightning's flash lit up the shore ahead. The glimpse she had, of a long deserted beach, confirmed its barrenness.

'Not much longer, I reckon,' Tostevin said. 'And when she do blow again, she will blow hard, eh?'

The calm continued but thunder crashed again, with lightning following sooner after. Sarnia recalled her mother's fear of thunderstorms, and how as a child she had felt that fear herself. She had none now.

Thunder and lightning, and the unending slap of waves, but otherwise no interruption to the calm. Then Tostevin said:

'She's on the turn.'

'Are you sure?' Peter asked.

'Certain sure.'

'How far back do you think the tide will take us?'

'Back through the Russell if we get no wind. But we will get a wind.' The lightning flashed nearer. 'See that, eh? We will get a wind.'

She felt against her face, unmistakably a puff of air.

'The wind!' There was another, stronger puff, the beginning of a breeze. 'Here is the wind you looked for.'

They did not answer her. She saw their faces in the light from the ship's lantern, intent and considering. Tostevin bent forward over his compass.

It was certainly a wind, gusting stiffly now. She was surprised they did not show their satisfaction. Peter said:

'Which quarter, Emile?'

'East of south. Maybe east of south-east, eh? Look to the tiller, while I take in sail.'

She went aft with Peter. She said:

'Do you not want the wind now you have got it? That you should take in sail?'

'Not this wind.' The tiller was swinging until he steadied it. 'It blows from a different quarter, from the south-east. It takes us the way the tide already runs, back on our course.'

'To Guernsey?' She felt for the first time a flicker of alarm. 'Must we return there?'

His free arm embraced her. He had meant to grasp her shoulders, but took her waist as the boat rolled.

'Not to Guernsey. But we shall have to wait for a change in the wind. We may have to spend a night at sea.'

She said contentedly: 'I shall not mind that.'

This storm, at the outset, was less violent than the other had been, with the wind not so extreme and the rain less torrential. But steadily it grew in force, and the waves lifted higher. The boat began to be tossed more savagely, and Sarnia was obliged to hold on to a rope to avoid being thrown from her place. Peter crouched by her, supporting her with his arm. He shouted, above the howling of the gale:

'Guernseymen build their boats to ride out far wilder storms than this. We shall be all right, I promise you.'

She nodded, and felt his face against hers, cold and wet but comforting. How much better here, she thought, than in that room at Les Fauxquets.

He produced a flask of brandy, and persuaded her to take a draught. Choking over the burning spirit she thought of Dr Falla's medicine also. All that was over. The brandy warmed her. How long a time, she wondered, since the second storm began? An hour? Or longer? She still had no fear of it.

Peter went to speak with Tostevin, and returned to her.

'I believe it is lessening. Emile thinks so, also. How are you feeling?'

She smiled. 'I am all right.'

He sat close and held her. 'I cannot tell you how greatly I admire your courage. I know few men who would have shown such spirit in conditions like these.'

She looked at him in the shifting light of the lantern, swinging with the mast to which it was lashed.

'It is thanks to you.'

She knew her voice had declared more than the words.

He said: 'When all this is over …'

He broke off as the boat heeled in a gust whose savageness exceeded anything yet. He cried: 'Hold on!' and gripped her to him. There was a tearing creaking sound, like that of a tree being uprooted, and though the boat itself began to come back from the roll she saw the lantern still dipping further away. She heard Tostevin cry something; in the *patois*, she thought, but his words anyway were lost in the shattering crash with which the broken mast struck the far gunwale.

A wave, like a wall of wetness, came at her, covering and drenching her, and ripping her from Peter's hold. She heard him call to her, but that was lost as the wave took her out. She prayed.

XXIV

SHE WENT UNDER, choking, and thought she must sink and drown at once. But she came to the surface again, and gulped in air. Something was buoying her up, and she had a fantasy that it was Peter, that his arm was supporting her. She tried to call to him, her voice lost in the black chorus of wind and water. It was not Peter, she realized, but air trapped in the oilskin; and as it bubbled free the buoyancy went, replaced by a clinging dragging heaviness. The reprieve had been no more than temporary: death was certain.

Then something struck her at the back of the neck. The boat, she thought confusedly, but it was something much smaller. She had reached out convulsively towards the object, and her arm fastened round it. A plank of wood; one of those which had been fastened loosely along the side of the boat. Her arm was slipping and she felt the plank being wrenched from her by the tug of the waves, but she succeeded in getting her other arm about it as well. A wave crashed over, smothering her, and she managed to hang on until she and the plank bobbed back to the surface, and she could breathe.

There followed a timeless agony of being battered by this monster, which swallowed her into its cold wet maw, then spat her out, only to swallow her again. More than once she thought she had lost her hold on the plank; many times she felt she was only prolonging for herself a torment which could have but one end. Would it not be easier and better to let go and slip quietly down into the heaving depths?

In the end she wanted only to do that, the desire a positive thing, a longing for peace even though in death. It was not her will, nor any conscious attachment to life, which made her aching muscles keep their grip, but a mindless refusal to accept defeat – even defeat from the senseless and indifferent waves. Yet, if senseless, rocked by God's hand, a part of His destiny? Even to that, she could not submit.

Suddenly the plank, her only ally, itself turned on her, striking at her as it had done before. It was too much, and she was too weak – the blow knocked her away. She sank down again through water, admitting an end to the struggle, but struck something else. Her feet touched substance, and her grasping hands scrabbled in the shifting looseness of sand.

She struggled weakly to stand, and at last succeeded. The water came almost up to her neck, but she was on solid ground. Another wave engulfed her and threw her off balance, and she was forced to labour again to recover a footing. But it had thrown her several yards forward as well, and the water scarcely reached her chest.

She stumbled on, belaboured and urged by the breakers. She was desperately tired; even now there was an impulse to collapse and cease her strivings. But with each weary step the sea was shallower – at last, incredibly, was no more than a ripple of froth about her ankles. She took another step forward, two, three; and dropped exhausted.

She slept and woke, hearing her own voice crying weakly for Peter. The storm raged, but less fiercely. She tried to get to her feet, but the drag of wet clothes and the oilskin were too much for her remaining strength. She tried to undo the oilskin's buttons, to rid herself of it, but her fingers faltered and failed. Peter, she thought: help me! Then tiredness once more became oblivion.

The next she knew was that something was plucking at her sleeve. She opened her eyes. It was day, with big clouds moving across a blue sky, and the sun warm on her face. A boy was bending over her; his fingers had tugged at her sleeve. He spoke, in the *patois*. Helplessly, she shook her head. He said something else, turned, and went away. She watched him go up the beach and disappear into higher ground.

Dazedly she took stock of her surroundings. She lay on sand more white than golden, in which were intermingled hundreds of small shells, most broken into fragments but some whole: the sand itself, she perceived, was for the most part made up of tiny bits of shell. In one direction the beach stretched away to a spit of land with sea beyond it; in the other to a hill, or hills. A warm light wind blew in from the sea behind her, where the waves, though less mountainous, were still high.

She looked for the boat, or for any sign of life. There was nothing. She thought in misery: how could there be? Her own salvation had been little short of a miracle. Had the tide taken her a hundred yards further she would have missed this landfall and drifted on to her death.

She had no idea what the landfall was: whether Guernsey or one of the other islands. There was the bulk of an island out across the sea – dark at its base but sunlit at the crest. She tried again to undo the oilskin and this time, slowly and with many halts, succeeded. She peeled it from her and attempted to stand up. Her dress clung tight and wet about her legs, and she could not manage it. She tried again and failed again; then lay back helplessly on the hot sand.

The sound of voices roused her, and looking in that direction she saw a figure break the skyline further up the beach, followed by others. There was the boy who had first found her, trailing respectfully behind someone whose clothes proclaimed him a gentleman; behind them again two working men bore a wooden hurdle. She thought she ought to call to them, but was too weak and indifferent to make the effort. In any case, they immediately saw her, and the small procession moved down the white sands towards her.

The gentleman was in his later middle years. He had grizzled curly hair, a round cheerful face. He quizzed her with an eye glass.

'Are you all right, ma'am?' He stooped to lift her, and supported her as she stood. 'The boy seemed unsure whether you were alive or dead.'

She said faintly: 'I believe I am all right.'

'But you are quite exhausted.' He had a quick strong voice. 'We must get you to a warm bed and nourishment without delay.'

She tried to walk a step, but her limbs faltered. The gentleman spoke sharply to the two men, who came to take her arms. Then he stripped off his coat and, laying it over the hurdle, eased her down to lie on it. She sank back gratefully.

The men picked up the ends of the hurdle and carried her up the beach. At the top there was close-cropped grass, studded with flowers. She saw what looked like wild roses, growing not on bushes but along the ground like daisies. The gentleman walked beside her. On her left the small hill she had seen from the beach was thick with fern, sharp-edged against blue sky. On her right she could see an end to land, with sea on three sides. She was more alert, and could think more clearly. Was this Guernsey? And if so, might there be a warrant out for her arrest, lodged by the Jelains?

The gentleman looked at her, and she said: 'Can you tell me, sir, where I am?'

'On Herm island, ma'am.' He managed a small bow as he walked. 'May I introduce myself? I am Ebenezer Fernie, Proprietor.'

She closed her eyes. 'Thank God.'

The Manor House stood at the centre of the island, on high ground. From its windows one saw the entire chain of islands: Jersey in the south-west, Sark with its appendage Breqhou in the same quarter but nearer, Jethou, nestling close beside Herm, Alderney far off to the north, beyond the rocky islets which Mr Fernie said were called the Humps. And, past Jethou, bulking so large as to take up almost the whole western horizon, Guernsey.

She felt no desire for food, but drank hot milk with brandy in it while a maid prepared her for bed. She slept the day through in utter exhaustion, waking to find the sun going down behind the hills of Guernsey, lighting them with an aureole of bright gold. The maid who came when she rang told her in broken English that it was almost seven; and although that was the hour at which Mr Fernie usually dined he had given instructions that dinner be held back until she was ready to join him. Water was being brought for her bath, and clothes had been laid out to replace those which the sea had ruined.

Sarnia had her bath and dressed as quickly as possible. Her limbs were leaden and she had no appetite, but she was concerned not to keep her host from his table. When she went down, though, he showed no sign of impatience. He asked if she would take some sherry wine, and she begged to be excused, pleading light-headedness. He said:

'It is food you need.'

He drained his own glass. She protested:

'I am not hungry, sir.'

He smiled. 'You think not, but it may be different when we try you.' He offered her his arm. 'Let us go in.'

Her belief that she had no appetite did not survive her first mouthful of the soup, a rich thick lobster bisque. Fish followed – a sole not from Dover, Mr Fernie explained, but from these local waters – and a saddle of beef. She ate ravenously, and drank the claret he urged on her as an accompaniment.

He asked her about the shipwreck. She answered only that she had been one of a party on a fishing boat from Guernsey which had been caught in the storm, and told how the boat had been dismasted and she herself cast into the sea. He asked if she lived in Guernsey and she told him no, that her home was in London.

She was conscious of an awkwardness in her replies, due to reticence, and was relieved when Mr Fernie changed the subject. He talked of his island of Herm, with great pride. He had travelled throughout the world and found nowhere more beautiful – even in Italy. She asked if he minded the isolation, and he laughed.

'Mind – why, I welcome it! Living here, always in sight of the cleansing sea, I am free of the cheatings and connivings of society. The world is wicked, as the gospel tells us, and a community as large as that of Guernsey does not escape such wickedness – I am not sure it is not worse than metropolitan places. But this is my small Eden, and morning and evening I thank God for it.'

He spoke with earnestness and vigour, and went on to talk with affection of the inhabitants of his tiny realm: honest fisherfolk, whose simplicity was a kind of holiness. He was very conscious of his duty towards them. That was why he had brought in a teacher, Mr Palmer, to instruct the children in reading and writing. Simplicity did not have to include ignorance.

Sarnia was struck by his sincerity, by the obvious benevolence of his intentions. She came, as he talked, to a conviction that she could trust him. When an opportunity offered she began, haltingly, to recount her own story in full. He listened to her, at first with interest, later with shocked amazement. She told him of her father's death, of the plot against Michael, of her incarceration and the deprivations she had suffered at Les Fauxquets, and of the events leading to the shipwreck. She wept when she spoke of that, and Mr Fernie said:

'It is a terrible thing, a terrible thing!'

'Will you help me, sir?'

'I will indeed.'

'If you could assist me in taking passage on a ship to England …'

'Do not worry, child. I will help you.'

The seas were still high the next day, and the day after that: too high to embark on a small boat. During the morning Sarnia wandered out to explore the island. From the Manor House a path led south between cultivated fields to a wild place of bracken and flowers where a patch of lawn, its edges riddled with rabbit holes, contained a group of fallen stones, relics of some very ancient edifice, their granite surfaces worn by more than a thousand years of sun and rain and winter gales.

Sitting there she thought of Peter. She could not believe him to be dead. If she had survived, a weak woman, was it not much more likely that he had done so? He might even now be sitting in Guernsey as she sat here in Herm, and mourning her death. The miracle of her own salvation required that other miracle to make it worth-while – even to make it real. She gazed out over the intervening sea – smooth-looking from this height but streaked with the tell-tale white of breakers – and thought of the Jelains, and Troutaud and the treacherous Bourgaize. If they lived, surely Peter could not be dead. It would be too gross a cruelty.

She found Mr Fernie when she returned, very much concerned over her absence. She must not, he insisted, speaking in a kindly voice but with great firmness, go out again on her own. She asked him why: was this not Eden, as he had said?

'An Eden for the soul, Miss Lorimer, but it is not without physical hazards. The cliffs are dangerous in places.'

'I will keep well away from the cliff edge.'

'Nonetheless, you must not wander about unescorted. No, do not protest! While you are here, you are my responsibility and in my care. I will accompany you on your walks in future.'

She was obliged to acquiesce, though she would have preferred solitude. In fact the walks with Mr Fernie were not unpleasant, once she grew used to his treating her as a child. He showed her pretty views, and told her interesting things of the island's history and its present life.

The community was largely self-sufficient, growing its own grain and potatoes and raising its own cattle for beef and dairy products. Two or three times a week a boat was sent to Guernsey, taking fish to the market and bringing back such things as oil and soap, wine and coffee. When, as now, the seas were too rough, messages could be conveyed by his pigeons, for which he kept a loft in St Peter Port as well as here.

He shook his head. 'Though in general I have little need for such communication, and small zest for it. This plot serves well enough for me. Do you find that you like it?'

They were at the northern extremity of the island, not far from the place where she had been cast ashore, and looking out to the distant cliffs of Alderney. Sarnia said truthfully:

'I like it very much.'

'Then you must visit it again in other, happier times. I promise you will always find it a solace for body and soul alike.'

They set out next morning, with a tide and a fresh south-easterly. Mr Fernie's boat was larger and better kept than Tostevin's, a two-masted ketch newly painted green, with a crew of two men and a boy. They sailed between reefs of rocks and left the smaller isle of Jethou on the port side. On the starboard Mr Fernie pointed out a tinier island still, a mere rib of granite but topped by a round stone tower. Built, he told her, to command the Russell straits and the approach to Guernsey in the days of conflict with the French, but now abandoned.

'As one would hope all artefacts of war some day will be.' He shook his head. 'But the world grows worse, not better.'

They passed the guardian Castle Cornet and came into Guernsey's small harbour. To the south-east, beating up from Jersey, Sarnia saw the mail packet on which, in less than an hour, she was to embark. The tide was high and the ketch was easily able to make harbour and head, with a single sail, towards the south-west corner. Several vessels were tied up alongside the quay, but the granite slipway there was empty except for a few figures at the top. The usual loiterers, she thought, who stood watching the traffic of the harbour.

The ketch drifted in, and one of the crew leaned out with a boathook to hook a ring. The figures on the slipway were nearer now, and clearer. She could see they were not common idlers: two, by their dress, were gentlemen, two others policemen.

The suspicion was immediate, yet unbelievable. No boat had travelled between the islands since her shipwreck: how could they have known? Then as a gull slipped squawking through the air above them, she knew – Mr Fernie's pigeons. They had carried word of her survival, and brought back accusations against her; accusations which Mr Fernie had believed. At that instant she recognized who the gentlemen were: Edmund and Dr Falla.

She said to Mr Fernie in a low voice: 'You have betrayed me.'

He looked at her with compassion. 'Child, I am sorry for you. The clouding of a mind is the worst misfortune to afflict our human condition. But I have no means on Herm to care for you, or even protect you from yourself. You need the ministrations of a physician, the wardship of your friends and relations.'

'I am not mad!'

He put a comforting hand on her shoulder. 'You will soon be well. I am confident of it. And I shall ask your cousins to bring you to visit me in Herm then. I greatly look forward to that.'

There was no point in further protest, and to resist the custody Edmund and Dr Falla claimed, would seem only another mark of insanity. She stared helplessly ahead as the boat touched shore.

XXV

She sat on the same bed in the same room in Les Fauxquets, listening to the same dog barking shrilly in the distance, the same chatter of hens and faraway clamour of geese. Nearer, inside the house, there was a murmur of voices. She saw the iron bars across the window, green of trees and blue patch of sky beyond.

It was as though no real time had elapsed since the night when Peter had awakened her – as though all that followed had been incidents in a fleeting dream. She was here, and in the Jelains' power. If Mr Fernie had taken their word against hers, what reason could there be to think anyone else would take a different view? Even Peter, when he first rescued her, had thought her crazy. The Jelains were respectable people, known throughout the island. It was she who was the foreigner, the unknown and therefore the mistrusted.

A bee buzzed and fretted against the window. She watched it in blankness and melancholy. Poor creature, she thought, I would release you if I could. The pane of glass she had broken in calling to Peter had been replaced. Mr Bourgaize was a worthy man, who saw to the repairs of his tenancy.

Her unhappy meditation was interrupted by footsteps on the stair, the turning of the key in the lock. It was Edmund who came in, and stood by the door, looking at her. On their way from the harbour, accompanied by the constables, she had said nothing, and he too had been for the most part silent. Now he said:

'I believe you have had a hard time of it, cousin, since taking such imprudent leave of this place. If Mr Fernie is to be believed, you are lucky to be alive.'

She made no answer. He came and took her chin in his fingers, raising her face to examine it more closely. His mouth smiled, but the blue eyes were cold.

'You look better than one would expect, after such an ordeal. I am glad of that. No, do not turn your head away.' His fingers tightened. 'Your escapade has made you famous. The poor mad girl who seduced young d'Aurigny into capturing her from her loving relations, and thereby caused not only his death – which some might say his folly merited – but also that of Emile Tostevin, a fisherman well known and liked. His body was washed up yesterday at Petit Bot, less than a mile from the cottage where his widow grieves. There is feeling over that which runs high. If it were not for your madness, which must excuse your conduct, one would fear for your safety.'

She could not remain silent.

'And Peter?' He looked at her with raised brows. 'Mr d'Aurigny – what of him?'

He said indifferently: 'The sea does not always give up her dead; and when she does it is not always in a place, or in a condition, which permits identification. Had he been cast up alive on one of the islands, as you were, it would have been known by now. The fool is dead, and deserved his death.'

She said nothing to that. Edmund said:

'Did you grow fond of him during those few hours you spent together? He is handsome enough.' He smiled. 'Or was. Now that the fishes have nibbled at him, I do not think he would be likely to take your fancy.'

She shook her head.

He said: 'Do you not believe him dead?'

Again she gave no answer. Tostevin's body had been found, but not Peter's. Edmund had said it would have been known if he had been washed ashore on another island, but that might not be true. She would not believe it true.

'It does not matter, anyway, what you think. All that matters, sweet coz, is that you yourself are living. I would not care to think of that warm lovely body battered and bloated by the sea.'

She stared in silent hate. He laughed.

'Take your time. There can be no hasty wedding after the notoriety you have acquired. But fortunately we have gained much sympathy on your account, so the urgency is also less great. We will see this summer through in happy anticipation; and in your case in seclusion. An autumn wedding would better meet the needs of propriety, and very likely has its charms.'

He let go his hold, and she turned her head away. Edmund said:

'I will visit you frequently, as is also proper, and give out reports of your progress. It will be seen what concern I have for this poor sad creature; and it is well known that sympathy can be a stepping stone to warmer feelings. Though I do not doubt that there will be those who suggest my interest is more provoked by your fortune than your person; for who could honestly love a girl whose mind is unsound? After all, you will besmirch my name by taking it. But it is the kind of bargain that has been struck often enough before. Even if people talk, they will recognize it as sensible.'

He stood in the doorway. 'Reflect on it, cousin. Meanwhile, your luncheon will be brought up to you shortly. We must maintain your health of body, even if your health of mind is impaired.'

There was in fact no return to the old restrictions. Food was brought to her at regular intervals, plain but of good quality, and she was allowed toilet articles and hot water. Fresh linen was provided for the bed and for her person. Although still a prisoner, she was now a well-tended one.

Yet this change in conditions gave her no reassurance. Previously they had been using ill treatment as a means to break her will. It seemed that they no longer felt the need for such coercion, being entirely confident of their victory. Dr Falla's medicine was offered to her, but when she refused it was not administered by force.

After lying awake, night after night, she was almost prepared to ask them for it. Sleep, other than in fevered snatches, became an object of even more intense longing than freedom. She felt herself growing old with the crawling passage of wakeful wretched hours. In the mornings she looked in the glass and half expected to see an old crone reflected.

She tried to console herself with fantasies of Peter, imagining him concealed somewhere on the island, biding his time to come again and take her away. In the small hours, watching the flickering flame of the night-light, she listened for sounds, and built them into promises of his return. The creak of timber, as the old house settled in the cool of the night, was his footstep on the stair, causing her to gaze at the door in trembling hope. Once she was so sure of his presence that she got out of bed, and whispered his name into the dark.

But with the passing of days the hopes grew fainter, the fantasies less convincing even to a mind drowsed with want of sleep. A week after she had been brought back, Edmund paid his usual call. He asked after her health, and when she did not reply said:

'I have news for you.'

She did not look up. No news that came from him could be to her advantage. 'Tostevin's boat.'

She looked up then, and saw him smiling.

'It has turned up – or rather, the remains of it. It floated into the harbour with this morning's tide. It is badly smashed but the fishermen know it, and the name is on it still. *Annette*. He called it after his younger daughter, who died when she was five. A man of sentiment, Tostevin. And the discovery of his boat has reawakened sentiment in the island: in his favour, cousin, but not in yours.'

She told herself that the boat did not matter. Peter could not have stayed with it so long; if he had been saved it would have been, as she was, through being cast up on a shore. But the news forced into her mind that consciousness of the passage of time which she had been rejecting. It was ten days since the shipwreck. He could not possibly be living still. She bent her head and wept, knowing this to be defeat at last.

'Do not fret,' Edmund said. It was a sneer. 'Their memories are short. No one will stone you as you come out of church.'

Thereafter a new kind of melancholy clung to her: not wild or anguished, but settled into a deep uncaring despair. She ate little, and lost interest in her appearance. Her hair went unbrushed, uncombed even. She scarcely touched the food that was brought her; not as a protest or defiance, not even from distaste, but out of sheer indifference.

Dr Falla came one day with Edmund, and she stared at him with lacklustre eyes, her hair bedraggled and her face unwashed: the water had cooled untouched in the bowl which Helene Bourgaize had filled that morning. Dr Falla put questions to her and she answered them blankly, too listless to be mute.

He told her she must eat. Food was brought – breast of roast chicken with bread sauce, potatoes, green vegetables – and she looked at it. She must eat, Dr Falla repeated. If not they would be obliged to feed her by force, with eggs beaten up in milk. She did not really feel she would mind if they did, but to refuse to eat after so direct a command would be defiance; and defiance was at an end. She ate the food while they watched her.

Afterwards Helene brought fresh warm water and with a soaped flannel washed Sarnia's face. The two men watched that also and she felt nothing: not even shame. Then the girl brushed her hair while she sat uncaring on the side of the bed.

Edmund did not visit the next day, but his mother came. Sarnia heard the rattle of wheels along the lane, the coachman crying whoah to the horses at the gate, but lay unmoving. She did not rise when Bourgaize brought in Mrs Jelain.

Mrs Jelain said: 'Leave us.' She came to the bedside and took Sarnia's hand, which lay limply in her grasp. '*Chérie*,' she said, 'I cannot tell you how distressed I am to see you so low.'

Her voice sounded sincere. Why did she bother to act a part, with no audience but this helpless and empty one? Yet that question too was trivial. She saw the face that bent over her, with an expression of concern on it, and could not be troubled even to turn her own head aside.

'You think ill of us, I know,' Mrs Jelain said, 'to have kept you confined here. But it was for your good, as Dr Falla advised.'

For my good, she thought, that your son should have forbidden me water to wash with? That he should have restricted my diet to bread and water? That he ... her mind shied from the recollection of final horror. It was past, as her resistance was.

'I wish that I had come to see you myself, but Edmund would not sanction it. He was strong-minded as a boy, and as a man is much more so. I least of all am capable of setting myself up against him. He insisted that everything should be left to Dr Falla and himself, that my visiting would do you more harm than benefit. I had no choice but to accept it.'

Could that be true? Had all the evil part of it been Edmund's, his mother no more than a weak and ignorant accomplice? What would that bland face show if she were to speak of the degradation she had endured? But who believed the accusations of a mad woman? And what would it matter, anyway, if she did?

'But now Dr Falla has been speaking to me about you. Your melancholia, he says, has changed from its previous form. It is quieter, and no longer has the seeds of violence in it. There is no need now for retirement, but instead for diversion and society. He agrees that you should not remain here, but return to Les Colombelles where I myself can care for you.'

Vaguely she wondered what this meant. Were they concerned lest her decline should prove so rapid that the grave might loom before they got her to the altar? She closed her eyes in weariness.

'My dear, all will be well, I promise you. We shall very quickly get the roses back into your cheeks. You have had so many distressing things happen, but all that part is over. In no time you will be back in society, laughing and chattering and dancing at balls.'

The Assembly Rooms ... Peter's smiling arrogance and his

flushed face turning white when she slapped him … and Peter beside her in the boat with the storm raging but his arm about her shoulders … A dry sob racked her.

'All this dreadful business will be forgotten. You are young, and the good things in your life lie ahead. Mr Jelain constantly asks after you. Although he does not express himself well, he is very fond of you. We have both loved you from the moment of finding you in London.'

A lie, or truth, or part of each? She did not know – wished only to be free of this voice running on, of everything. Coaxingly, Mrs Jelain said:

'Open your eyes, *chérie*.' She opened them. A warm smile met her. 'That is better. Now, let me help you up from your bed. And put your shoes on.' She knelt at Sarnia's feet and buttoned them for her. 'You do not need anything from here. We have all you require at home.'

They went downstairs together. Sarnia looked at the passage along which she had crept when first seeking to escape. How long ago that seemed. The clock ticked in the hall, counting pointless seconds. In the kitchen the ginger cat lay curled asleep on a chair – the chair in which Elizabeth Bourgaize had sat and knitted, watching the foot of the stairs. How very long ago.

Bourgaize came to bid her goodbye. He helped her into the landau, a little smiling man, and hoped for her swift return to health and spirits. She thought of his hands holding her while Dr Falla's medicine was forced down her throat. Could it truly have happened, or had her mind conjured it up in madness? But the memory was too real. Then was she mad now?

The coach rolled through the tunnel of green and up the hill towards sunlight. Mrs Jelain sat opposite her, regarding her with what looked like affection.

She said it because it seemed appropriate, an acknowledgement of surrender which, for all her indifference, might give her a kind of peace.

'I will marry your son, madam, if he still wishes it.'

Mrs Jelain reached forward, smiling, to pat her hand.

'That makes me very happy, *chérie*, as I know it will him. And his happiness will accomplish yours. I will vouch for it.'

XXVI

DAY PASSED INTO NIGHT; to day, to night again. The days turned into weeks. At Les Colombelles Sarnia was well cared for. She was pampered as an invalid: delicacies were pressed on her. She ate them because it was easier to do so than refuse. Mrs Jelain's maid saw to her hair and helped her with her toilette, and for duties and errands above that there was the little Marie, re-engaged into the household. She did not speak of her dismissal, nor very much of anything; but of course she had always been timid and quiet. She attended to Sarnia's wishes, or would have had there been any, but her eyes fixed on the housekeeper or Mrs Jelain whenever they were in the room.

What would the child say, Sarnia wondered, were she to ask her to post a letter? Had she been inclined to mirth, the notion would have made her smile. She herself received letters from Aunt Maria and Mr Merton. They said much the same thing: they were grieved to hear from Mrs Jelain of her illness. They trusted she would soon be quite restored to health, and meanwhile were happy she was in such good hands. Mr Merton added that a banking colleague of his had recently retired to live in the island of Jersey, and was warm in praise of its beauty and temperate climate. She did not reply to either. There seemed little point in doing so – in doing anything.

The summer faded. The wedding would be in October, she was told: a quiet ceremony with few guests. She nodded in apathetic agreement. No more had been said of her proposal that after the wedding, after Edmund had gained control of her fortune, she should leave the island. She did not raise the matter herself because she no longer cared. She loathed Edmund with a loathing that nothing would ever eradicate, but that deep hatred did not touch her will. She felt she had no will.

She was offered outings, and would have accepted them if pressed. But she had no inclination for picnics or tea parties, and Mrs Jelain and Edmund seemed content for her to remain in the house. Although she made no visits, a few people – close friends of the family – called on her. She would sit, in the garden or the drawing room, silent except when directly quizzed. She gave bare but civil answers then, in a low monotonous voice. Sometimes she saw glances pass between the guests. She took their meaning but they did not trouble or even interest her.

But one afternoon in September, with the wind blowing leaves against the window, a different caller was announced. Sarnia was sitting at embroidery with Mrs Jelain when Mrs Perret came in to the parlour.

Mrs Jelain asked: 'Who is it? I heard a horse ride up.'

'General d'Aurigny, ma'am. Begging the pleasure of Miss Lorimer's company.'

Mrs Jelain was flustered. 'I do not think …' She put down her embroidery and stood up. 'I will see the General. He is in the drawing room? Tell him I will be out directly.'

Sarnia laid down her own work. 'He asked to see me, I believe?'

Mrs Jelain put an arm about her shoulders.

'I will explain you are not yet well enough to receive callers.'

She spoke with affection but positively. It was the sort of thing in which Sarnia daily acquiesced rather than go to the trouble of objecting. But she said:

'I am quite well enough to receive the General, and should like to do so.'

The firmness of her own voice surprised her, and appeared also to surprise Mrs Jelain, who looked at her in hesitation. Sarnia thought she might refuse permission, but she said at last:

'We will see the General here, Perret. Show him in.'

He seemed older than on their previous meeting; but then, she thought, had not the whole world aged in those few months?

He said to Mrs Jelain:

'I am honoured you should receive me, ma'am. And you, Miss Lorimer. I trust I find you well?'

Mrs Jelain answered for her: she *had* been ill but was lately much recovered.

The General nodded, and spoke again to Sarnia.

'I hear tell, Miss Lorimer, that there is to be a wedding in the near future – that you are engaged to Mr Edmund Jelain?'

Again it was Mrs Jelain who replied, before Sarnia could say anything. The wedding had been fixed – a quiet affair – they were all very happy about it – she herself felt blessed in the prospect of gaining so sweet a daughter-in-law.

The General directed his gaze on Mrs Jelain. He said:

'The illness you speak of, ma'am – it has not made her mute, I hope?'

Mrs Jelain laughed nervously. 'Why no, General. It is just that I …'

The General turned his attention back to Sarnia. He went to her and took her hands in his.

'My dear young lady, I would have called on you earlier but for this illness I was told of. You have had a terrible time since coming to this island, and it is plain that the experiences have left their mark on you.'

He paused, holding her hands still.

'I was anxious not to distress you, and still am. But I wish to express my sympathy for all you have suffered.'

She stared at him in desolation. 'I caused his death.'

'Not so. He almost caused yours, I fear, in this hazardous expedition he took you on.'

'No! He did it for my sake. He was so …'

Sobs welled up from her heart, for so long dry, and grief and misery which she thought indifference had killed, were alive to ravage her again. In the storm of weeping which possessed her, she heard Mrs Jelain's voice excusing her and saying that she was still prone to fits of melancholy, not ready yet for ordinary society. Mrs Jelain put a hand on her arm, but she retreated from it.

The General's voice steadied her. He said:

'I am truly sorry that my visit has so upset you.'

Sarnia lifted her tear-blotched face. 'No. Please do not think so. I am very glad you came.'

Mrs Jelain started to say something, but the General cut across her words.

'You are a brave girl. I guessed so when I first met you, and now I have no doubt.'

He turned to Mrs Jelain. 'I will take my leave, ma'am. But before I do … When I had the pleasure of calling on you in the summer, I suggested you bring Miss Lorimer to the Manoir during her stay with you. I made no particular invitation, and unhappily the thing never came to pass.

'But I repeat that invitation now, and more precisely. I hope that Miss Lorimer, accompanied of course by you, your husband, and your son who is her fiancé, will do me the honour of calling tomorrow evening at six.'

His tone corresponded more to command than invitation. With a small embarrassed nod, Mrs Jelain said: 'We shall be very happy to do so, sir.'

The General said to Sarnia, in a softer voice:

'You will come, Miss Lorimer? You do not think it will disturb you?'

'No.' She shook her head. 'It will not disturb me.'

XXVII

Le Manoir d'Aurigny stood in the parish of St Martin, no more than half a mile from the main thoroughfare but deeply hidden in woodland. The entrance to the grounds was by way of tall iron gates, worked with the shapes of cormorants which were the family's heraldic bird, and adjoined by a trim porter's lodge. From there the drive wound through the trees, emerging into a circular lawn with the house behind it.

At first glance it was not so impressive as Beauregard, principally because it was less elevated. Where the other house stood proud on its hill, this one seemed to clutch at the earth and bury itself deep in it. The architecture was Jacobean but there were additions of later date, an entire wing coming unexpectedly into view. It had a look of age and accretion.

They were shown through a hall hung with portraits in oils to a large room at the rear of the house, where the General greeted them. He was formal in his manner to the Jelains, gentler towards Sarnia.

She had been instructed by Edmund to say little – nothing beyond what politeness required. It had not been necessary: she had so long passed the stage of protest or rebellion, or any hope of help from others. Even so Edmund had disliked the notion of the visit, and had been minded to reject it. His mother had reminded him of the General's position in the island: such a discourtesy to him might have unfortunate effects. It was better to go, and make an excuse for leaving early. He had agreed reluctantly.

The General offered them sherry wine, which Sarnia declined but the Jelains accepted. Mr Jelain, sipping his, praised its quality, but the General cut through his compliments. He said to Sarnia:

'I would wish to talk of my son, Miss Lorimer – my son, Peter. When I saw you at Mr Jelain's house, you were distressed by my mention of him. If you would prefer to retire to another room, I will arrange to have you attended there.'

She shook her head. 'I would rather stay.'

Edmund said: 'Miss Lorimer is not a well person, sir. I am surprised that you, as a gentleman, should consider introducing any subject which you know might distress her. I beg you to keep this discussion for some other time.'

He spoke boldly. The General looked at him for a moment, before replying.

'I am indebted to you, Mr Jelain, for your guidance as to the conduct of a gentleman. I am quite aware that Miss Lorimer is less well than one might hope. And I am concerned for it. If Miss Lorimer wishes to retire, arrangements can be made. If she wishes to place a veto on discussion of my son, I will respect that also.' He looked at Sarnia. 'The decision lies with you.'

Sarnia said: 'It does not distress me. And I would prefer to remain present, and not retire.'

He smiled at her. 'I am glad of that. And I will not abuse your consent if I can help it. But I must talk of my son. You understand?'

She nodded. 'I understand.'

'Peter was not my first son, either in birth or preference. He was a bright, a spirited boy, but lacking in the discipline to which my family have been accustomed. From his earliest days he got into scrapes, and the scrapes grew worse as he grew older. He drank and gambled – was altogether wild. My remonstrances seemed only to increase that wildness, and deepen the division between us. I think now that I may have been at fault there. He was young, and the young are wilful and often ignorant. The responsibility of keeping them from folly lies heavier on their elders.'

Mrs Jelain said brightly: 'You do yourself an injustice, General. I am sure …'

His hand motioned her to silence. 'I will listen to you at

another time, madam. Pray give me leave to speak for the present. As I say, Peter was wild as a boy, wilder as a young man. Miss Lorimer herself is a good witness to that. In her first public engagement on this island, as a young lady unacquainted with our society and therefore the more in need of its protection, she was forced to take extreme measures to reprove him.'

Sarnia said: 'He meant no insult. I misapprehended his intention. I was too hasty.'

'You are generous to pardon him. But on any account his behaviour was bad; and not on that occasion only. Our family is one which has claimed some respect as its due in this community. The claim is one which exacts standards of behaviour yet more rigorous. *Noblesse oblige* is a Norman saying, and if we are not noble we are very certainly Norman.'

In the corner of her vision she saw Edmund smile, and realized he was enjoying the General's indictment of his son. She said, conscious of anger for the first time in many weeks:

'I found him worthy. No, much more than that!'

'The strange thing,' the General said, 'is that he should have behaved as he did in relation to you. Wild, as I say, and undisciplined, but not a cad.' He shook his head. 'To take a young lady out of the care of her relations, using a pistol to intimidate those to whose protection she had been entrusted, then to expose her to the hazards of a sea journey in a fishing boat, with the weather uncertain … I had not thought so ill of him.'

Her indignation was increasing. 'He did it in answer to my plea! I begged him to help me.'

'But to take you from a home where you were being well cared for …'

She said passionately: 'He found me wretched, degraded, close to starving! I had nothing to eat but bread and water. I was not allowed water to wash myself, nor clean linen – a drug was forced down my throat morning and night to make my mind confused …'

The General turned to Edmund: 'Those are serious charges.

What do you have to say to them, Mr Jelain?'

He said with calm confidence: 'Only that my poor cousin has been sadly disturbed in mind, and still is. The shock of her father's death began it. The hazardous expedition on which your son took her made things worse.'

'That is a lie.'

But she spoke with less vigour, her spirit failing in the conviction, enforced on her for so long, that her testimony counted for nothing. Why should the General believe what she said? Or anyone?

The General said to Edmund: 'You say there is no truth in her accusations? The diet of bread and water, the refusal to permit her to wash herself … these are fabrications of madness?'

'Indeed they are.'

'And she was not kept locked in a room in conditions of squalor?'

'Locked in, yes – for her protection. In her madness she might have injured herself or others. But she was well looked after and well fed. She had all the facilities for comfort.'

She protested: 'No …' But faintly.

'There is a conflict of evidence,' the General said.

'Do you think so?' Edmund asked. 'On the one hand Dr Falla, the Bourgaizes, myself. On the other, a poor crazed girl.'

How true it was. The General looked from Edmund to her, his face impassive. He walked across the room and pulled on the bell-rope by the fireplace. He would be summoning a servant, perhaps to end the interview. The old feeling of helplessness and despair came back.

'If Miss Lorimer had someone to confirm her story,' the General said, '– one person, even.'

'But she has not,' Edmund said. He spoke quietly, careful to keep the triumph out of his voice. 'How could she have?'

The door had opened while he was speaking. A man's voice said:

'You are mistaken, Jelain. I am that person.'

The shock of hearing merged into the greater shock of sight. Peter stood in the doorway. She swayed and started to fall, and he came forward quickly to support her.

He helped her to a sofa and sat beside her, chafing her hands. The General said to Edmund:

'Well, sir? What do you say now? I have already spoken with my son. The foul conditions in which he discovered Miss Lorimer correspond exactly with the charges she has made. Far from having the comfort you spoke of, she was confined in a filthy room and in extreme privation.'

Edmund said sullenly: 'I deny it. I do not know how your son came to be here, but it is plain he is as crazy as she is.'

'Do you say so? He is ready to lay a charge against you in the Royal Court. We will see who convinces the Jurats.'

'Will he do that?' He stared at Peter and Sarnia. 'He might do well to think twice, if he has Miss Lorimer's interests at heart.'

'You speak of her interests – when she was imprisoned in a state far worse than one would keep a beast?'

'For her good, as I have said.' Confidence was returning to Edmund's voice. 'We have done our best to protect her, both for her sake and that of the family, but it seems the truth must come out. Her father's death unhinged her. From grief – or guilt?'

'I am listening,' the General said. 'Guilt for what?'

'He is said to have died of food poisoning. She prepared his food.'

'A bad shellfish. Is she to feel guilty over that?'

'But perhaps it was a different poison. Not long before his death she ordered fly papers for the house: far more than were found afterwards. If this is told to the Royal Court, they must take note of it. And it might be that when her father's body is exhumed, they will find arsenic in it.'

Peter gently released her hands, and stood up.

'You speak persuasively,' he said, 'and I am sure you are right.

They will find arsenic. But Miss Lorimer is not responsible for it being there.'

'Tell the Court that! Only she and Troutaud were at the house, apart from the old man. And Troutaud had no reason to do murder. The will that was made in the afternoon offered him no advantage; but it doubled her expectations.'

'A cogent argument,' Peter said. 'And it might even be that Troutaud would testify that he saw her boiling up the fly papers – perhaps even saw her putting something strange in the dish her father was to eat?'

'I would think it possible.'

'It seems you rely heavily on Troutaud.'

'He was her father's manservant for twenty years. His word is to be relied on.'

'I am glad you say so. Perhaps I should tell you that I have not just today returned to the island. I have been here several days. I thought it best to disguise myself on my arrival, and came here to my father without anyone else knowing. This story of her father's murder, and the threat that she would be accused of it, was told me by Miss Lorimer when I was helping her to escape.'

'It makes no difference if she spoke of it,' Edmund said, '– or if you say she did. It lies at her door still.'

'On Troutaud's evidence. But what if he has changed his story?'

'He will not!'

'When he was a young man,' Peter said, 'Troutaud went to sea with old Jelain. He was very likely stalwart in those days, but age and the life of a manservant have dragged him down. It did not take much to get him to confess.'

'You may have forced him into lying – that is all.'

'Lying?' Peter took a piece of paper from his pocket. 'A promise to pay one thousand pounds to Roger Troutaud, by the year's end. Signed by Edmund Jelain.'

Mrs Jelain gave a small moan. Edmund said:

'That means nothing.'

'Nothing? A thousand pounds is a lot of money – ten times what his master left him in his will. You had borrowed it from him, maybe, and were promising a repayment? Your own need of money is well known. But where would a man like Troutaud get a thousand pounds to give you?'

Edmund for the first time was silent. Peter said:

'That is not all. You say you yourself were not at the house. Nor were you, publicly. But Troutaud says you came clandestinely. And there is a cottager who will testify to seeing your horse, that fine black gelding with the white blaze, not a hundred yards from Beauregard that evening. You came to the house. You had a purpose in doing so. Knowing the old man's will to have been changed that afternoon, you thought him better dead so that he could not change it back or foil your plan to marry Miss Lorimer. Troutaud refused to commit the actual murder, and it was you therefore who put the poison in the dish. The promise of money was so that he should not inform on you.'

'He lies!' His face was dark no longer, but a dreadful grey, and he pulled at his cravat with his fingers. 'It is all lies …'

'Everyone lies but you, it seems,' Peter said. 'I have not long come from the Commissioner of Police. An order for the exhumation of old Jelain's body has already been made. If there is poison in it …'

He pulled the bell-rope. 'You will be shown out. I should have liked to thrash you, but my father persuaded me against it.' He smiled. 'He says I am over-rash. I beg that you leave, before he is proved all too correct.'

A servant opened the door, and Edmund and Mr Jelain went towards it. Mrs Jelain looked at Sarnia.

'*Chérie* …'

'Miss Lorimer will stay here,' the General said, 'if she so chooses.' He glanced at her in inquiry, and she nodded quickly. 'You will have her night attire sent here at once, and her other things in the morning.'

The lawn behind the Manoir was even better kept, of still more ancient tending, than the one in front; but where that had a circle's regular shape, this stretched out among cypresses and gnarled magnolias until it merged into woodland. That was on either side. In front the view was open, to the sea and rocky cliffs that ended in a jagged group of huge granite teeth: the Pea Stacks, the General had told her.

The best outlook was from a rustic summer-house close by the tall blue-green candle of a spruce, and Sarnia sat there on a sunny autumn day. She had a book with her, but was not reading it. His footsteps were soft on the lawn, but she heard him coming and looked up.

Peter said: 'Tea will be sent out shortly. May I sit with you?'

She nodded, and made room. After three days it was still difficult to believe in his physical presence. She wanted to stare at him, but instead looked away.

He had told her the story of his escape from drowning – how he had clung all night to a rope of the upturned boat and in the morning, drifting somewhere between Guernsey and Alderney, had been sighted and picked up, on the extreme edge of exhaustion, by a vessel bound for South America, for Port of Spain. He had thought her dead, as she had him, and had made a vow to bring Edmund Jelain to book. Because of the need for secrecy which that involved, he did not try to communicate news of his survival even after they reached port. Instead he shipped as crew for the return journey.

He had told her all this and she had listened and marvelled, thanking God; and yet she could not believe it. She had a need to touch him that was like the needs of hunger and thirst. She felt it again now, but did not yield to it. She pulled away the fold of her dress that lay close to him on the garden seat.

'There is news,' he said. 'They have been arrested: Troutaud and Jelain both. They accuse each other very readily, digging a deeper pit with every word. Not that it matters whose hand put in the poison. The evidence of their conspiracy is enough.'

'They have not tried to escape, then?'

'Escape? How? This is an island, and unless you are a ten times better swimmer than Leander, you must depart from it by boat. The harbour was watched, and the fishermen were warned. Not that they would have helped him, for any reward, once the story got about.'

She was silent. He said:

'It is an unpleasant business, and best forgotten – though I fear that may not be easy for you.'

She said: 'I shall never forget all you have done for me; nor ever be able to repay it.'

'You can do so very easily.'

His eyes were on her face and she looked away, her heart thumping. He found her hand.

'I love you. I believe you know it. My father says it shows in every look I give you. Will you marry me, dear Sarnia?'

'You pay me a great honour – far greater than any I have known or could know.' She heard her own voice, low and calm. 'But my answer must be no.'

'Sarnia …'

'Please do not press me further.'

His hand let go of hers, and faintness almost overcame her. He said only:

'I will not. You mean to return to London soon?'

She nodded. 'By Friday's packet.'

Figures emerged from the house and crossed the lawn: the servants, bringing tea.

XXVIII

THE MANNER OF THE PORTER at Merton House was entirely changed. He greeted Sarnia with an almost obsequious civility, then rang for Joey, the office boy, and peremptorily commanded him to escort Miss Lorimer to Mr Merton's room. Mr Merton had said she was to be sent up at once.

Mr Merton himself rose and came round his desk to greet her with a warm clasp of the hand.

'My dear Miss Lorimer! How good to see you again. Pray be seated.' His eyes studied her keenly. 'You look tired. This must have been a terrible ordeal for you.'

She had written to him briefly, telling only of her cousin's apprehension on the charge of murdering her father – information which in any case had been printed in the newspapers. She said now:

'It was a shock.' She attempted a smile. 'But I am all right.'

'A very great shock, indeed,' Mr Merton said. 'But we shall soon have you back to health and spirits. Time does heal. You may find it difficult to believe that, with all your life ahead of you; but I, with so little time by comparison, know it to be true.'

'I am sure you are right.'

'You are staying at present' – he consulted the heading of her letter on his desk – 'at the Royal Suffolk Hotel?'

'Yes, but I intend to find a place of my own, in the suburbs perhaps.'

He nodded. 'And you wished to consult me on a business matter.' He smiled, the small eyes lighting up. 'You are not asking for your old employment back, I take it!'

Sarnia smiled also. 'No, though I was happy in it. The business is somewhat different. You know of the fortune which is to come to me from my father's estate.' He nodded. 'There is an attorney in Guernsey who looked after my father's affairs and will see to mine also. I am sure he is in every way a capable and worthy man. But I feel I shall need an adviser closer to hand. I have no male relations and no friends. I wondered if you could recommend someone here in London who would see to things for me.'

He said approvingly: 'You are wise to seek help. A woman alone is too often and too easily exploited. And however honest your Guernsey attorney may be, some overseeing will not come amiss, especially with such a distance between you. You do not plan to live in Guernsey?'

The display in his fireplace today was of large yellow chrysanthemums. There had been yellow chrysanthemums in the garden of the Manoir, but bigger than these and more deeply golden. She said:

'No, I do not expect to return to the island.'

'Then certainly you must have a local man. I know a fellow in Gray's Inn who will do capitally. And if you will permit me, I should be very happy, on a purely informal basis, to offer my own advice on any points in which you are in doubt.'

'You are very kind.'

'Not at all. I shall be delighted not to be losing entirely the pleasure of your acquaintance. You must come and have dinner with us some evening, Miss Lorimer. I should like to have my daughters meet you.'

She smiled and nodded. He had an unmarried son, too, but she acquitted him of any designs in that direction. She must, she thought, almost with despair. Life on a basis of such universal cynicism and lack of trust was not worth the living.

They talked for a while, and she excused herself. He asked if a hackney coach should be sent for, but she refused the offer. The Royal Suffolk Hotel overlooked the river, between the Temple and Charing Cross, and was in easy walking distance. Mr Merton pressed her hand again when she left.

'I perceive you are unhappy, my dear Miss Lorimer, and there is good reason for it. Your father's death – and then the discovery of the complicity in it of your cousin, the man to whom you were engaged.'

'I have come into a fortune, have I not?'

'And it is small consolation. I have dealt in money all my life, and know what it is worth. But I promise you that you will forget all this.'

'You are very kind, sir.'

'Nor will you always, or even for long, lack the warm and loving support of a man you can love in return. You have been cruelly disappointed in your cousin, but that disappointment will be made good. Nothing is more certain.'

She smiled. 'I shall do my best to believe you.'

On the way downstairs she called in at her old office, and spoke with Mrs Mallay and the girls. It was a conversation that was constrained on both sides, and she soon felt obliged to take her leave of them. The stool in front of her old desk was empty.

She descended the two remaining flights, accusing herself. The constraint had been inevitable, but it had been her duty to overcome it, to put them at their ease. But she felt, as nowadays she so often did, tired, drained of energy. The effort had been too great to make; but all the same she should have made it.

The room in which Michael worked was on the right at the foot of the stairs. She passed the door, thinking of him, and then stopped. He was standing by the porter's desk, looking at her.

Her thoughts went back to that terrible morning in the farmhouse when she had learned that he had abandoned her. How long ago it seemed – the earlier days of their friendship in London were less remote. She went towards him, and put out her hand.

'Hello, Michael. How are you?'

He took her hand and held it tightly. His face was strained and nervous. He said:

'May I talk to you?'

'Here?'

The porter was watching and listening to them. Michael said:

'Perhaps you would walk out with me for a few minutes?'

Autumn had turned briefly back to summer. It was a rich September morning, heavy with London heat and dust. They walked towards the gardens of Lincoln's Inn. He did not speak at first, and she was silent too. Then he said abruptly:

'Can you ever forgive me?'

'I have done so long ago.'

'The charge that was laid against me was false – you know that?'

'I had no doubt of it.'

They walked in silence again and turned in through the gates of the Inn. As they crossed the courtyard, he said:

'It makes no difference. I cannot forgive myself. It will shame me all my life.'

His misery was transparently from the heart. She put a hand on his arm.

'You must not dwell on it. You were cruelly trapped.'

'I did not know what to think, what to do. I cannot describe how I felt as the ship took me away from the island. I wrote you a letter and posted it in Southampton.'

'I did not receive it. They kept it from me.'

'I did not know. I thought you might not have answered from contempt. I knew your cousin had behaved villainously towards me, but that was out of his desire to marry you. If I had known that he was a man capable of murder …'

Like Mr Merton he knew nothing of her imprisonment and all she had suffered at the farm. And she did not wish to talk about it. She said:

'It is over and done with. Thank God.'

The trees were autumn-coloured, belying the softness of the day. A group of black-gowned attorneys walked across the lawn near them, heads bowed and muttering. Michael said:

'I failed you. That is the essence and whole of it. Whatever excuses I make, or you make for me, it comes back to that. It is something that will always be with me.'

Time, Mr Merton had said, was a healer. Of grief and injury, true, but of pride? A decent man's discovery of his own falling short from his ideals – could time make good that bitterness? Could anything? And he was a decent man. She felt deeply sorry for him; so deeply sorry that she almost loved him.

She said: 'You must not let it be.'

They had come into the Fields. Her way lay south, towards Temple Bar. And he must retrace his steps and return to his office stool. They stood and looked at one another.

He asked: 'Shall I see you again?'

She looked into the grey eyes, wrinkled now not with mirth but with anxiety and self-doubt. Yes, a decent man, a generous man and, in his way, a strong one. She had need of such strength, such generosity, such decency – God knew how great a need she had!

She shook her head. 'No, Michael.' She saw him wince. 'It is not because of that. Please believe me.'

But she knew he did not. He said:

'God bless you, anyway. I will pray for your happiness.'

She left him quickly, because she must. She kept back her tears until she had turned into Searle Street; then they could be checked no longer. A gentleman passing looked at her curiously as she held her handkerchief to her face. The tears flowed faster: she did not know if she was weeping for Michael or for herself.

XXIX

ON A COLD BUT SUNNY MORNING in December, Sarnia sat in the parlour of the villa which she had rented in St John's Wood. Her view was out into the garden, where the gardener was sweeping the paths clear of leaves blown down in the gales that had swept across this snug suburb earlier in the week. The trees that marked the garden's end were bare and black in the sun, but the privet hedge effectively screened off the villa beyond. High hedges ran all round. When she walked along the neat paths she could be certain of being unobserved.

She heard the doorbell ring, and wondered who it might be. The doctor, possibly, though he had not said he would visit her today. Her curiosity was not great. It could be no one that she wished to see.

When, after a quick knock, her door was flung open, she was totally unprepared. She began to rise, then sank back. With a stifled feeling in her breast she saw Peter standing before her. In confusion, she said:

'Mr d'Aurigny, I beg you ... My maid has orders ...'

Annie had appeared at his side.

'I told him you were not at home, madam. But he would not listen!'

'I beg your pardon.' He loosened the top of his overcoat. 'But I have come a long way to see you, and I was not willing to be put off.' He smiled. 'May I remove my coat?'

She was embarrassed, angry, at the same time dizzily happy. And there was a debt which could never be repaid. She said to the maid:

'Take Mr d'Aurigny's coat, Annie. And bring us tea.'

She still did not get up but asked him to take a seat, pointing to a chair on the far side of the room. He said:

'I am very glad to see you looking so well.'

She replied awkwardly: 'You look well yourself.'

He laughed. 'You should have seen me yesterday! The crossing was vile. But a night's rest has done me good.'

'You are staying at an hotel? Will you be long in England?'

'I do not know.'

His eyes looked into hers. There was a trembling in her limbs which she hoped did not show itself. She thought of asking him if he were here on business, but was suddenly shy of the answer, of any communication between them. She waited, and he said:

'You have read the report of the trial? And the verdicts? That Edmund Jelain and Troutaud were both condemned?'

She nodded. 'Yes.'

'Dr Falla was fortunate not to be charged as an accessory. It would have required you to give evidence, of course, which was not necessary in the cases of the other two. But his complicity is known, and he is disgraced. He no longer practises as a physician.'

She was silent. None of it mattered. As though aware of her thought, Peter said:

'I did not come, though, to talk of villainies and miseries of the past. I have a better purpose.' She looked at him quickly, and looked away. 'When you were in Guernsey I put a question to you. Your answer offered me no encouragement. Yet I am here to put it again; and this time I hope with better success.'

'No.' She shook her head. 'Please …'

'It was pride that caused me to lack persistence then. And you had been subjected to such coercion on the same subject by that murderous cousin of yours. I am a younger son, after all. I did not care to have you think I too was hunting your fortune.'

'I did not think so; nor ever could have done.'

He said cheerfully: 'Good, but I came over prepared this time to take the risk. Will you marry me, Sarnia?'

'I cannot. It is quite impossible.'

'I have told you I am ready to be persistent. I have put down my pride. Will you do the same?'

She looked at him for some moments. Then, slowly, she rose from behind the table and showed him her full figure. She did not know what reaction she expected, but the reality shocked her. He rose also and, coming swiftly across the room, put his hand to the curve of her belly. His eyes close to hers, he said softly:

'You see, it is not so hard.'

She tried to turn from him, but he held her.

'Listen,' he said. 'Jelain did me a good turn at the end, though without meaning it. I saw him in his cell after he was condemned. He was bitter but had found a strange comfort. His avarice is beyond understanding. His child would get the money at least, he declared: the child he had fathered on you by force.'

She closed her eyes in pain. Peter said:

'I knew then why you had refused me. Look at me, Sarnia.'

She did so reluctantly. She said:

'And why I must refuse you still. You know it. You cannot marry me: no man of honour could.'

'No?' He laughed. 'Then I am not a man of honour! I have often suspected it.'

'Your family …'

'My father knows, and I come with his blessing. Though I would have come as surely without it.'

His hands were on her still, and she wanted to he held, wanted to believe in a miraculous rain of hope after the long months of drought. But she said:

'Listen. You have seen how secluded this villa is. I do not go out now, but only walk in the garden. No one sees me except my servants. So I conceal my condition. But this is not, as you may think, in order that the child can he quietly fostered when it is born. I shall keep it with me.'

'I had not imagined you would do anything else.'

'Then how could you marry me, taking not just me but my bastard – the child of such a father!'

He shook his head. 'A violator is not a father. Fatherhood is a care and a duty.'

'It is easy to say now. The doing might prove a different thing.'

'The Jelains,' he said. 'Did they never talk about the d'Aurignys – about my mother?'

'No.'

'Gossip has a long life on Guernsey, but even it grows old in time. And they would be wary: a man was run through with a rapier by my father once, and lay a week at death's door. But we have a thing in common, dear heart. My mother also ran away from the island, though not because of coldness or infidelity or brutality. She left with an officer of the garrison. A month later she returned, and eight months after that I was born. She died in giving me birth.'

He shrugged. 'Maybe I am my father's son, but it is a thing to which neither he nor I could ever swear. I do not have his looks, certainly. But another thing is certain also: that my father has never made an atom's difference between my brother and me. There is no way in which he could have been more of a father than he has.'

'Even so ... There is a difference, surely, between a child of folly and one of wickedness – the child of a man hanged for murder.'

His hand pressed her body. 'After he made that boast – he would not have lived to be hanged had I been able to come at him. I would have killed him there in the cell, if two warders had not dragged me off. But however the seed was planted, it is in your womb that the child is growing. It will be your child, and I shall love it almost as dearly as I love you. Do you think I lie?'

She stared at him a long time. He said softly:

'Well?'

It moved in her like a tide: hope, sureness, happiness. She said:

'No. I do not think you lie.'

'Then will you marry me?'

She smiled at last. 'Willingly. More willingly than I could ever hope to tell.'

He kissed her. She surrendered to the embrace but drew back at the knock on the door.

'Annie …'

He kept hold of her hands. 'She must become accustomed to our domesticity – the whole world must.'

Sarnia shook her head. 'I never shall. And do not want to.'

He wiped the tears from her face with his handkerchief as Annie came in with the tray.

Printed in Great Britain
by Amazon